SOUTHERN ECHO

Abhinav Ramnarayan

Copyright © 2022 Abhinav Ramnarayan

All rights reserved.

ISBN: 9798362640224

For the sleepy, vibrant and endlessly surprising city of Chennai, to which I owe everything

Prologue

The blow was a surprise when it came.

The old man dropped his book and slumped onto the table, trying to blink away the spots that appeared before his eyes, and his mind struggled to compute the intense pain that hit him like a thunderclap.

When he was finally able to think, his first thought was how *stupid* it all was.

Anger, frustration, injured pride — what did it all mean? Why did it move and motivate people to do so much harm?

To commit murder?

His fingers fumbled feebly for the old desk phone on the table, but already, his body was not responding to his brain. The message was going out, but the lines of communication were breaking.

"I was only... was only... trying to help... to do good," he managed, his lips shivering.

It appeared that someone disagreed.

They say your life flashes before your eyes before you die. For the old man, it was more a messy mulch. Even though he was fading, he tried to make some sense of what his life had meant. And then, one face appeared in front of him, clear as a bell. His daughter. His heart filled with unexpected joy and he smiled.

Footsteps. An intake of breath. And then a rough voice spoke.

"Oh my god!" it said.

He recognised that voice. He blinked, and a small trickle of energy flowed back into his body. He looked up into a pair of luminous black eyes.

"You!" he managed, feebly. "It... was... you?"

"No. I hated you, but no. It wasn't me. I just came in."

'Hated'; already the past tense, he noted.

The eyes hesitated and then the voice said: "How are you feeling?"

Despite himself, he smiled.

"Oh... abso... fine... small... headache... that's all..." the old man said, struggling to get the words out.

Suddenly, a weariness came over him, and he stopped speaking.

A surprisingly tender pair of hands lifted his head slowly, and the rough voice spoke again, this time into his ear.

"*Om shanti, shanti, shanti-hi,*" it said.

He nodded. He wasn't religious, but this mantra went beyond religion, beyond life. It was a call for peace. And indeed, a delicious, blissful sense of peace came over him. He didn't have to fight any more. At last.

The old man closed his eyes.

1. Salman Rushdie

Harsha laughed loudly and insincerely at the joke before he turned away to try and stop a waitress who was walking past. She smiled mechanically and presented a plate to him.

"What is this?" he asked, as politely as he could, staring at a plate of unappetising looking canapés — little cubic blocks of unrecognisable food items stuck together with toothpick skewers.

"Pineapple, cheese and olives, sir," she said.

He tried not to blanch and picked one of them up. "Thank you," he said and looked up at her. For a second, he paused — her North Eastern features immediately reminded him of his old friend Richard, and he felt a tug at his heart strings before she smiled and walked away.

Harsha sighed and returned to the elderly group he had been talking to. One of them was now talking about the time when the remote control to their front gate had been broken.

"And then we had to actually go out through the garden door and get an auto rickshaw! Can you imagine?" she finished, one hand gripping the fabric of her gold-trimmed sari and giving a theatrical shudder.

There was a burst of laughter. "Hard to imagine you in an auto, Mallika! Did you have to have a rose petal bath afterwards?" one elderly man asked jovially.

Harsha muttered something, walked away from the group and turned to look out onto the veranda of Madras Club at all the socialites, film stars, wealthy industrialists and, of course, the photographers.

To be fair, it was a beautiful sight to any but the most jaundiced eye. People in colourful clothes, their jewels twinkling under the bright ceiling lights — a sharp contrast to the drab colours of London — fringed by a beautiful, tropical garden dotted with large copper vessels containing fragrant lotus blossoms. There was the clink of glasses, the buzz of conversation, and some soft, undefinable sitar music playing through it all.

Harsha's eyes were pretty jaundiced. He downed the disgusting skewer in one bite and then walked up to Anwar, his photographer, who was standing in one corner and looking benignly out at the teeming veranda.

Anwar grinned at Harsha, who asked him wearily: "Did you get a picture of Salman Rushdie? And especially Padma Lakshmi? That's the one the old crow wants."

Anwar grinned, his neat little moustache turning upwards over his pearly white teeth. "Harish *bhaiyya*, why waste time with some old novelist — look at the talent around here!"

Harsha sighed. "Anwar, have you just been taking pictures of all the women, you pervert! Come on man, get that picture, I'll get a comment and we can both go home!"

The man looked at him in disbelief. "Go home, Hari? What is wrong with you? Look around you! There's nothing but beautiful women, all of whom are dying to meet an eligible bachelor like you. Just chill and enjoy!"

Harsha turned to look at the veranda once again, involuntarily scanning for signs of Anwar's so-called "talent".

Off to one side, the great Indian novelist Salman Rushdie and his beautiful partner Padma Lakshmi were holding court. A group of people surrounded him and Harsha could almost taste the excitement among them. Of course, celebrities came and went in the South Indian city of Chennai — it was a cultural hub, after all, even if it wasn't as big or bustling as Mumbai or New Delhi — but Rushdie was still quite a draw.

"What about her," Anwar said, nudging Harsha and cocking his head towards a beautiful young woman in a low-cut dark blue dress and a pearl necklace. "You go talk to her, ask her if she is an actress or a model."

"Anwar, are you... are you actually telling me what pick-up line to use?"

"No, no — just want to take pictures," Anwar said, grinning, and Harsha shook his head in disbelief. The photographer quickly added: "Ok don't do it, but we need to go back with *some* pictures or Namritha is going to be upset! Come on Harish *bhai,* you can do it! This is for the party page — we need some glamour shots!"

Glamour shots. Party page. Harsha had had a steady job working for *The Times* back in London. One extraordinary episode in a resort in India the year before had somehow convinced him that he needed to come back to his homeland, that he had some noble calling back here. He was going to expose the dark underbelly of Indian society and alleviate the lives of his downtrodden fellow countrymen and women.

Except that he was doing none of that, of course. He had

applied for a number of news reporting jobs in Chennai, Bangalore and even Kolkata, where his parents lived. But there seemed to be some sort of unwritten rule in Indian journalism that the kind of assignments he craved — crime, politics, news — were reserved for the more "working-class" reporters. Harsha, who was awkwardly bucketed in the middle class category by virtue of his excellent English, was only repeatedly offered reporting jobs in features, culture and (he shuddered internally) business and finance.

Finally, he had caved and taken a job on the features desk at *Southern Echo* in Chennai, an exciting new daily newspaper covering the four southern Indian states — Andhra Pradesh, Kerala, Karnataka and Tamil Nadu, where his mother was from. The idea was that he would get his foot in the door and then pitch stories with social and political significance. The day before he joined, his head had been buzzing with excitement at the possibilities.

But instead, his editor Namritha kept sending him to interview B-list celebrities and to cover society events. He watched in frustration as other reporters — some of whom were admittedly very good at their jobs — went off to cover the kind of stories he would have loved to write. Meanwhile, he, Harsha, was…

"She is pretty tasty, eh?" Anwar said lasciviously, cutting into his thoughts.

At this moment, the young woman in the deep blue dress turned and gave Harsha a bright smile — prompting Anwar to nudge him furiously — and he reflected to himself that a surefire way of wiping that smile off her face was to go over and tell her he was a journalist with the *Southern Echo*; could he please have a picture of her for the paper?

But it was either that or Rushdie and Lakshmi, so Harsha gloomily prepared himself to say those fatal words.

A waitress was passing by with some glasses of champagne so he grabbed one, downed it rapidly, slammed it down onto a nearby table and turned purposefully towards the woman.

At this moment, a large lady in a pink sari and a permanently happy expression came bustling up to the two of them and said: "Harsha Devnath? From the *Southern Echo*? Duh-lighted to meet you! Duh-lighted!"

"Er..."

"I'm Damani, you know, I put this little shindig together." Understanding dawned on Harsha and he stammered out some words of gratitude for the invitation that she brushed aside.

"Nammu is an old friend, and she told me that I *must* make sure you get some airtime with our star guests," she said, giggling slightly. "And is this your photographer? What is your name, my man?"

"Er... Anwar," the photographer said, taken aback at being addressed by this glamorous woman.

"Duh-lighted to meet you, Anwar!" she declared, holding out a hand. A hunted expression coming over his face, Anwar quickly shook her hand and then retreated slightly.

"Well then, Harsha, come along! Come along, Anwar!"

"Thank you so much!" Harsha said, this time with absolute sincerity. Not having to push his way through that admiring mob was a genuine boon. He dutifully followed Damani, not looking to see if Anwar was following, and managed to pull together a plastic grin of some sort in anticipation of meeting the great novelist.

Should he say something about Rushdie's novels? He had a vague recollection of *Midnight's Children*, which he remembered admiring for its beautiful prose — but it had been too pessimistic about India for his taste. *Or perhaps not pessimistic enough*, he thought, looking around gloomily at this posh gathering.

He switched back to reality and watched with envy at the polite way in which Damani got through the crowd. A touch of the shoulder here, a laughing greeting there, and suddenly Harsha and Anwar were standing and blinking in front of Salman Rushdie and Padma Lakshmi, who were indeed standing there like king and queen, an ornate chandelier above them and a table full of books on the other side.

"Oh Salman," Damani trilled. "I'd just *love* for you to meet one of our young up-and-coming journalists, Harsha Devnath, who is just *so* keen to have a few words with you."

She stepped aside and the novelist came into view. Harsha thought he looked a little bit bored. But at the mention of a journalist, this seemed to vanish so quickly that Harsha wasn't even sure he had seen it in the first place, and suddenly, he was being charmed by one of India's greatest ever English novelists.

Unfortunately, it was at this moment that the champagne kicked in, and the world went blurry.

"How can I help you, young man," Rushdie said, stepping forward and putting one arm on Harsha's shoulder.

"Ummm... just a few words on why you are here, in... er... Chennai! In Chennai. Why are you here in Chennai, and then Anwar here will take the picture," Harsha said, vociferously signalling to his photographer, who stepped forward with alacrity, his eyes on the resplendent Padma Lakshmi.

Salman Rushdie said something and Harsha squinted his eyes, trying to focus.

"Oh!" he said, suddenly and scrambled in his backpack

for his notepad. "Just a minute," he said.

He suddenly found he was being guided to the table with the books by Rushdie, and he dutifully peered at the books.

"Er..." Inspiration hit him. "So what message do you want to give to the world with your new book?" he asked.

The rest of the interview was even more of a blur and he suddenly looked up to see Anwar plucking at his sleeve. "It's time for the photo!" the man hissed.

"Yes of course," Harsha said, flustered, and stood aside. He felt a tremendous sense of relief that the ordeal was over and started to walk away.

"Some more champagne, sir?"

"Oh god, no," he said instinctively, and turned away to watch Anwar taking some pictures of the couple before scuttling over to his side.

"All done, Harish *bhaiyya*!"

"Thank god!" Harsha said, fervently. "Let's get the hell out of here."

The man looked at him in consternation. "We can't go now! We have to get at least three more pictures of beautiful people. You talk to them, I snap them."

"Bloody hell!" Harsha groaned, causing a couple of nearby women to start and stare at him.

Would the ordeal never end? Was this why he had come back to India?

What the hell had he done?

2. *Home sweet home*

"Alright, enough of this — you get up and shower, put on some nice cologne, and I will pick you up in 40 minutes. *Capisce?*"

"Dude, I am wiped. I am completely, completely wiped! I just need one night at home!" Harsha pleaded into his mobile phone.

"What wiped and all?" said the tinny voice on the other side. "All you've been doing since you came back is one big party, *machan,* and you're telling me you won't go out with your oldest friend?"

Harsha sighed and rubbed his eyes. He stared out from his bedroom window onto the tranquil beach in front of him, trying to allow himself to be soothed by the rhythmic crashing of the waves on the shore and the distant sight of a fishing boat bobbing against the blue horizon.

"Azhar, I..."

"Listen, get your butt into the shower now, and I'll be there in 30 min max. Go, go, go!"

The phone went blank and Harsha looked down at it in exasperation. He had been out every night this week so far, covering one event after another, and this after a full day of work in the office, and now he was having to go out with Azhar to god knows where.

Why didn't his oldest and closest friend get the fact that they weren't 21 anymore? Harsha would celebrate his thirtieth birthday in a few months, and it was an event he was dreading more than any other. The fact was, he was almost exactly back to where he started when he had left university.

In the intervening years, he had gone to England, done a Masters, worked for *The Times* in London, and had an incredible adventure in a small resort in a rural Indian village that he thought had changed his life.

But now here he was, back in Chennai, in a meaningless entry-level journalism job, about to go on a night out with Azhar and very likely have some highly embarrassing encounters with women. It was hard not to feel like he had made absolutely no progress in his life.

He sighed and went back into his room to try and remind himself that all the events of the past few years had actually happened.

He passed by the framed copy of his university degree: a Masters in Journalism from City University London. Beside that was a neatly cropped copy of his best (and only) front page story for *The Times* — a news story on how the new Conservative government's curbs on foreign students was impacting the university sector — and then there were some framed photos of him with some of his favourite classmates on graduation day. He picked it up and looked at it. Rhonda was working for Channel 4, on the production team for *Dispatches,* an investigative TV show. Phil was a culture reporter for *The Guardian*; Jenny was an editor at *The Telegraph*, and moving up the ranks; Dave was Manchester football correspondent for *The Mirror*, and was followed by thousands of people on Twitter (a confusing new metric for journalistic excellence), and Jackie was freelancing and writing an investigative book on the British postal service.

And what was Harsha doing? Taking pictures for the party page for the *Southern* fucking *Echo*.

He sighed and climbed over the unmade bed, trampling on the beautiful embroidered sheets his mother had given him as a homecoming gift, and continued his perusal of his life so far. On the far side of his bedroom, by the door to the bathroom, there was a framed version of the news article he had written after that extraordinary episode two years before, when he and his friends had helped bring a murderer to justice.

"Rural Killer: Remote Village Rocked By Vicious Murder", the headline read.

Harsha felt that now-familiar churning of the stomach when he thought of how he had sat just opposite the person responsible for the grisly killing of an unusual and lonely young woman. Disgust turned to pleasure when he thought of his notes and how they had led to a great number of articles and a bit of international attention. He had even been shortlisted for the Ramnath Goenka Award for journalism. Had he won, his life would have been different, but some other character had won for an article on the Narmada dam. *As though that story hadn't already been done to death for nearly a decade,* Harsha thought bitterly to himself.

He shook his head to try and discard such unworthy thoughts, and instead picked up the framed photograph next to the article and looked at it. He felt his heart well up.

Azhar, Junaina, Shane, himself — and Maya. All stood arm in arm outside Azhar's resort in the aftermath of their adventure. It was a carbon copy of a picture from university — except that they were all a decade older. Azhar, looking even slimmer and more handsome than back in the day, if such a thing were possible; Junaina looking odd without her nose and lip rings and her Black Sabbath T-shirt, but otherwise similar; Shane a bit bloated and faded compared to the tall, cheerful boy that Harsha remembered from college; and Maya — older, moodier, but even more desirable and attractive, at least to Harsha's eyes.

Harsha spared a second to look at his own image in the picture. He was certainly a good-looking enough man, even if he said so himself, but what stood out to him was how hopeful and content that Harsha in the picture looked, even though he was only two years younger. When he put down the photo frame and looked up at the mirror in his wardrobe, he thought he looked far more world-weary and aged with worry, and had a sense that his life was slipping by. He stared unblinkingly at his own reflection for a bit, and then sighed and headed to the bathroom to get ready for a night out he desperately wanted to avoid.

Twenty minutes later, he came out of his bedroom and into the living room. He nodded to his flatmate, Paul, who had taken up his usual reclining position on the sofa, laptop on his lap, the evening light shining down on his neatly parted hair and chiselled features.

Paul looked up at him, sniffed, and said: "A bit dolled up for a session of *Alien vs Predator*, aren't you?"

Harsha clapped his hand on his forehead. "Oh Paul, I'm so sorry, mate — I completely forgot. My friend Azhar is insisting on taking me out tonight."

"You look pretty depressed for a man about to go and paint the town red," Paul said, giving his odd barking laugh.

"Believe me, Paulo, I'd much rather play AVP with you here and order a pizza."

"Probably a good thing. With the amount of cologne you've got on, you'd probably scare all the aliens away; they'd all be fleeing back to their home planet by now," Paul said, barking with laughter again.

Used to his flatmate's odd sense of humour, Harsha gave a perfunctory grin.

"This shirt ok?" he asked, more out of habit than anything.

Paul looked at Harsha's navy-blue shirt, thick brown leather belt and faded jeans combination. "Looking like Shah Rukh Khan!" he declared, without making clear whether or not this was a compliment.

Harsha smiled briefly and then went towards the kitchen to get some water. Much as he agonised over where he was in his life, his living situation at least was very good.

He had been introduced to Paul through the grapevine of the Indian community in England. A Tamil Christian and an IT engineer working for an exciting new challenger bank in England, Paul had been emotionally blackmailed back to Chennai by an authoritarian set of parents — particularly by his domineering mother, who resembled some sort of giant praying mantis in Harsha's imagination.

Paul had complied. But in his passive-aggressive way of rebelling, he had followed instructions to come back to Chennai, but stayed in his own place and refused to see his parents. In fact, Paul barely went anywhere at all, living his life through his high-end laptop and Playstation, only reluctantly trundling out to Tidel Park every weekday to fulfil his day job as a coder for an IT firm.

All of this suited Harsha right down to the ground,

especially now that his own parents had shifted back to his father's original hometown of Kolkata in West India, leaving Harsha without a home in the South Indian city where he had grown up.

And when he had first walked into Paul's flat in Neelankarai, just off East Coast Road in the outskirts of Chennai by the beach, his breath had caught at the sight of the beautiful balcony and window views out into the Bay of Bengal. The beach was literally just outside the balcony — if you didn't mind a storey's jump — and he went for long walks along the ocean, looking out into the beautiful gardens of the beach-side homes, throwing out greetings to the bare-bodied fishermen who hauled in their catch from their catamarans every evening.

This was when he could spare the time of course, with the *Southern Echo* taking up 16 hours of each day and Azhar seemingly taking up the rest.

As if on cue, his phone ringtone -- the opening riff of London Calling by *The Clash* — blared out, causing Paul to jump in his seat. Harsha downed his glass of water, picked up his phone to see Azhar's name flash on the screen, and cut the call.

"It's time to go party," he sighed and walked towards the door, as though he was heading towards some great doom.

3. Azhar

"Looking good, buddy!" Azhar said excitedly from the passenger seat, as Harsha opened the door to the car and stepped into the back seat. "You ready to rumble?"

Harsha nodded resignedly and looked at the man who was arguably his closest friend in the world. Azhar still looked absurdly good despite having passed his 30th birthday; bright eyes, chiselled features and a sensuous pair of lips meant he could have stepped straight out of a Bollywood movie into the teeming streets of Chennai. If anything, he was only just coming into his prime, a few lines adding character to his face and the somewhat sleepy look replaced by a glint of intelligence that came with a productive career and sense of self-worth.

"Hello Harsha!" said the driver, cutting into his thoughts.

"Selvam!" Harsha said in surprise, recognising the driver's eyes in the rear view mirror. "What are you doing here? I thought you hated Chennai?"

"Had to go to the hospital for surgery to reset my nose. But soon I will go back to Pahaar Resorts!" the man said, forcibly reminding Harsha of that horrible episode where Selvam had been beaten by the police during their investigation into poor Lakshmi's death. He felt a pang. For Harsha, it had been a career-changing event, but for Selvam it would appear that the consequences had been far more negative.

"Ok, Selvam, let's go and then we can keep talking," Azhar said. The driver eased the car into gear, and Harsha heard the familiar crunch of rubber on gravel and sand as the car eased its way through the side alleys that led to Harsha's little getaway in the outskirts of town.

"Don't worry, Harsha! I am doing fine! Azhar sir is paying all my bills and helping me with my family and everything. I am fully healthy now!" the man said, smiling into the rear view mirror.

"That's good to hear, Selvam!"

The car reached the entrance to East Coast Road, the narrow little highway that connected Chennai to the historic village of Mahabalipuram and, beyond that, the erstwhile French colony of Pondicherry. Selvam waited patiently for a break in the long stream of cars that were moving in both directions.

"What about your flatmate? Does he not want to come?" Azhar asked.

"Paul? Nah, he hardly ever socialises. He's a really lovely guy but also really shy. Never been able to convince him to join me at any of these parties, even if they're free," Harsha said, lazily watching the traffic with the air of a man who doesn't actually have to navigate it.

"Sounds like a bore," Azhar said, losing interest.

Selvam suddenly revved the car forward to take advantage of a slight pause in traffic caused by a hesitant uncle in a scooter, triggering a chorus of horns from all sides. Azhar put on the music, turned up a song by Daft Punk and started dancing in the front seat, pumping his hands up and down.

"Yeahhhh. We're up all night to get luckkyyyy," he yodelled. Harsha shook his head half in amusement and half in exasperation. "Isn't that right, Selvam?" Azhar asked his driver.

Through the rear view mirror, Harsha saw Selvam grinning affectionately at his employer.

Harsha signalled for Azhar to turn the volume down and said: "Mate, I'm absolutely starving; can we get some food first?"

"Oh of course, dude, we're going to have dinner first. You need to meet this girl I'm dating. And a friend of hers is coming along as well."

"The girl you're dating? This is a new revelation!"

Azhar waved his hand as though it was an unimportant detail. "Just dating, bugger, we haven't tied the knot or anything. But you will like her friend."

Harsha doubted it, but decided that it was pointless to discuss it.

"And then where? Bike and Barrels?" he asked, remembering the bar they used to frequent back in university.

Azhar clapped his hand on his forehead. "That dump! It used to be cool ten years ago, dude, please don't embarrass me by mentioning that! *Bike and Barrels*," he repeated, shaking his head.

"Then where?"

"10D or maybe Speed," Azhar said, casually.

"10D? Is that a new place? Not a very exciting name,"

Harsha said, a little nettled at Azhar's vociferous put-down of his suggestion.

"Nah, it's cool man. It's short for 10, Downing Street."

"And that's supposed to be a cool place?" Harsha asked derisively, shaking his head. He tried to imagine what his friends back home — back in London, he should say — would have thought of the idea of using the British Prime Minister's address as the name of a trendy bar in India and cringed a little to himself. The idea was ridiculous.

"We gonna meet some sweet girls there, you'll see!" Azhar said reassuringly.

"Isn't your girlfriend going to be there?"

"Not my girlfriend! And no — they're only joining us for dinner. Then we're free! Man, I'm so stoked you're back! Can't wait to get out there and be your wingman!"

"Really, Azhar," Harsha said quickly. "I'm not ready for that right now. Give me time."

Azhar turned around fully in his seat. He looked seriously at Harsha and said: "You're not still hung up on Maya, are you?"

"No! Azhar — no," Harsha said forcefully, and something in his voice must have got through to his friend, who nodded and dropped the subject.

After a brief silence, Harsha asked: "Where are we going for dinner?"

"New place called Phuket. It's a Thai restaurant. It's in the new Cloud Nine hotel, should be good fun," he said.

It took them 40 minutes in the evening traffic to get to their destination, during which time Azhar ran through his collection of Daft Punk, M83 and a host of other artists on the car stereo, and seemed to be charging himself up for a really big night out, a fact that made Harsha extremely nervous. It looked like the only way to get through this night would be to get steaming drunk — and who knew what the consequences of that might be.

Finally, they stepped out into the evening air at the entrance to a grand new designer hotel. Selvam waved them goodbye, and the pair of them made their way into the place, Harsha looking around with curiosity at the funky designs and light effects below the glass floor. This was a side to Chennai that either hadn't existed while he had grown up here, or of which he had been unaware.

"Here's the place," Azhar said, and led Harsha into a beautiful, sparsely-lit restaurant with glass walls that looked out onto a garden filled with palm fronds surrounding a little pond. By the entrance a (presumably) Thai woman was sitting gracefully on a divan and was busy carving a raw pumpkin into flower shapes. A tinkly, Far Eastern-style music played discreetly from hidden speakers.

Azhar looked around and then waved to a table by one side where a pair of women were sitting. He marched towards them, navigating the space between the tables recklessly. Harsha's heart beat unnaturally fast as he followed Azhar. This was as close to a date as he had got since coming back to India, and a very rare one after the Maya episode a couple of years ago.

"Hey Rads, how's it going?" Azhar asked, casually, leaning over to kiss one of the women on the cheek, and then turning to nod at the other one.

"You're nearly half an hour late, Azhar!" the woman said, looking at him with slightly despairing eyes that suggested that whatever he thought of their relationship, she was anything but casual with him. She looked appraisingly at Harsha and then said: "I'm Radhika, and this is Seema."

The second woman stood up and smiled at Harsha. He was relieved to see she was dressed in a simple red T-shirt and jeans. Radhika was wearing a spangly, silvery dress that blinded Harsha when he looked directly at her.

There was a moment of confusion where Harsha didn't know whether the right greeting was a kiss on either cheek — as was customary in Europe — or a handshake, and so he ended up doing an awkward half hug with Seema. Radhika then took matters into her hands and kissed him on one cheek and then sat down and turned her attention back to Azhar, who was perusing the menu, a slight frown on his face, though at this point he did look up.

"Oh, sorry! Nice to meet you, Seema," he said, giving the new woman a charming smile before flicking his eyes back to the menu.

Harsha sat down and gave Seema a slightly embarrassed grimace, though he was not sure what for. He realised with a slight jump of nerves that she was extremely attractive — quite tiny, probably not above five feet tall, with lovely, long hair and a shy smile. He couldn't figure out if the shyness was put on or genuine, but she glanced at him from under her lashes and gave him a smile at that moment, leaving him clearing his throat and reddening slightly.

"So, Harsha," Radhika said brightly, finally turning her attention to him. "You ready for this double date? Seema is one of my closest friends, you know? Only the best will do for her, as far as I'm concerned. Good thing is, you're good-looking. Not very tall, but Seema isn't either," she added.

Harsha reeled at this direct attack and went into a fit of coughing, which brought over a concerned waiter, who asked solicitously if he would like some water.

"Yeah, let's get some for the table. Sparkling *and* still,

thank you," Azhar said authoritatively, and the waiter scuttled away.

"Nice to... er... meet you, Seema," Harsha said.

"You're a journalist, Harsha?" Radhika cut in again. How the hell was he supposed to be on a date with Seema if this woman wouldn't let either of them talk?

"Yes, for *Southern Echo*."

"Oh god," Radhika said, clapping her hand on her head. "Bad start!"

"Why, what's wrong with *Southern Echo*?" Seema asked timidly, and Harsha felt pathetically grateful for even this low level of support.

"*Arre*, all they write about are sex scandals and crimes! Real gutter journalism! What are you doing there, Harsha? If you're a serious journalist shouldn't you be working for *The Hindu* or at least *Times of India*."

Harsha gaped at Radhika. He was so used to England, where people tended to be far more polite, that he had no plan of defence at all for this. What was most galling was that Radhika didn't even seem to be trying to attack him in particular. All of this was delivered in a conversational tone that suggested this was just the way she talked.

He turned to Azhar to see what his friend thought of this, and found him still deeply involved with the menu.

"What's all this *kheng ped redang ped* rubbish? Where's the Thai red curry?" Azhar asked.

"That *is* Thai red curry. Written in, you know, Thai," Harsha said sardonically.

"Hmmm, well at least you're intelligent," Radhika declared, to Harsha's immense irritation.

Dinner was an awkward affair during which Harsha felt like his life was taken apart by Radhika and examined piece by piece. Out of consideration for Azhar, Harsha restrained himself from retaliating in kind, though to be honest, he wasn't sure if he would have been capable anyway.

Seema seemed friendly enough, but Harsha's mind was beginning to wander back to a resort on the border between Tamil Nadu and Andhra Pradesh as he toyed with his spring roll, when a slight movement caught his attention from the corner of his eye.

He turned to look curiously and saw two of the restaurant staff standing in the little garden outside, seemingly accosting a young woman in a plain *salwar kameez*. He started at this unusual sight and turned fully to look properly at what was happening.

The rest of the group turned to follow his gaze and Radhika said: "*Arre*, what's going on there? Is it some kind of assault? Azhar, why aren't you doing something?"

"Do what?" Azhar asked. "It doesn't look like assault. They are pushing her away."

On second glance, Harsha realised Azhar was right. The two staff members did look like they were pushing the woman away, though the manner in which they were doing it wasn't particularly friendly.

Seema spoke up for once and said: "Are you sure it's a woman?"

All four of them squinted and then Radhika said: "Oh my god, it's a *chakka*! A transgender! These people are everywhere! Begging for money, harassing people. They should all be put in jail."

More than one restaurant guest had noticed the commotion now as it got slightly more violent. One of the two men gave the person a proper push and she fell over on the concrete pathway, hitting her head in the process.

23

"Come on," Harsha said to Azhar, standing up and dropping his napkin to the floor.

"What? What come on? Don't... Harry! Don't start your Tintin stuff again now!" Azhar shouted after him in genuine alarm.

Harsha was already halfway towards the side exit of the restaurant.

"C'mon, Snowy!" he called out over his shoulder.

4. Gita

Harsha stepped out into the garden. He felt a sudden rush of warmth and humidity envelop his body, and heard the sounds of conflict replace the soft strains of East Asian music. The two men were yelling as loudly as they could at a person on the floor, who was dressed in a faded *salwar kameez* and sobbing quietly as she tried to get up. Every time she got to her feet and walked towards the hotel, one of the men pushed her back down to the floor.

"What's going on 'ere?" Harsha asked, doing his best impression of an English bobby (he was never sure afterwards why he did that) and the two men jumped and then turned to him. They were both dressed in the same uniform as the other staff in the hotel.

The really shocking thing was that they were both so young and pleasant-looking. One of them looked at Harsha with a mixture of defiance and deference, but the expression of the other, who was slightly older-looking, darkened. He said sharply: "This is none of your business, sir! Get back in the restaurant!"

It's a funny thing, conflict, Harsha thought to himself. We

all like to think of ourselves as good at it. Standing up to the boss, telling the office bully to go to hell and so on. But when actually faced with a situation of conflict, it was actually extremely shocking and challenging to handle. He took a deep breath and said: "I will go in – if you just explain to me what is happening to this woman."

"It's none of your business, that's what's happening," the man said rudely and recklessly.

The first man shushed his colleague quickly and said to Harsha: "Sir, this is a matter of office policy; can you please just go back to your dinner, and this will be resolved very quickly."

"I just want to go back to work," said the woman quietly, a catch in her voice. She was splayed on the floor, legs akimbo, and Harsha thought he never heard a more pitiable, sad and submissive voice.

"If you don't leave THIS INSTANT, we will call the police!" said the sterner of the two men. The woman bent her head in a submissive manner, but did not move. Harsha thought he saw a trickle of blood make its way down her forehead.

At this point Azhar ran up. He was accompanied by a rotund man with a bristling moustache, a tight white shirt stretched over his belly. This new person took in the situation and his moustache seemed to bristle even more. Both he and Azhar began to speak loudly at the same time.

"You two! What the hell is going on here! Sir, what are you doing here? This is none of your business."

"Bugger, why are you getting involved in this shit! Are you trying to get us in trouble again?"

The two young hotel employees turned to this new man and started a rambling explanation in which the name

"Gokul" came up repeatedly. Harsha brushed Azhar's hand off his shoulder, walked up to the woman and squatted in front of her.

"Are you ok?"

She looked up at him, and he couldn't quite repress a shudder, because he couldn't tell if it was a man or a woman, even though she was wearing a *salwar kameez*. She smelled of jasmine and sweat. Reminding himself of his liberal leanings, he smiled and said: "You are hurt. Can I help you?"

She looked at him with tragic eyes and said: "I just want to go back to work."

There was an uncomfortable silence, during which Harsha tried to assess the situation and then said: "You used to work here? Have they fired you?"

She looked at him and then, to his great distress, two tears rolled down her eyes. "Yes," she whispered. "Yes, I used to work here."

The rotund man had clearly finished dressing down his two staff members, because at this point he came up to Harsha and said. "Yes, but he was…. She was…. *Gokul* used to work here! This man… person… he or she or whatever it is, doesn't work here! And even if I accepted you here, look at the scene you have caused! Scandal! Terrible for the restaurant!"

The whole group turned to see that all the people in the restaurant were looking out at them.

"I wouldn't take you back if someone paid me a crore of rupees! Get out before I call the police!" the rotund man finished triumphantly, as though he had proved a point.

"Well, the first thing you can do is stop shouting. That's what's creating a bloody scandal," Azhar said crossly. Harsha felt a rush of gratitude for his friend and gave him a smile, which wasn't reciprocated.

"I *beg* your pardon, sir, but I am the manager of this hotel and this is *my* job on the line, and..."

"Ho! Job on the line, is it? Well, it will be if you continue talking to us like this..."

Harsha tuned out the argument behind him, took a deep breath, and held out his hand to the woman sitting on the floor. This small gesture seemed to take her completely by surprise – Harsha felt another wringing in his heart – and she looked up at him, dried her tears quickly and prepared to stand up with his help.

The arguing behind Harsha stopped.

The manager stepped up and said: "Listen – please leave right away. You are not an employee of this place any more."

Harsha looked over at Azhar, who was looking troubled, but shrugged back at Harsha. What could they do?

The woman bent her head for a second, wiping away a trickle of blood from her forehead, and then nodded and turned to leave. The manager looked a bit smug. It was partly to wipe that disgusting smile off his face that Harsha turned to her and said: "Wait!"

He ran up to her and said: "Listen, can we be in touch? I am a journalist, and I..."

The manager's eyes popped open and he stepped forward. "I cannot allow..."

"What do you mean, you cannot allow?" Azhar roared. "The last time I checked, this was a free country! He is well within his rights to..."

Once again, Harsha tuned the argument out and took advantage of the time Azhar was buying him, saying: "Listen, I just want to make sure you are ok. At the very least I can put you on to any work that I know about..."

The woman hesitated and then said: "Who do you work for?"

"Er... *Southern Echo*," Harsha said, a little embarrassedly.

But she looked quite impressed. She nodded and then waited for him to take out his mobile phone before dictating her number to him.

"I'll do my best. Courage, my friend," Harsha said. "Oh, and... Gokul, is it?" he asked awkwardly, his fingers poised over the phone's keyboard.

She shook her head. "That's not my name anymore. Now I am Gita."

With those words, she turned and disappeared into the night.

As soon as she was out of sight, the manager gave them both a "hmph" before turning and marching away, flanked on either side by the violent young staff members. Harsha and Azhar were left standing there in that beautiful, balmy garden, with a gentle breeze bending the palm trees quietly around them. Harsha looked over at the restaurant and saw that the people were starting to go back to their food, the evening's entertainment over.

After a second's silence, Azhar said bitterly: "Harsha, you fucking dick. Why must you make life so difficult? We are here to have a *fun* evening. We were supposed to *drink*. We were supposed to *laugh*. We are here with two hot girls and..."

"Oh mate, come on," Harsha said, impatiently. "Your Radhika... I mean, come on."

"At least she actually is a woman! Fucking hell, Harry," Azhar said, throwing his hands up and walking towards the restaurant.

Harsha ran to catch him up. "Come on man, you don't mean that? Did you see how sad she was? Gita, I mean?"

Azhar paused on the doorway and turned to Harsha, and the two young men faced each other for a second. Finally Azhar said: "Yes, I... ok yes, I did feel sorry for her. But Harry, I was just happy to have you back, just wanted to go out and have some fun with my old friend! But you're always off fighting some cause like that Spanish bugger! What's his name?"

"Don Quixote," Harsha said, knowing the way his friend's brain worked. "But listen, this is who I am and you have to accept..."

"Harry! I don't have that many friends here, man! No one like you! Everyone sees a Muslim, or a Hyderabadi or..." Azhar's hands flailed about and then, seeing Harsha put his head in his hands, he stopped and waited a little warily.

There was another silence, and then Azhar asked a little nervously: "You ok, man?"

Harsha took his hands away from his face. "Just tired, dude. Listen. You're right. This was supposed to be a fun night. I promise, I'll be a good friend, I'll even be nice to..."

Radhika's from the doorway to the restaurant cut sharply into the conversation. "You boys coming in or what? Typical men! No consideration at all! And what happened to that *chakka?*"

Harsha and Azhar gave each other a long, agonised glance before turning back towards the restaurant.

5. Southern Echo

Harsha walked into the offices of the *Southern Echo* newspaper in his usual, slightly resigned fashion. He worked such long hours and often well into the weekend, so that Monday blues became irrelevant. He nodded to the security guard, who jerked awake and nodded back at him, and then ran up the stairs and nearly bumped into Jeevan, the office boy, who greeted him cheerfully.

Why a newspaper had an office boy, whose primary job seemed to be to make sure journalists had coffee ready on their tables, he didn't know. He felt it was wrong somehow, and yet, to have a steaming cup of coffee — packed with caffeine if not flavour — served at his desk periodically was magic.

Jeevan was always smiling and cheerful, though, and was a popular figure in the office. Harsha reflected to himself for the millionth time that the indomitable spirit of India's working class was one of the most incredible things about the country.

When he arrived at his desk, he looked around and nodded at Sandhya and Nritya (known behind their backs as the "ya ya" women, both because of their names and their habit of agreeing with everything the boss said) and gave a more genuine smile to Kalyanasundaram, who had set up camp next to him.

Kalyan was a short, barrel-chested man with a thick Tamil accent, and was one of *Southern Echo*'s leading news correspondents. Though the news desk was situated further down the office, Kalyan had decided to sit with the features team nominally to improve his English. But Harsha suspected he preferred the company to the news desk, which was a bit more backstabbing by nature — and that Kalyan also liked the diverse feel to the features desk, which had more people from the North of India. The fact that there were more young women in this part of the office probably didn't hurt either.

In turn, the women in the features desk all adored Kalyan and teased him gently, which he took in good spirit.

Nritya, a slender, dark-lidded girl dressed in a tank top came up to him and half-sat on his desk as he plonked himself down onto his chair. She crossed her arms and said without preamble: "Harry, you better watch out."

She nodded towards the glass office where their editor said.

Harsha winced.

"Old Nams is on the warpath?" he asked, and she nodded. Kalyan snorted with laughter behind them.

"Harsha, better go take your dose now itself," he said, taking his eyes off his own computer, blinking at the strip of navel visible beneath Nritya's tank top and hurriedly looking at Harsha. "Get it over with."

"What dose?" Nritya asked, her brow furrowed in confusion.

Harsha sighed and said: "He just means she is going to give me a bollocking. That she is going to yell at me," he added, seeing her continued confusion. "Was it the Salman Rushdie piece?"

"She hated reading it. She was complaining about it when I came in," Nritya said, not without some relish. "Said you were to see her as soon as you came in."

"Well, I didn't exactly love writing it either," Harsha said, but he did swing himself out of his chair and took a deep breath before heading to his manager's office.

There had been editors in the past who had filled Harsha with dread. Namritha was not one of them. True, she handed out "doses" often and seemingly at random, but he felt nothing but irritation as he walked up to her office. It would have been too much to say he held her in contempt. But she certainly did not command his respect. It wasn't that she didn't know news. She knew news very well. It was more about her management style.

He knocked on the pane of her glass door and walked in. "Hi," he said unenthusiastically. She continued editing a page for a second and he stood there resignedly until she looked up at him through her plastic rectangle-framed glasses.

She looked at him for a few seconds with what he assumed was supposed to be a piercing gaze, before saying: "What is this rubbish you filed?"

He didn't know what to say to that, so he didn't say anything.

She held out a page and said: "This is not what I expect from you! You were educated in England! You worked for *The Times*! How can you produce something so sub-standard?"

She would have gone on indefinitely in this vein, so he

cut in and said: "Can you tell me what specifically you had an issue with?"

She raised her hands as though to heaven and gesticulated speechlessly for a second and then said: "Everything!"

Classic Namritha. This sounded like a dose just for the sake of it. She must have seen his slightly scornful expression because she quickly added: "It sounded like you absolutely hated the event and that you disliked Salman Rushdie and Padma Lakshmi. You sound so contemptuous about socialites — this is supposed to be perky and cheerful and you sound as though this was the seventh circle of hell you attended, not a party!"

Harsha reeled. Unexpectedly, Namritha had actually hit him with a valid criticism and quite an insightful one at that.

"You worked at *The Times*, for goodness sake!"

Why did she keep bringing that up?

"Well Namritha, I didn't do features there, I was working on political news. You need to give me some time to get used to…"

"How much time?" she barked out. "Nritya does a *fabulous* job of editing the teen page. She has established a group of contacts and turns out solid pieces regularly. Sandhya is a whiz at culture. Ricardo…"

Here it begins, Harsha thought, tuning it out. Namritha's management style was to yell at them all individually and point out how flawed they were in comparison to their peers. It made absolutely no sense at all — how could they all be rubbish and amazing at the same time?

Finally, it was done, and he nodded and then walked back to his desk. He dumped himself down onto his chair and turned on his computer.

"*Enna pa*, good dose or bad dose?" Kalyan asked, jovially.

Harsha just shook his head, unable to speak, such was his frustration. Kalyan seemed to sense that his companion wasn't quite in the mood, so instead he signaled to Jeevan, who came over and delivered Harsha a steaming cup of coffee, smiling at him.

"Thank you, Jeevu," Harsha said, unable to remain depressed in the face of the office boy's unrelenting cheerfulness.

He stared at the screen blankly for a while, trying to think of how he could change his copy, when Sandhya came bustling in and said: "Oh my god, how was it?"

"What? Who?" Harsha asked, looking up in confusion at the tall, rather bird-like woman in front of him. She was the very picture of organised chaos, her long hair trailing down the side of her designer *kurta* and her cloth bag overflowing with books and papers, her face carefully made up to accentuate the softness of her features.

"Padma Lakshmi of course! So beautiful and so glamorous! Can't believe I had that stupid niece's birthday party to go to. What was she wearing? And of course, Salman Rushdie as well, of course," she added a little begrudgingly. "What were they like?" she asked, cocking her head to one side and intensifying the bird-like impression.

Harsha mumbled something and went back to his work, and Sandhya looked at him in astonishment for a second at his lack of enthusiasm before exchanging glances with Kalyan and then returning to her desk.

Silence reigned for about 20 minutes before Kalyan said. "*Pa*, is there no such word as 'acknowledge'? Is it a foreign word?"

Harsha wheeled his office chair over to Kalyan's desk

and corrected his spelling for him, and briefly glanced at the headline before asking: "Is this about the new hydropower station in Kovalam?"

Kalyan smiled sympathetically at the envy in Harsha's voice. "Yes," he said, simply.

"Interesting subject," Harsha said. "What is your view? Do you think it is fair to displace those people who live on the site? Will that MP get into enough trouble for pushing ahead with the project? The opposition party is already..."

Sandhya tutted loudly from behind them. Harsha turned around quizzically and she said: "Trust you to find some power station more interesting than *Padma Lakshmi* or *Salman Rushdie*."

She was still shaking her head when Harsha turned back to Kalyan, who was grinning at him. Kalyan said: "Be patient, *pa*. Your time will come."

Harsha was still thinking of these words when he went into the 11am editorial meeting and sat round the table in Namritha's office with Sandhya, Nritya and Ricardo, who had just lounged in at that moment, wearing a hideous red shirt with little *chakras* all over them, unbuttoned to show his clean shaven chest. He smiled lazily at Namritha, who fluttered her eyelashes at him before turning to Nritya.

"Oh Nittu, I have to ask you — how was your dinner with that boy? Will there be a second date?" their boss asked, giggling.

It always amazed Harsha how Namritha could be so unpleasant and then an hour later turn on the charm and behave as if nothing had happened.

The meeting was a dreadful affair, a mixture of story intentions and gossip. Finally it was Harsha's turn to speak. They all looked at him, Namritha's friendly manner flickering, but remaining in place.

"So, there's this piece I was looking at on the sudden spike in skateboarding in Chennai. There's quite a few clubs and groups now and even some competitions. Could be very picture friendly," Harsha said, knowing full well how well this would go down. A buzz of approval went around the group, to his complete lack of surprise, and they excitedly discussed this earth-shattering new development in the city for a full fifteen minutes, dissecting the possibilities.

"We need good pictures. We need a really talented guy to do some flips or whatever you call it, and then a really hot girl showing some skin, doesn't matter if she can't skateboard," Namritha said authoritatively, by way of conclusion. "Oh. And you can write about 600 words," she added as an afterthought. "Talk to some people, make it exciting. Great idea, Harsha. Glad to hear you're thinking in the right way at last."

A wave of relief went through the group, but Harsha licked his lips nervously. He had only come up with this idea as a sweetener for what was to come.

"Anything else?"

Harsha cleared his throat. "So, I wanted to do a deep dive into the transgender community in Chennai. Did you know there is quite a varied community already? Many of them face tremendous levels of violence and are fighting for their right to work. They even have the support of some government figures..." he trailed off as Namritha looked at him as though he had suddenly started smelling of something particularly nasty. The others had gone silent. Sandhya was looking at him in bewilderment while Nritya was smiling a little to herself, no doubt enjoying his demise to come. Ricardo was looking at him expressionlessly.

"Transgenders, Harsha?" Namritha asked, putting one hand to her forehead, her good mood evaporating. "Seriously, I don't think you even understand what we're trying to do here! This is supposed to be a *features* desk! It's supposed to be something people read for relaxation, not to feel even more depressed."

Harsha didn't say anything, instead he just bowed his head. What was even the point of sticking around in this stupid job, being so unhappy? The salary, yes, but surely he could do something else?

"Look," Namritha said, catching wind of his mood and perhaps not wanting to take the wind entirely out of his sails. "I do get it. You want to do social affairs stories. But this is the wrong place for that. Once you're on the news desk — you can explore as many of these stories as you like."

"Why not... why not just let me explore this? And maybe you could have a look at it and see if it's newsworthy? Or recommend it to the newsdesk?" Harsha implored, trying to ignore the catch in his throat. "I could do it in my free time," he added, thinking of the two waking hours each day in which he was not working.

Namritha was already shaking her head. "I want you to focus on the skateboarding story and not get sidetracked by this. Unless you want me to give Ricardo the skateboarding piece?" she asked, grinning menacingly.

If this was intended to be a threat, it fell completely flat.

"By all means! I think he is much better suited to it than I am," Harsha said brightly, giving Ricardo an insincere smile.

"No! No!" Namritha said, putting her hands up. "Harsha, I am not discussing this further. You go do the story that you are being paid for. That's that."

She turned to her computer, a sour expression on her

face, and her team trooped out silently, not speaking to each other. Harsha could sense that he had upset them all by implying that what they did was not meaningful, and he felt a bit sorry for that, but not that much. He wasn't judging what they did for a living. It's just not what he wanted to do himself, it really was that simple.

When he went back to the desk, Kalyan threw him a shrewd glance and said: "Want to go for a cigarette?"

"You don't smoke, Kalyan. And I gave up as well."

Kalyan did an about turn. "Wow! Well done *pa*. For how long? Anyway, that doesn't matter," he added quickly. "Come, let's go for a tea and a *bajji*."

Harsha followed Kalyan out into the street, feeling about as depressed as he ever had been since he had come back to India. It was ironic. He had spent so many sessions with a therapist back in London about becoming happy, and that had eventually led him back to India — where he was now even unhappier than he had been in the first place in London.

All he wanted was some sense of job satisfaction. And of course, to be well-known and successful and all those things. But basically, he wanted job satisfaction. He saw all these young journalists out there writing incredible, groundbreaking stories, and he was being left behind. In his 20s, he'd had exactly one big story to his name, and that had been a total fluke — he had been in the right place at the right time. He didn't have that much time to do more before he was on the scrapheap, or so it seemed to him.

Kalyan didn't say anything until they reached the little roadside stall outside the office which was flanked by an old shed on one side and a grazing cow on the other. A group of men and women had surrounded the tea maker; they were grabbing their brew in little glass cups and having their *bajjis* delivered in little strips of newspaper, the oil soaking through the lettering. Harsha noticed with vicious satisfaction that the papers in question were from a copy of that day's *Southern Echo*.

They sat down on a crumbling wall with their tea and *bajji* and Kalyan gently began to tease out Harsha's issues. He listened quietly while Harsha unburdened himself and then passed judgement.

"Since day one since I came to sit near that desk, you have been very sad," Kalyan said, solemnly. "You should not take life so seriously, *pa*. You are very lucky to have a good job, doing something that you love. So many people are worse off."

"But that's exactly it, Kalyan! So many people are worse off and I'm sitting here writing about skateboards and Salman Rushdie!" Harsha said, his voice breaking with emotion and barely-suppressed rage. "Honestly, I don't think I have any other option other than to quit!"

"You think it will be different at another newspaper?"

"Surely I have to try? I can't just accept the *status quo*?"

Kalyan sighed and shook his head. Then he put his tea cup down on the wall and said: "Look here, *pa*. You have to understand one basic thing about editors, otherwise you will never be happy in any newspaper job."

Harsha waited for a second, and then said: "What?"

"They are all complete fools."

Harsha snorted with laughter, spraying tea out in front of him, and lifted his hand in apology to a passerby who had jumped out of the way.

"What do you mean, Kalyan? I mean, I don't disagree, but..."

"Editors all think — what story will our readers like? Then they ask you to go write that story. And if you tell them, that is not the reality, they will tell you that reality is wrong. So, then you get two types of journalists." He paused and took a sip of his tea, his eyes twinkling at Harsha from above the rim of the glass.

"Go on," Harsha said, interested despite himself.

"One type of journalist is a scoundrel who changes their story and gives the editor what he wants, never mind reality. It is very common, unfortunately! You can see them everywhere — people who will — how you say it in England? Sell their grandmother for a story! Huh? And then the other type of journalist is like you, always frustrated. Never getting anywhere. Finally writing a book of poems that nobody is reading."

"Great," Harsha said, bitterly, putting his tea glass down vigorously on the wall. "Thanks for the pep talk, Kalyan."

"*Ille pa*, wait, wait. There is also a third type of journalist," Kalyan said, putting one hand reassuringly on Harsha's shoulder. "He is a clever one. He knows that life is full of stories that people will want to read, that don't need any extra *masala*. So even though editors don't understand this, he is smart and knows a way of getting his story out there."

"How?"

"Well first you need to have the story. These trans... what? Transgenders, ok, you already decided there is a story there," Kalyan said, biting into his snack. Munching, he continued: "Now just go write the story you want to write!"

"Namritha won't allow me!"

Kalyan took a great swallow and then said indignantly: "What is this 'allow'? Are you a child? Nobody can stop you if you want to write a story, *pa*."

Harsha blinked and looked at Kalyan open-mouthed. "Do you mean…"

"I mean write your story!"

"What's the point of a story if they won't publish it?"

Kalyan sighed and then said: "Do you know why I joined this paper?"

Harsha shook his head.

"I am not saying this to show off, *pa*, but I was extremely well read at *Dinathandi* where I was covering government politics before. And it is the best-read Tamil paper *in the world*, my friend. I was the king in my patch. So why do you think I came here to break my head over this crazy English language?"

"Better pay?" Harsha hazarded, waving his hand slightly over his mouth. The *bajji* was extremely spicy.

Kalyan shook his hand derisively. "If I want to make money, I will start a political party, man. I came here because the owner, Jaishree Verma, convinced me. She wanted me to write about Tamil Nadu politics in a new way, in a true way and bring something new to journalism in Chennai." He leaned forward and said in a conspiratorial manner: "She *understands*. Jaishree. She *gets it*. You write your story, man, and we will find a way to publish it."

Harsha looked encouraged for a moment, but then his face fell again. "But Kalyan, Namritha keeps me busy with all sorts of other shit! Parties, skateboarding, all kinds of horrible assignments that turn your brain to dust!"

"Your brain must be already full of dust if you think you have to do them all," Kalyan said, drily.

Harsha turned on his precarious seat on the wall and looked fully at his companion. "What do you mean, Kalyan? I can't just not do what she tells me, no?"

"*Ayyo*, all you middle class types — you've spent too much time studying and writing exams and trying to make teachers happy! Think outside the box, *pa*. What can she do if you don't write this skatebread story or whatever it is? Nothing! Fire you? Don't be silly! They can't just fire you. They have to have a reason."

Harsha looked out into the distance in a daze, his mouth open slightly. Then he shook his head and said: "It's too much of a risk, Kalyan."

Kalyan clapped his hand on his head. "An educated, intelligent fellow like you, talking about risk! There is no risk, man! That is the big illusion that these corporate bastards want you to believe! If you lose this job you will be fine! You will find a better one! Go do what you want to do now, and for God's sake stop complaining without doing anything! Go do your story and *then* complain!"

Kalyan downed his tea in one gulp and jumped down from the wall. "Let's go back. And don't you dare talk to me again until you have started working on your transgender story."

Harsha jumped down and followed him, still feeling slightly dazed at the severe talking-to. But he also suddenly felt much, much lighter, and the catch in his throat had vanished.

6. *Advocate*

Harsha was pleasantly nervous as he stood outside the Madras High Court building, waiting for his interviewee to arrive. He looked around appreciatively at the old colonial era building and tried to calm his thoughts by wondering what sort of cases would have been heard here back in the day under the Raj. Would the judges and magistrates all have been British? It was something to look into maybe, he thought idly, as he stared at the beautiful neem trees that ringed the garden around the building.

He snapped out of his reverie when the courtroom door banged open and a group of middle-aged to elderly men came bursting out, lawyers looking slightly ridiculous in their long flowing black cloaks (Harsha was a bit disappointed by the total absence of wigs) and some other men looking smart in their suits.

One of the latter came confidently up to him and said: "Harsha Devnath?"

Harsha stood up immediately, looked over his interviewee and smiled. "Hello, sir, how are you?"

"I'm Gopu. Short for Gopinath," the man said smartly.

He took Harsha's proffered hand and shook it firmly. "Let's go get some coffee," he said, and started walking at a brisk pace down the old corridor.

Harsha struggled to keep up and took a second to process his first impressions of Gopu. He was a tall, wiry man with large square spectacles that were slightly tinted so that they gave a dark aspect to his eyes. His hair was greying and thin but combed smartly across his head. He was probably well over 60, but still stood erect, marching down the corridor with a sprightly step.

Harsha liked him immediately but also felt slightly scared of him — adding to his overall nervousness of this situation. He reminded himself of Pipal Resorts and the far scarier encounters he had had there to give himself some courage.

They arrived at the high court canteen, which was buzzing with friendly chatter, and Harsha asked politely: "Are you participating in a case here, sir?"

Gopu shook his head and then waved to one of the waiters and then they sat down in a table in one corner. "Not this time. I used to be a lawyer for many years, but now I am just here as an observer for the government — as the business secretary of the state of Tamil Nadu. The Sevillon case."

Harsha nodded, as he pulled out his notepad, put it down on the table (after checking it was clean) and tested the point of his pencil. It was a high profile case indeed — the European pharmaceutical giant wanted Indian companies to stop manufacturing "generic" versions of its far more expensive drug. If it got its way, many poor Indians would be priced out of certain treatments.

"What is your view on the case, sir?" Harsha asked,

curious. "Just between us of course — I am not reporting on this," he added, hurriedly, pointedly putting his pencil down.

"Officially, the TN government is against Sevillon preventing Indians from accessing drugs essential to their health," Gopu declared. There was a pause as the waiter came up, and they both ordered coffee.

"And unofficially?" Harsha persisted.

Gopu's eyes twinkled. "Well, unofficially, and this is not for publishing — Sevillon spends millions of dollars on research and development — we don't want to disincentivise them from doing that by not giving them their due. As usual, we will find a middle ground — probably some sort of fee that the Indian producers can pay Sevillon. There was a time when even that was not possible in India. But we become stronger," he said, forming a steeple with his fingers and looking over them at Harsha. "But that's not why you are here, is it, Harsha?"

Harsha shook his head. "I am here to talk about transgender people, sir. And I am particularly interested in why you have taken up their cause."

Gopu leaned back and looked around the packed canteen, a slightly sardonic smile on his face. "Taken up their cause! Strong words!" he said, finally, turning his gaze back on Harsha. "What cause is that, my friend?"

Harsha looked confusedly back at him and then said: "Er, the cause for transgenders, I suppose?"

Gopu nodded and then stared at the tips of his fingers, clearly considering his words carefully. "You see, we are not talking about a cause. We are talking about science. Sometimes a man is born in the body of a woman. Sometimes a woman is born in the body of a man. You only have to look at the scientific evidence. And then they have a choice —

either they accept they are in the wrong body, or they try to change it."

He looked up to see Harsha taking notes furiously, leaning over his notepad, and smiled at the young man's bent head.

"Is that shorthand? Very impressive. Anyway," Gopu continued, "It is not in the purview of the government to argue with science. I am just adjusting our policies accordingly. Thank you," he said to the waiter, who had arrived with two cups of coffee, and both interviewer and interviewee stepped back and breathed for a second. Gopu looked across at Harsha with a slight, and it seemed to Harsha, a self-satisfied smile. But who would begrudge him that?

"You say it is science. Is that a fact?" Harsha asked.

"Oh yes. Do you know about... well, have you read anything on this topic?"

Harsha shook his head, feeling irrationally underprepared. But you couldn't read books before every single interview as a journalist, or you would never get anything done.

"I have several books in my office. I keep them there so I don't antagonise my wife," Gopu said, chuckling. "Come by sometime, you can borrow them anytime."

"And so, what exactly is the rule change that you have overseen, sir?" Harsha asked, after the waiter went away.

"Call me Gopu. The rule change is very straightforward. I've just reiterated to the civil service that we cannot discriminate against people in government employment on the basis of gender. That rule already exists. All I've done is put it down on record that this also includes discriminating on the basis of *trans*gender. A very small change," he said.

"A small change with big implications."

Gopu nodded benignly and then said: "The principle is simple, Harsha. Do you know what the Canadian government said when they legalised homosexuality?"

Harsha shook his head.

"They didn't go on about equality and human rights or any such grandiose thing. They simply said: the government has no business deciding what people do in their bedrooms. I would extend that statement here to say: the government has no business deciding what can and cannot go on within people's underclothing." He gave a dry cackle at his own statement and Harsha couldn't help grinning in response.

He briefly thought to himself that lawyers — or former lawyers as in this case — always made for a slick interview; they certainly had a way with words. They could, however, also slip out of answering questions equally well and sometimes turn them around on the interviewer, making it a bit of a mixed experience for journalists.

"Let me ask you something, Harsha," Gopu said, on cue. "How long have you been a journalist?"

"Uh... for a few years, sir. I worked at *The Times* in London before coming here to take up this job about a year ago," Harsha replied. "But I wanted to ask..."

"London! Ah," Gopu said, smiling. "Now why don't you tell me, Harsha, what is the attitude towards transgenders in the UK? One would imagine it is a more advanced country in terms of human rights?"

Harsha thought deeply about it and then said: "To be perfectly honest, I had no idea about it until I did some research this week. From what I can see, there seem to be some arguments between feminists and transgender people. Well, more like fights. It's a different problem to the one here, in my view. But it can be pretty ugly as well."

Gopu nodded. "We in India are still at a stage where many people find the whole concept disgusting, or against our principles. Not all of us — but many." He leaned forward and put one hand on the table and fixed Harsha with his eye and said: "But what if I tell you we can skip a whole stage, learn from how the West has gone about it and do even better? We can develop our views more rapidly and skip all the painful fights they are still having over there? Technology, and the indomitable spirit of Indians, the warmth of our culture, these things we can use as weapons in the fight for human rights! We can become the best in the world — better than England or anywhere else!"

Harsha was getting dragged into Gopu's enthusiastic view of the world and was struggling to maintain his journalistic professionalism, so he decided to get back down to earth. He looked down at his list of questions for inspiration.

"And have there been any transgender employees in the government, Gopu?" he asked, going for the most direct one of them all.

"We had a couple of recruitments in the Secretariat, but they didn't make it through probation. But — it's a start," Gopu said.

"They didn't make it through probation?" Harsha asked, pausing and looking up with a slight frown.

A shadow fell across Gopu's face. "I think you have to understand, Harsha, that these things take time. We recruited some people. That was a great start. It did not work out, but we learn and we move forward." Gopu stopped talking, blew lightly on his coffee and took a tiny sip, his little finger poking out daintily as he held it.

"Can you put me in touch with them?"

"I'll have my secretary look into it. But I'm not sure we can send you too many details — data protection," Gopu said, urbanely.

Harsha would have loved to have drilled down into this a little bit more, but it looked like Gopu was unwilling to elaborate, and Harsha's confidence as a journalist wasn't yet at a level where he felt able to persist further.

Instead, he also took a sip of his cup and luxuriated in the glorious taste of South Indian filter coffee. It, along with *dosai*, was one of the great pleasures of coming back to live in Chennai. He took another sip and then said: "Was it difficult to get this through the civil service? Didn't the politicians object? Surely members of parliament aren't going to stick their necks out for such a controversial cause? I even heard some of them call you 'the pervert'."

Gopu shook his head at this.

"Some of them do. But others are open to hearing the arguments — you may be surprised at how open many of them are. You must not have outdated ideas about Indian politicians," he said sternly.

"I promise you, I have an open mind, sir," Harsha said.

Gopu drank his coffee, his eyes on Harsha and said: "Can I talk on background?" Harsha nodded and put his pencil down. "Politicians are politicians," Gopu said, leaning forward and dropping into a conspiratorial tone. "This country is modelled on the British system. It is run by the civil service. I have been a lawyer for three decades and a civil servant for one. I think I know how to get things done."

Harsha smiled and then said: "And how does your family feel about all this, sir? Gopu?"

Gopu laughed softly. "Harsha, if I wanted to make my

family happy, I would have retired years ago, sat on my rocking chair, fallen asleep over *The Hindu* crossword and played bridge every evening at Mylapore Club," he said, shortly. "My wife thinks I am growing old and that she should have fed me more *murungakkai* back in the day to prevent my premature senility. My daughter thinks I am going mad and keeps telling me to go to the Ashtalakshmi temple to pray for my brains to come back."

Harsha chuckled and looked up at Gopu's bright eyes. Certainly he could detect no such signs of senility. In fact, the man looked bright, alert and fit. Harsha wouldn't have been surprised if he stood up and ran a marathon right then and there.

"Seriously, though? How do they feel?" he asked, insistently.

Gopu shrugged his shoulders. "Every day is another step in the journey," he said diplomatically. "And not just for my family — for me as well. I learn something new about the subject every day, by talking to new people or reading new books."

"What are you reading at the moment, sir?" Harsha said, asking the question closest to his heart at all times.

Gopu smiled. "It is not a scientific book — it is called *I am Vidya* — a new English translation of a memoir by a transgender person from Chennai."

"And is it good?"

"It is excellent — very gripping. The first few pages describes her journey to Mumbai to get a sex change operation. Hard hitting," Gopu said. "If you come by my office I will lend it to you once I am done with it. Just don't let my wife know that I am spreading propaganda like this," he finished, laughing.

"Is it that bad?" Harsha asked.

"It is marriage — so yes!" Gopu responded without pausing for breath.

Harsha grinned in response, though he thought he caught an undertone of seriousness to Gopu's remarks.

"Is it worth it, sir?" he asked, frankly.

Gopu looked at him directly and for a length of time before saying with conviction: "Absolutely."

The waiter wandered over with the bill. Gopu waved Harsha's offer away and said instead: "Would you like something to eat? They have fantastic *dosai* here. I always feel uncomfortable if I meet a journalist and don't at least attempt to bribe them a little."

Harsha laughed again and said: "Certainly, Gopu."

"One plain *dosai* and one onion *uthappam*. Just cut it in two and serve it in separate plates," Gopu said to the waiter, who bobbed his head vigorously. "You must try both," he added, to Harsha.

"Thank you Gopu," Harsha said sincerely. "I have really enjoyed meeting you. I expected this to be quite a serious meeting, but I like your sense of humour!"

"Young man," Gopu said, leaning forward and looking at his companion seriously. "If there's one thing I've learnt in life — it's that you must always keep your sense of humour. Life has ups and downs. But your ability to laugh — that will always be there with you, like a superpower."

Harsha felt a gush of affection for the man sitting opposite him and then tried to quell it to maintain his professionalism.

"What brought about your interest in this story, Harsha?" Gopu asked with a slightly avuncular air.

Harsha briefly told him about the incident at the

restaurant and his subsequent encounter with Gita.

Gopu nodded gloomily. "For some reason, this issue is rife in the hospitality sector. I think many of the transgender community tend to be working there," he said. "What was the name of this person?"

"Gita, and I think her name before was Gokul," Harsha said.

"Gokul... Gokul..." Gopu said, tapping his lip with one finger as he searched his memory. "Oh of course! Very sharp — quite intelligent. Not going down the route of begging or drug abuse like some others. Too intelligent for menial jobs of course, but impossible for her to aspire to... well," Gopu said, with a wry twist of his lips. "If it had been her who had got one of the first few jobs in government, it might have been different."

Harsha sat up at this, struck by an idea. "I believe she is looking for a job now. Do you think she might be able to apply for any positions here?" he asked.

Gopu looked slightly uncomfortable, but he smiled and said: "I don't believe we have any vacancies at the moment, but I will keep you posted," he said finally. He fished in his pocket and pulled out an old leather wallet, leafed through a few business cards and finally fished one out and gave it to Harsha. "Try Mithra, she works for the Aravanigal Society of Chennai. A charitable trust. She may be able to help."

"Aravanigal?" Harsha asked, taking the card and frowning at it. His Tamil had improved substantially over the past year as he reacquainted himself with one of his two mother tongues, but that word was still unfamiliar to him.

"*Aravani* in Tamil means transgender, or near enough," Gopu explained. "There are a couple of groups in the city, such as ASoC and the Tamil Nadu Aravanigal Association that does great work in helping bring some of these people into mainstream society."

Harsha absentmindedly toyed with the card as he wondered how to ask his question without sounding rude. "What *happened* with the first few transgender employees, sir?" he asked finally, deciding not to beat around the bush.

"Oh, every time a new project begins, there are bound to be hiccups," Gopu said evasively. "But listen," he added, leaning forward. "The hospitality industry. I would start asking around there, especially if you have any contacts at all in that sector."

"I do have a friend who works in the industry," Harsha said, smiling to himself as he thought of Azhar's likely reaction if he asked for his help on yet another investigation. "But I'm not sure how helpful he will be."

"Why not? It is a worthy subject, is it not?"

"Oh no, Gopu, it's not that — I... well... I've already dragged him into a massive row in the past to do with my job, which ended up with his hotel being cordoned off by the police and whatnot."

Gopu looked intrigued, but at that point the waiter came by with the steaming plates of *dosai* and *uthappam,* adorned with *sambar* and an assortment of chutneys. Harsha's mouth watered.

"*Enna* Dorai, that arrived suspiciously early," Gopu said to the waiter in Tamil, a twinkle in his eye. "Are you sure it is freshly made?"

"Sir, we made it extra quick for you, specially. VIP treatment," the waiter said, with a flourish and a slight grin.

"I must be so important that you changed the laws of physics for my sake — thank you!"

The grinning waiter left and Harsha tucked into the *dosai,* which was divine even by Chennai standards.

"So what was the row you dragged your friend into?"

Harsha laughed, swallowed a mouthful of *dosai* and said: "There was a murder in this resort which my friend runs in the Tamil Nadu-Andhra border, which obviously I had nothing to do with. But I happened to be staying there at the time and then I tried to do some amateur reporting into the case and somehow got involved in the investigation, along with other friends and, well…"

He paused, looking up at Gopu, who was watching him closely and said: "I'm not explaining myself very well. Let me just say that it ended with the police descending upon us, and some extremely dramatic events right on his hotel property. It was quite crazy, in the end," he said, reflecting briefly on the incredible events in Pipal Resorts about two years ago.

"And I guess that's how you have ended up here, and not in London?"

Harsha looked up at the man, and realised that Gopu had understood him and his motivations extremely well.

Almost as though to confirm this, Gopu then said: "You know what, Harsha? I have a feeling the transgender community here will end up being very grateful for having you on the case."

7. *Friends*

"Move, idiot! Go to the left. THE LEFT!" Harsha yelled at the television, while Paul amusedly bypassed Harsha's Porsche Cayman with his own lime green Ford Mustang and then raced off into the distance, leaving long dark skid marks on the tarmac road on the screen in front of them.

"How is this even possible? I'm the one who introduced you to this game and already you're better than me?" Harsha said in irritation.

"Maybe if you relaxed a bit more?" Paul suggested. "Right now you're as prickly as an English porcupine," he said, giving that odd little laugh again.

"Fuck this game," Harsha said, flinging his controller down.

"Woah, hang on — careful with that controller!"

"I'll buy you a new one," Harsha said, moodily, crossing his arms and sitting up on the sofa.

Paul chuckled, paused the game and put his own pristine controller down on the coffee table. "Maybe *Need for Speed* isn't our game. Let's stick with *Alien vs Predator*. I think you are more in your element when you're blasting monsters into tiny pieces," he said.

The doorbell rang and the pair of them looked at each other in surprise. "Expecting anyone?" Harsha asked. Paul shook his head.

Harsha jumped down from the sofa and went to the front door and looked through the little viewing hole. It was obscured, so he opened the door a little cautiously.

"Surprise!"

Harsha's jaw dropped and the door swung wide open of its own volition. He stared out at the people crowded by the doorway, his heart lifting tremendously.

"What dude, why are you standing there like a fool?" Azhar asked, sauntering forward and tapping Harsha on the chest with his usual air of arrogance.

"Harsha's tongue is tied up in knots," grinned a tall, pudgy looking man in a checked shirt and jeans, a thin beard snaking its way around his round cheeks and a twinkle in his eye.

"Yo yo," said the third person, a dark-skinned woman wearing a black T-shirt that hung off her skinny frame. She gave him a casual nod of the head, though this nonchalance was belied by the delighted grin on her face.

"Shane! Juni!" Harsha turned to the man who was clearly the culprit for this night's escapade and said: "Azhar! Where did you unearth these clowns from?" Azhar was grinning affectionately at him, looking more like a college student than ever before, a Patagonia backpack straddling his powerful shoulders.

"Bugger, let us come in!" Azhar said. "We can't have a college reunion on your doorstep." He pushed his way past Harsha and walked into his living room, looking around with vague interest. "His flat has got a nice view," he said casually to the others.

Harsha led Shane and Junaina into his living room, and Junaina said: "Nice? This is better than nice! This is incredible!" She looked open-mouthed at the wide expanse of beach visible from Harsha's living room.

"It's good, isn't it?" Harsha said, modestly. "It's all down to Paul here — he's the one who found it."

Paul was standing by his bedroom door looking at all of them, a lazy smile on his face. Only intimate knowledge of his flatmate allowed Harsha to see the deep panic in the man's eyes as he surveyed this group of new people invading his home.

"Nice to meet you, Paul, I'm Azhar, an old friend of Harsha's. He has told me a lot about you," Azhar said, stepping forward and holding out a hand. Harsha smiled a little to himself. Azhar had an effortless charm that allowed him to make friends with almost anyone.

"Paul, this is Shane and this is Junaina, also known by everyone as Juni," Harsha said. "I went to university with these guys — and they are the ones from the resort adventure I told you about."

"Yeah, we were like the Famous Five," Shane said, giving his trademark chuckle that Harsha remembered so well, as he sat down on the arm of their sofa, one leg dangling in space.

"God, don't remind me of that madcap episode!" Junaina exclaimed, leaning against the wall and shaking her head in mock despair. "I turned up at this resort for a college reunion only to find these jokers knee deep in some crazy investigation into some jungle homicide or some such nonsense. Typical Azhar!"

"What the... I like *that*!" Azhar said indignantly,

thrusting out one arm dramatically toward Harsha to emphasise his point. "This fucker here was the one who insisted on dragging us all into that mad situation, even though I *repeatedly* tried to get him to stop, and then hello! *All* of you refused to leave when I expressly told you to get the hell out of my resort!"

"Harsha is as stubborn as a mule," Shane said, grinning.

"That he is!" Paul said, with a guffaw of laughter, as he edged further towards his bedroom. This instantly made Harsha jump slightly guiltily, as he realised that he had just assumed Paul would be all right with the invasion of his home in this manner.

"Is it alright if these guys hang out here for a while, Paul?" he asked, a little nervously.

"Oh please! Stay as long as you want... er... I'll just be in here," Paul said and ducked into his bedroom, shutting the door.

Azhar stared in surprise at the now-shut door and turned to the others, a look of comical surprise on his face. "I was just about to offer the guy a drink, where did he disappear off to?"

"That's his bedroom, fool, and he can do whatever he wants in his own house, can't he?" Junaina asked, pushing herself off the wall and coming forward to the sofa.

"What the... I *never* said..."

Harsha knew this would descend into an extended bickering session, so he cut in quickly and said: "Guys, I only have a couple of beers in the fridge. Azhar, do you think you could drive me down to the wine shop? We could get some..."

"Bugger, do you think we came empty handed?" Azhar asked, looking scandalised, and pulled off his backpack, and pulled out a bottle of Bacardi rum and some Coke, and a couple of large bottles of Heineken beer.

"Bacardi. Not bad," Junaina said, approvingly.

"Yeah, you'd have probably got Old Monk or some shit if I'd left it up to you," Azhar said scathingly.

"Don't be such a snob! Nothing wrong with a bit of Old Monk!" Junaina muttered defensively.

"I knew it!" Azhar declared before turning to Harsha, as though that argument were closed — as indeed it was, as far as Harsha was concerned. "All we need from you, Harry, is some ice and the way out to the beach here, so we can all sit down on your balcony and have a few drinks!"

"That I can do!" Harsha said happily.

"Does your flatmate want to join us?" Shane asked politely.

"Uh... I'll text him, but he's a bit of a lone wolf, and I don't want to disturb him," Harsha said a little uncomfortably. He knew that both Paul and he had tacitly agreed to have an "English" sort of relationship as flatmates — considering each other's room and personal space as sacrosanct, and he wondered if this mob would fully understand. To his relief none of them seemed particularly concerned.

Azhar did say: "He's quite a good-looking guy. Might be useful on a night out," but then seemed to lose interest in the subject.

"Speaking of which," Harsha said, and they all turned to him. "Are you guys sure you want to hang out here? I mean, it's pretty basic, nothing special and that..."

Shane smiled understandingly and said: "Azhar tells us you've been burning the midnight oil at your new job and with your new story, so we thought we would make life easy for you."

"Plus, who the fuck wants to socialise with the crowd in Chennai. Truly pathetic," Junaina said cuttingly. "The chances of meeting someone decent is less than zero."

"The chances of *you* meeting someone decent is zero, agreed," Azhar said as he banged Paul's ice trays violently on the kitchen countertop.

Harsha and Shane exchanged glances and grinned at each other. Azhar and Junaina would bicker under all circumstances — even if they were both caught in a burning building.

They went out onto the warmth of the terrace that overlooked the beach and sat down on the ramshackle patio furniture that Paul and Harsha had rustled up between them. They took sips from their drinks in peace for a second, enjoying the scene in front of them.

"Nice wind chimes," Shane said, ducking to avoid the little pipes dangling from the roof of the balcony, but looking at them with interest. They tinkled in the breeze just then.

Junaina put her feet up on the short wall that separated Harsha's terrace from the beach. "You could actually just jump straight off this onto the beach. Not that far up," she said, lazily.

"Are you mad? We're one floor up — at least 18 feet! You would break your legs," Azhar declared.

Harsha reflected to himself that he rarely — if ever — took full advantage of the beautiful apartment in which he lived, with its magnificent balcony looking out onto the beach. The ocean shimmered in the evening light and stretched out into the horizon, where it met the teal sky, a few thin, white clouds drifting across its rim. A few runners went by, jogging around one or two palm trees that waved in the breeze, and beyond them, a couple stood fully clothed and holding hands by the water, the edge of the woman's salwar kameez dipping into the oncoming waves. A bit to the right and in the distance, a group of fishermen hauled in the day's catch and dragged it up to the shacks that formed the little fishing village on the edge of Neelankarai.

"Stinks of fish," Azhar said unromantically.

No one paid any attention to him, and they chatted briefly of this and that, Junaina keeping them all entertained with her stories about working for an IT company in the United States. "Seriously guys, every American who works at Talent Technologies now can recognise the smell of *thayir sadam* and *vadu mankai*. Frikkin' Tam Brams have taken over the place," she said. "Even I can't bear it anymore and I'm Tam Bram myself! Thank god they allow me to work from the Chennai office sometimes. And then when the summer over here begins I quickly run back to the US!"

"Since when do you qualify as a Tam Bram! Tamil, maybe, but not sure smoking weed all day and listening to bloody Black Sabbath makes you Brahmin," Azhar snorted.

"Whatever, bitch, don't pretend you understand spirituality! Anyway, Harry, how are you settling into life back in India? I must admit, nice as it is to come back — it has its challenges!" Junaina said, smiling, and Harsha reflected that she had softened a lot since university. The caustic remarks were still there, but she let her warmth show a lot more these days.

He briefly considered confiding his deep sense of confusion and regret about the decision to come back to India and then decided to go for a moderated version of events.

"Well, you know, it's been a big challenge in many ways. But having this place helps," Harsha said, gesturing to indicate the terrace and the view of the beach. "Also, I've been working on a story that has given me some satisfaction."

Junaina cut in at this point, leaning forward from her chair and said: "Yes! Been meaning to talk to you about that! Azhar tells me you're off on another adventure! Trying to save some *chakkas* or something! Didn't you have enough last time round, when we nearly got killed off by that mob at our doorstep? Seriously, Harry you maniac, be *careful!*"

Harsha was both annoyed by her tone as well as touched by the note of concern in her voice.

"Can we not call them *chakkas*?" he asked finally, the annoyance winning out. "They are just people born in the wrong body, trying to be comfortable with who they are."

"Born in the wrong body? I mean, what is that all about? I can just decide to be a man tomorrow?" Junaina asked, shrugging her shoulders. "I guess I just don't get it."

An awkward silence fell over the group as the other two men sensed Harsha tensing at these words. The waves crashed against the shore and a few gulls cried out into the evening. Harsha took a deep breath and tried to think of a way to respond to this without patronising or lecturing Junaina in a way that would put her back up.

"I suggest you look up the science," he said finally, and realised by her expression that he had failed.

"I don't need to look up the science — I know a fad when I see one," Junaina said shortly.

"Seriously — a fad?"

"It's cool to be gender fluid or whatever they call it, isn't it? And now in the US they're starting to have all these gender neutral toilets. Absurd."

Azhar and Shane were looking from Harsha to Junaina

as they spoke, as though watching a tennis match. Harsha screwed his eyes shut and then opened them again to look at her.

"Junes — why would someone go through the trauma of changing their gender and facing all that discrimination and unwanted attention just for a fad?" he asked gently. "Also bear in mind that you're always telling us how hard it is to be a woman in a patriarchal society, and rightly so. Why would someone actively choose that?"

Junaina shrugged her shoulders. "Some people like attention and some people even like being victims," she said.

As he was considering his response, Azhar unexpectedly said: "I have to admit — I don't get this whole transgender thing either."

This was a body blow. Apart from the shock of Azhar and Junaina actually agreeing on something, Harsha was so used to being backed up by his best friend that this came as an absolute surprise. He turned to look at Azhar and found him looking apologetically back.

"Maybe it doesn't matter whether we *get it* or not. It's none of our business what gender someone chooses at the end of the day," Shane said philosophically and Harsha smiled gratefully at him. For a minute, he had wondered if any of his friends' views would align with his own.

"It's none of my business *until* someone with a dick wants to share my toilet," Junaina said in an irritated tone as she took a big slug of her rum and coke, the ice cube tinkling as they bumped into each other in her glass.

"Better not get married then. Not that anyone would want to marry you," Azhar said caustically and Harsha recognised that he was trying to lighten the tone of the conversation. For once, Junaina didn't take the bait, instead downing her drink and looking out into the ocean, which had turned a dark blue as dusk approached.

Shane leaned forward, looking at Harsha earnestly, and said: "To go back to the original point, I think we just want to make sure you're not getting yourself into trouble."

"Don't worry, guys, the only trouble I am getting into is with fashionistas and influencers — whatever that means — when our desk misspells their stupid names on photo captions," Harsha said moodily, picking up a cherry stone from his plate and flinging it out onto the beach. "I am yet to convince the news desk to publish anything on the subject of transgenders — so I'm just stuck doing stories about Deepika Padukone's latest hairstyle or whatever."

"Who the fuck is that?" Junaina asked.

"You don't know Deepika Padukone? Be more Westernised," Azhar said in an annoyed tone.

"The point is," Harsha cut in, "I am at a dead end, writing stories about fashion and rollerskates or whatever else the fuck."

So heavily did he say these words that a fresh pall fell over the group and they all fell silent, listening instead to the sound of the oncoming waves.

Finally, Junaina said: "Is there any more of that rum going?"

Azhar, who seemed to have taken over the hosting duties, went inside to replenish their supply of crisps and drinks. Shane gently turned to Harsha and asked in an off-hand manner: "Heard from Maya recently?"

Junaina froze in her position, staring out at the beach, but Harsha could almost sense her listening desperately for his answer.

But Harsha shook his head. "I know she is in Chennai,

but we agreed not to be in touch. So no. I don't even know what she's doing with her life."

Something of his pain must have come through in his voice, because Shane said, gently: "It was the right decision, Harsha. You were both very mature. She needed a bit of space to try and make her marriage work."

Junaina cleared her throat and they both looked at her. "Why are you looking at me?" she asked, looking slightly alarmed at their sudden scrutiny.

"Thought you were about to say something."

"Oh. Er… none of my business, but you know. I do think her husband is a bit of a loser."

"That's not the point, Juni," Shane said, giving her a rare frown, and she subsided. "If you must know, Harry, Maya is working for a charity on human rights. I think it's called Holding Hands or something."

"Good for her. At least she's doing something worthwhile," Harsha said, sinking further into gloom.

Fortunately, Azhar came out with a tray of drinks and snacks and the subject changed naturally. Taking a sip of his rum and coke, Harsha looked round at his old friends with great affection and gratitude. He may have been estranged from them for years, and they might infuriate him from time to time, but they always popped up when he most needed them. They almost made his crazy decision to come back to India seem right.

Of course, there was a big Maya-shaped hole in their gathering, but he shelved that for now. He would have to get used to that and get over her. And in the meantime, he had this trio, he thought to himself as he leaned forward to clink glasses with the gang.

8. Newspaper baron

Harsha sat gloomily in front of Namritha's desk — the place that was fast becoming his most hated spot in the world — and looked bleakly at her. She alternated between glaring at him and then at the monitor in front of her, as though trying to decide which made her angrier. Finally, she settled on him.

"The news desk forwarded me your story," she said, smiling, though it looked more like a grimace of sorts. "I must say, Harsha, I'm just a tad surprised you didn't come to me first," she said, with what sounded to him like an insincere titter.

"I thought you weren't interested," he said, listlessly. Kalyan had sounded so authoritative in his advice that Harsha should file his story about transgenders directly to the news team, but it had clearly got trapped in the political web and had sprung back to his own line manager.

And there it would stay, Harsha thought to himself, *irrespective of its quality*.

"Oh I am *interested*, of course; sorry if I gave you the impression that I wasn't," she said, tittering again. "A very worthy cause! Let me see if I can find space for it at some stage. It's looking a little busy at the moment. How's that skateboarding piece coming on?"

As Namritha's piercing eyes flashed at Harsha through her pointy-shaped plastic-rimmed glasses, it was easy to picture her as a spider in a web. She was clearly holding this transgender story over his head in order to get him to do the stories that she wanted him to do. What were the chances that one would lead to the other? Practically zero, Harsha thought gloomily. But what else could he do?

"I think Anwar already has the pictures, I just have to write it up. Which I shall do this afternoon," he said, privately realising that in the battle with Namritha, he had blinked first.

A slightly smug smile appeared on her bright pink lips, and she turned back to her screen.

"Shall we say in about an hour?" she said, not even looking at him, knowing the argument was won.

Harsha got out of his chair heavily and was about to leave when Chinmay, the graphic designer, suddenly barged into the office, breathing heavily.

"Chinmay! What…" Namritha began, half getting up, astonished by this gross breach of protocol.

"*Arre* Harsha *bhaiyya!*" the man said excitedly, and Harsha smiled, reflecting how absurdly young the graphic designer looked (and probably was) considering he worked in a full-time job at a newspaper.

"What is it, Chints?" Harsha was on great terms with all the non-reporters at *Southern Echo*, finding them much easier to get on with than his fellow hacks, barring Kalyan.

"The boss wants to talk to you! Now!"

"What boss?" Harsha and Namritha chorused, Harsha in confusion and Namritha in consternation.

"The *big* boss, *yaar*. Jaishree madam!"

Jaishree Verma was the owner and chief editor of the newspaper, and usually based in Bangalore, though she also spent time in the other main cities of the four Southern states — Chennai, Hyderabad and Trivandrum.

"Why on earth would she want to talk to me?" Harsha asked, in genuine astonishment. He glanced at Namritha and saw his own feelings reciprocated on her face.

"It's this Padmnabhan fellow! He was killed!"

"Are you raving, Chints? Or do you have the wrong person? I have no idea what you're talking about."

"*Arre*," Chinmay said, hopping on one foot and then the other. "Just come! Hurry! She wants you there now! You can't keep the boss waiting!"

Despite knowing that Kalyan would object to unseemly haste in the face of a summons from management, Harsha still hurried, picking up his folder and following Chinmay out through the glass door. He glanced back at Namritha and couldn't help grinning to himself at her look of baffled fury. The skateboarding piece would have to wait.

He had no idea what the boss wanted with him, but clearly it didn't make Namritha happy. And that in itself was enough to perk Harsha up.

Chinmay led him to the other end of the office to a glossy, full-length conference room that dominated one side of the newsroom.

Luxuriant plants dotted the massive office space, and a large screen loomed above a boardroom-style table, presumably to allow for power point presentations to be displayed at four times their usual size. This was where editorial meetings were usually held — Harsha was not senior enough to attend any, but he had seen Namritha surreptitiously check herself in her little mirror before putting on a smile and marching towards one of them.

To one side of this was a smaller wooden desk where the big bosses usually sat; on this occasion, Jaishree Verma was perched there, her square chin resting on one strong hand. Rahul Medappa, the chief editor of the publication, was with her. They were deep in conversation, Rahul's slim frame forming a sharp contrast to his boss's bulkier presence.

Chinmay gave Harsha a thumbs up and quietly slipped away towards his own section of the newsroom, and Harsha walked up to the glass doorway, his heart beating slightly.

He knocked on the door, and that odd, tinny sound of knuckle on glass filled the room as he pushed his way in.

Rahul looked up and smiled cheerfully at Harsha. "Come on in, Harry!" he said. Harsha hadn't realised they were on nickname terms — in fact he had only really spoken to him once: at his job interview, which was coincidentally also the only time he had ever visited this room.

He approached the desk with mingled apprehension and curiosity.

"Sit down, Harry," Rahul said breezily, and Harsha complied. He looked up to see the *Southern Echo*'s owner eyeing him speculatively, and he had a fleeting impression of intelligence behind those heavy eyelids. He knew only a little about the woman who was responsible for paying all their salaries. She was from Kerala, and had inherited a lot of property-related wealth — Kerala being one of the few Indian states where inheritance was matrilineal — and had then married even richer.

She had decided, of all the business enterprises that were available as options, to start a newspaper. Many people unfairly thought that her husband, an information technology entrepreneur, was the brains behind the operation, but everyone at *Southern Echo* knew better.

"You must be wondering why you are here," Rahul said, and Harsha turned to him. The chief editor was leaning back and toying with a pencil as he spoke. "The fact is — a rather incredible crime has occurred and it is connected to something you are working on."

Harsha felt a thrill of foreboding. Was it poor Gita? Or was it one of the skateboarders he had interviewed? Who was this mysterious Padmanabhan?

"It is a senior government official — M. L. Gopinath. I believe you met him recently?"

"I did, yes, Rahul. Is he alright?" Harsha's heart was thumping again. Clearly Chinmay had got the name wrong, and who was to blame him — all these long South Indian names sounded so similar.

"I'm afraid not — he died in his office yesterday. The police were keeping it quiet, but Sampath heard it from a source," Rahul said, referring to *Southern Echo*'s main crime reporter. "And it is a suspicious death as well, his source said."

Harsha did not expect the wave of sadness that swept over him at this news. Gopu had been a striking, intelligent and charming man. He pictured him striding to the canteen and ordering coffee from the friendly waiter, a slightly crooked smile on his face. Harsha bowed his head and stared down at the floor.

"In any case," Rahul continued, and Harsha's face jerked up and he looked bleakly at his editor. "You were the last journalist to meet him. We would like you to write something. Perhaps an obituary of some sort." He leaned forward and tapped his pencil on the desk as he continued:

"Gopinath was an important official. He was a strong advocate for human rights and environmental causes. He made a lot of people angry. This is going to be a *big* story. I believe you were writing something about transgender jobs in government? If you could broaden it out a little..."

Jaishree unfolded her arms and Rahul fell silent. Harsha had a brief moment in which his sadness was superseded by a thrill of pleasure that his story would run after all. This was then followed by a stab of guilt for feeling this way in the aftermath of a good man's death.

Then Jaishree spoke, and all other thoughts fled away. "Harsha — you did a good job in that Arasur murder case," the owner of *Southern Echo* said, and Harsha went red with pleasure.

Rahul's head snapped towards Harsha in shock and he said: "That was you? Oh, I didn't..." He saw Jaishree cock an eyebrow at him and he said: "Oh, oh, of course! I remember... just didn't make the connection immediately... a lot going on... thought it was your... yes, yes of course," he stammered.

Harsha didn't have much sympathy for Rahul. It was in this very room that he had mapped out his credentials and had talked extensively about the story that had changed his journalistic career. How had the editor completely forgotten? Or perhaps he hadn't been listening at all?

Jaishree shook her head ever so slightly, before mastering her exasperation and saying to Harsha: "It was a good bit of journalism. Do you think you could help with a similar project here?"

"I ... ye... absolutely, Jaishree!" Harsha said, stumbling over his own words in his excitement.

"You see," Jaishree continued, her eyes boring into

Harsha again. "Sampath tells us an old friend of yours happens to be in charge of this investigation."

"An old friend of mine?" Harsha asked, thinking wildly of Azhar and Shane and wondering what on earth anyone like them could have to do with this. He was bewildered for a second and then light dawned. "Not Inspector Palanivel?" he asked incredulously.

"*Detective* Inspector Palanivel. His success with the murder case that you know so well earned him a promotion and a return to Chennai."

Has anybody not come back to Chennai? Harsha asked himself.

Rahul butted in and said: "Sampath has good contacts with the police but he doesn't know this fellow, as he has been away from Chennai for some time. It's a real bonus to us that you have a relationship with him." He nodded encouragingly, as though this had been his plan all along and that he hadn't completely forgotten this crucial detail about Harsha's usefulness to the paper on this story.

The problem, of course, was that Palanivel was an unpredictable character, but Harsha's ambition and desire to write something meaningful was too great for him to make such an admission. Instead, he found himself saying: "I feel certain that he will be happy to resume our relationship. He was a reliable contact and an intelligent man."

Jaishree was scanning him carefully, and Harsha had the uncomfortable feeling that she could see through his bluster, but all she did was put her pudgy fingers together and sigh before saying: "I will be honest with you, Harsha. *Southern Echo* is struggling to get a foothold here in Chennai. The old timers read *The Hindu* or *Indian Express* and all the young folks read *The Times of India* or *Deccan Chronicle*. What we need is a big scoop — a really juicy story that gets everyone talking about us and a story that gives us an *identity*. This could be that story. Gopinath was extremely well connected in government — both in Tamil Nadu and in Delhi — and across the top law circles. This story is *big*. And you would be helping to put *Southern Echo* on the map as a newspaper that does serious politics and does it *fast*. A newspaper that captures that zeitgeist of the times — and does not shy away from controversy. You can have no doubt that you will be very well regarded if you succeed. What do you say — will you help us?"

Harsha almost stood up and saluted, such was the gentle force of Jaishree's rhetoric.

"I'd be delighted, Jaishree," he said, instead.

Jaishree nodded and then said: "You'll work with Sampath on this story. I will have a word with Namritha and ask her if she can spare you for a few days."

Despite everything and all the conflicting feelings going through Harsha at the moment, the one unalloyed bright spot was the glorious thought of not having to work with Namritha for a few days.

9. Fort St George

It was a strange thing, Harsha thought to himself, that he had grown up in Chennai, but never visited its birthplace – until now.

The company car ran smoothly up Anna Salai, passing between the statues of Periyar and King George glowering at each other from across the bridge, and past the snaking arms of the Kuvam river towards Fort St George.

A towering flagpole was the first thing that Harsha saw, with the Indian tricolour rippling in the salty sea breeze. Back in the day, it would have flown the Union Jack, or the French tricolor, depending on which of India's many colonisers were enjoying success at that point in time.

Fort St George itself had been built by the British in the 17th century and the town of Chennai had grown around it, unlike many of India's other historic cities that had been repurposed by the British rather than developed by them.

But it was so much more than just one military building. In its heyday, it had been a little town within itself, with a mint, police station, barracks, hospital and a house where Arthur Wellesley, later to become the Duke of Wellington and the Prime Minister of Britain, had once reportedly stayed.

True to form, many of the old buildings had been repurposed or fallen into disrepair. The complex now housed the secretariat, where many of Tamil Nadu's civil servants worked; this was Harsha's destination.

As they approached one of its several entrances, St Thomas Gate – so named because it led to the erstwhile Portuguese settlement of Santhome further south – Harsha saw that it was crawling with security personnel. Harsha couldn't quite picture anyone getting in who wasn't supposed to be there.

He cleared his throat and turned to Sampath, *Southern Echo*'s crime reporter, who was sitting next to him in the back of the car. "How on earth would anyone have got in here?" he asked.

Sampath shrugged. "We don't know anything about this matter yet," he said.

Sampath was a short, trim little man with thin hair and an impressive moustache, which formed a little curtain over his teeth when he smiled, which was often. Harsha had liked him on sight but was sure he detected a sense of reserve.

There was a class divide between them, but Harsha suspected it was more to do with the fact that this story was in Sampath's patch, and he couldn't have liked having an extra reporter foisted on him, particularly given what notorious back-stabbers journalists generally were.

Harsha wished he could express to him that he had no desire to supersede Sampath in the editors' affections; he simply wanted to be part of the story, and not dominate it.

But there was no way of bringing this subject up without any provocation so Harsha just tried to be as nice as possible to Sampath, which, to be fair, was not hard.

Their car was waved through security mainly thanks to the large "Press" sticker lodged on the windshield and they went through into the fort complex.

Harsha looked around at the streets in awe, feeling a little thrill at the air of dilapidated grandeur that still hung around the place. He had just enough time to take in the spire of the 17th century St Mary Church – the largest Anglican church east of the Suez Canal – before they drove up to the main square that stood in front of the gleaming white building that was the original hub of Fort St George.

A chill went down Harsha's spine as he looked at this ancient edifice. It seemed to symbolise the Raj in every way. Would he have ever gone to live in England if this episode in history hadn't happened? Would he even be speaking and thinking in English?

"Let's go before the police officers take their lunch break – who knows when they come back from that," Sampath said, cutting into his thoughts. "Thank you, Ramu – we won't be long," he added and scrambled out of the car.

Harsha hastily followed him, slamming the door shut after a quick nod of gratitude towards the smiling driver, who then manoeuvred the car under a large tamarind tree, turned off the engine and leaned back in his seat with the air of someone prepared to wait indefinitely.

"So, we have not published anything yet, Sampath?" Harsha asked as they walked up towards the Secretariat, which was situated in an entirely different, much more modern building with large glass panelling, elaborate pillars and a neat lawn at its feet.

"No, we decided to hold the story until we found out if it was a murder or not. All my source was able to tell me was that Gopinath had died in his office and Detective Inspector

A. Palanivel had been assigned to look at this case. We still don't know if it is a homicide case," he said.

"Oh!" said Harsha in surprise. "Rahul said it was a suspicious death?"

The expression of distaste on Sampath's face spoke volumes of his opinion about their esteemed chief editor. Harsha's insides jumped. What if it was just a normal death, a heart attack or something? He felt that familiar mix of contradictory emotions – relief from a personal standpoint and disappointment from a journalistic point of view.

"There is a small risk that some other papers may find out before us about the Gopinath death, but still that's fine if they get that story and miss the bigger story that it is a murder," Sampath continued, wiping his face vigorously with a handkerchief as they made their approach to one of the main doors that led into the fort. It was an extremely warm day, and both of them were sweating within minutes of leaving the air-conditioned office car that Jaishree had ordered to be left at their disposal.

"Let me do the talking," Sampath said confidently as they approached the guards at the entrance, and Harsha was more than happy to concede this point. He was completely out of his element here.

The guards at the entrance to the Secretariat had that ultra-vigilant air of security people everywhere in the immediate aftermath of a breach in security.

Sampath exchanged pleasantries with one of them, who was clearly an old crony.

Harsha was a bit too nervous and excited to pay attention, but he soon cottoned on that they were discussing some Tamil movie he hadn't seen, and he felt this was something he needed to remedy, if only to have something to talk to people about.

"Typical Vimal! He always gets the best new actresses to work with..." Harsha tuned out again, but then his ears pricked up when Sampath chortled and then casually nodded his head towards the inside of the building and said: "Any chance we will get a quick look?"

The policeman was mid-chuckle, so the pair of them waited until he subsided and then he said: "Ok, ok, but only ten minutes. Tell them I said you are ok."

Sampath nodded his thanks casually but Harsha couldn't help but thank the man effusively, earning him a slightly concerned look from both the guards. Harsha tripped on the stairs as they made their way towards the door of the building, where a policewoman scanned their press passes and then waved them in.

They walked through a crowded but silent foyer towards the section of the building indicated by the guards. Harsha scanned the nearby doors and windows for entry points, with a vague recollection of James Bond movies and playing the *Hitman* video game. He finally concluded that there were probably a million different ways to break into this building that he hadn't even considered, and gave up.

A receptionist pointed them towards a long corridor, and they quickly headed in that direction.

There was a buzz of activity as civil servants and police all marched up and down the corridor, talking to each other and carrying papers to and fro. Harsha proceeded along the stone floor as confidently as he could and said: "Looks like anyone could have got in here. I was doing some reading up, and there are these groups that wanted Gopu's blood for..." Harsha trailed off as Sampath stopped in his tracks and turned to him. "What is it, Sampath? Did I say something wrong?" he asked concernedly as he faced the smaller man in the middle of that long, echoing corridor.

Sampath looked to either side to make sure no one was listening — no one seemed even to acknowledge their existence — and then said: "Harsha, do you mind if I give you some advice?"

"Of course not."

"When you are reporting on crime, it is very tempting to try and *solve* the crime. But that's not our job. That's not what we are here for. We are only here to report what we see and hear, and to try and get information that other papers don't have. It's not a novel where the journalist is a crime fighter." He seemed to realise that he was sounding a little patronising, because he stopped and said: "Don't take this the wrong way. It is just my little advice to you."

Harsha nodded and put one hand on his colleague's shoulder and said: "Sampath, I appreciate it a lot. I am here to learn from you and you have already taught me a valuable lesson."

Sampath gave his trademark grin and the two of them continued their way towards the entrance to a cordoned-off room where all the activity seemed centred.

"From the press," Sampath said in a bored voice that Harsha felt sure was cultivated, while they both flashed their passes.

A hefty, expressionless policeman said: "Press can't go in. Please wait here, and the inspector may be free to brief you later."

"We have written permission," Sampath said in an insistent manner, though he didn't raise his voice an iota.

The policeman just shook his head again, but Harsha at that point caught the eye of someone he recognized passing by the doorway inside the room.

"Constable Gautami!" he called out, and a policewoman reappeared in his line of vision and looked out of the doorway curiously. Her eyes met Harsha's. She looked exactly the same as Harsha remembered her from his resort adventure, with her snub-nose and her bored-looking eyes, but the drab brown police uniform had been replaced with a more formal pant suit that better showed off her slim frame, and she had one button undone on her crisp white shirt, showing a little triangle of brown skin.

Gautami's eyes widened and Harsha wondered for one panicked second if she would blank him completely, but instead she came out of the room and looked at him carefully, before saying formally: "Good morning, Mr Devnath." Her face then relented into a smile and she added: "Why should I be surprised that you would pop up wherever there is a murder?"

Sampath and Harsha had been waiting outside the room for maybe twenty minutes when finally the door that said "M. L. Gopinath, IAS" opened and the man who had been in Harsha's thoughts for the last two days stepped out and looked resignedly at the two journalists.

Harsha thought that, if anything, Detective Inspector A. Palanivel looked even trimmer than he remembered. In fact, there was a hint of gauntness about his cheeks. But the moustache was as neat as ever and he was immaculately fitted out in a shirt and khaki trousers, complete with a thin leather belt. Only his slightly scuffed shoes showed any signs of wear.

"Mr Devnath," he said, resignedly. "Gautami was not joking." There was no trace of humour on his face as he said this.

"Good to see you again.. uh… *Detective* Inspector," Harsha said, scrambling up from the narrow bench where the pair of them had been sitting, and holding out his hand. "This is…"

"Sampath Kumar," Palanivel said smoothly, transferring his hand from Harsha's to Sampath's. "Used to work for *Dina Thanthi*. Then got poached by an English paper, what was it? *Southern Echo*? Interesting."

"Pleasure to meet you, sir," Sampath said, and Harsha envied him the confidence of his manner. Sampath sounded like (and was) a seasoned journalist.

"How can I help you today, gentlemen?"

"We were just hoping for a few more details on the murder, sir," Sampath said, in that same offhand tone, flipping open his notebook. "When did it occur?"

Harsha was full of admiration for this tactic but could have told Sampath that Palanivel was too sharp for that.

"Who told you it was a murder, Mr Sampath?" the policeman asked, his brows contracting.

"The other lady. Gautami, I think?" Sampath said, nodding to Harsha.

Palanivel paused for a second and then said: "I think Gautami was referring to the last time we encountered Mr Devnath here. It was during a murder investigation. We have not made any such decision about this case."

"Quite a lot of police here for a straightforward death," Sampath said, mildly.

"He was a senior government official; we have to be thorough and check for any suspicious circumstances," returned Palanivel, his face completely deadpan.

If Sampath was frustrated at not getting the confirmation he needed, he didn't show it for a second.

Instead, he asked: "Can we get five minutes in the room?"

Palanivel pursed his lips as though puzzled. "It is just a room, Mr Sampath. There is nothing special about it."

Sampath nodded, as though agreeing, and said: "I know. But our boss wants us to be able to tell him we saw the inside of the room. If you just let us have a quick glance, we will be on our way. Then you can confirm or deny if it is a murder investigation at a later stage."

Palanivel hesitated for the first time, then turned to Harsha instead and said: "Well, Mr Devnath? Is that what you want as well? Just to look into the room?"

Harsha's insides jangled. Clearly the policeman felt he could read him better than he could Sampath, and his beady eyes were now boring into Harsha's skull, it felt like. What could he say that was correct?

"It doesn't have to be both of us, sir. We are going to file a story and just want to get as much detail as we can," Harsha said, and then, glancing at Sampath, he felt he could risk a little bit more. "One way or another, we are going to write a story, inspector. We might as well just write one that's as accurate as possible."

It was a calculated risk, but the offer to let Palanivel have some control over the story must have been a tempting one, because the inspector pursed his lips again and then cocked his head towards the door and said: "Five minutes."

Harsha felt the adrenaline pumping through his veins, but he arranged his expression into something resembling a professional one and nodded. He followed the inspector, though Sampath did give him a tiny wink before inviting him to go first with a dramatic sweep of his arm.

10. Crime scene

Harsha had a sudden and horrible worry that Gopu's body would still be in the room, and he briefly felt his gorge rise before stepping into the room and sighing with tremendous relief upon realising that it was empty of any dead bodies. There was a stale smell to the air that he decided not to think too much about.

There were plenty of living people, though. On one side, two people in hazmat suits were busy scanning one corner of the room, using what looked like cotton buds to take out little bits of dust. It looked like a scene out of the American crime series CSI, and it surprised Harsha with its level of sophistication. Maybe he had underestimated the level of advancement of Indian policing.

On the other side, Constable Gautami was deep in conversation with a uniformed policeman, who was nodding and taking notes as she spoke, and Harsha smiled to himself, remembering the crucial role she had played in bringing Lakshmi's killer to justice with her undercover acting. It had genuinely been like something out of a spy film.

Palanivel was now leaning against a table with another

policeman and the two of them were contemplating the room. Sampath sauntered over to the pair of them and leaned against the same table, seemingly oblivious to the slightly frosty reception. Harsha heard him make some casual remark, still keeping the same relaxed air which was clearly his *modus operandi* as a journalist.

This left Harsha slightly at a loose end, but he took out his notebook, leaned against the door and made some notes on the room. It was a beautifully furnished office, with an ornate teak desk and built-in teak cabinets with old doorknobs. From some of these hung little placards which Harsha assumed were somehow connected to the investigation. A more modern lamp sat on the desk. Some papers and an old letter opener were strewn across it, as was an old bell. Such was the old-world feel to this building that Harsha could well believe the bell was for summoning some clerk or the other.

There was a bookshelf on one side, and Harsha gravitated towards it as though by habit and looked at some of the titles. A rather large book called *Taking a Stand: The Evolution of Human Rights* was given great prominence on the top left-hand side of the shelf. Harsha thought of the *Collected Works of Shakespeare* that held a similar place in his own bookshelf – mostly untouched — and grinned to himself. A lot of the other books were on similar human rights themes, and there were a few familiar-looking biographies such as *A Long Walk to Freedom* by Nelson Mandela and *The Art of Happiness* by the Dalai Lama.

Harsha was also surprised to see some unusual fiction books. *To Kill a Mockingbird* was perhaps standard fare, but Toni Morrison's *Beloved* and Margaret Atwood's *Oryx and Crake*? Harsha somehow pulled up an image, with great difficulty, of Gopu sitting back at his desk and tucking into a dystopian Atwood novel, and felt a surge of affection for the man. How many layers each human being had!

Further down the shelf, there were also books on Dalit leader Dr Ambedkar, then Mulk Raj Anand's *Untouchable,* and then, finally, the ones that Harsha was really looking for: the transgender section. At least eight books on transgenderism and transgender lives. Harsha pulled one out at random – *Transgender History* by Susan Stryker – and started leafing through it.

"Oy! What are you doing? You can't touch that!" Harsha started, briefly dropping the book before catching it again. He looked up to see a policeman bearing down on him, a frown on his face, and Gautami behind him, looking on in slight embarrassment. Harsha put the book back, trying not to look too sheepish. He apologised before resuming his scrutiny of the room. The policeman huffed and then went about his business again, and fortunately the incident didn't seem to have caught anyone else's attention.

After the designated five minutes, Palanivel looked up and nodded to Harsha and Sampath, who reluctantly got up and walked to the door. The inspector accompanied them. Then Sampath asked: "Do we know how he died?"

"Those details are still being established," the inspector said with finality.

Sampath nodded, as though this were the most natural thing in the world. "I understand. These things take time! Can we be in touch, sir? So we can check with you once you have made more progress? And of course," he added, laughing, "In case it becomes a murder investigation?"

Palanivel gave him a thin smile and then said: "What are you planning to write today?"

Selvam didn't hesitate for a second. "We will cover the

death of Mr Gopinath, add a little bit of detail, and we will say that it is being established whether or not it is a murder investigation. Nothing more than that."

"Really?" the inspector returned, sceptically.

"Why do you doubt it?" Sampath asked as they went out onto the crowded corridor once again. The place really was a hive of activity, Harsha thought, as a woman brushed past him with a tray of food, making his stomach rumble.

"I have had some experience with the press before," Palanivel said shortly.

Sampath allowed a couple of blue-shirted assistants to squeeze past him before saying: "We at *Southern Echo* want to maintain certain standards, sir, our owner is very keen that we stick to our principles no matter what."

Harsha rubbed his nose in embarrassment, but clearly the newspaper's reputation hadn't spread widely enough to reach Palanivel's ears, because he nodded, seeming impressed. He then said: "I don't know enough about *Southern Echo* and what it stands for, but I am trusting in your own reputation as an honest journalist. That's what my colleagues tell me. Next time onwards, you will have to go through the press office, and it will be easier for everyone concerned if you stick to the facts here."

Sampath bowed his head in acquiescence and then, as Palanivel turned to go away, raised his hand to stop the man and asked: "*Can* we get in touch with you in a few days to find out the progress?"

The inspector stopped, turned briefly and then said: "You will have to arrange that with the press officer."

"Sir!" Sampath said, pleadingly. Palanivel turned again, frowning slightly this time. "Your press office... well, I don't know if we will ever get through them to you. In my experience they usually give us ... confusing messages," Sampath said quickly, and Harsha was full of admiration for the way in which the man said exactly what he thought of the police press office without being offensive.

The detective hesitated, then nodded towards Harsha and said: "He has my number."

A relieved smile broke out on Sampath's face and the two journalists chorused their thanks. At that point Gautami came up to say something to Palanivel and gave Harsha a little smile over the inspector's shoulder as they left.

Sampath grinned at Harsha as they walked down the corridor. He waited until they were out in the open before saying: "That was a very productive morning! Good work!"

"Was it?" Harsha asked, frankly astonished. "All we got was a five-minute look at a completely normal room and no details at all on how the death happened. Did old Palanivel tell you something while I was away?"

Sampath shook his head, but his grin still refused to fade. "All we needed to know was that they are exploring the *possibility* of a murder investigation. Not only from their words, but from what we saw inside the room. That is our story."

Harsha stared at his companion as they ducked under the police cordon, and waited until Sampath had bade his farewell to his policeman friend before bringing him back to the matter at hand.

"And what if it turns out to just be a normal death? Won't our story look foolish?" Almost as soon as he said this, he smiled a little sardonically and said: "Oh, of course. People will believe it's a cover up or something."

"That is not our problem," Sampath said impatiently. "We are here to report the facts of what we saw and heard.

And there is more than enough there for a big story. Probably front page. Yes, we are ready to sign out," the last bit was to the security guard at the exit, who flipped open a tattered old ruled notebook and pointed to their names. They both signed, nodded at the man and made their way back to their car.

Once they were sitting in the comfortable upholstery and luxuriating in the cool burst of air conditioning, Harsha, who had been collecting his thoughts, said: "Sampath, forgive me, but the story still seems a bit thin to me. All we know is Gopinath died and that there is a possibility of a murder investigation. Is that really enough?"

Sampath grinned, looking out at the beach to his left, and said: "We can add some background about the man himself, there's plenty out there. Then we will have to add some more colour about the scene itself."

Harsha thought with some trepidation of the sparing notes he had written about the appearance of Gopu's room.

"You were taking some notes, looking at his books and so on, no?"

"Yes," Harsha said, with some apprehension.

Sampath turned and patted Harsha's hand reassuringly with one rather hairy paw and said: "Then, my friend, this is where your English training comes in. Between us, we will write a great story, don't worry!"

"Between us? I'm not sure I have that much to contribute!"

"Eh! You are the one who got us into the room! You are the one with the policeman's number! You have more than done your part."

It seemed that Harsha had actually met that rare breed of journalist who was willing to collaborate and share credit.

He stopped worrying about the story and stared out at the Chennai streets, thinking instead about Gopu and his eclectic collection of books.

11. Double date

"Yo, yo, you ready to head out?" Azhar said, barging past Harsha into his apartment, the smell of his cologne wafting across their untidy living room. "Hey Paul. You coming out with us?"

Paul stared blankly and open-mouthed at this whirlwind of a person, a pizza slice dangling from his hand, before shaking his head.

"What's all this?" Azhar asked indifferently looking at the screen, on which a man could be seen climbing halfway up an ancient Italian building.

"*Assassin's Creed*. A video game," Harsha said shortly, as he dropped the controller of the Playstation down onto the sofa, not bothering to elaborate further, knowing Azhar's limited knowledge of the genre.

"Oh right," Azhar nodded. "Like Super Mario or something," he said, and Paul and Harsha's eyes met briefly in agonised despair before Harsha said: "Something like that."

Azhar nodded, then stuck his hands in his jeans and looked around with a slightly bored air and said: "Looks like you ... oh hang on!"

He strode forward purposefully and picked up the newspaper lying on the table, which had a picture of the Secretariat building basking in the sunshine plastered all over the front page, and then said jubilantly: "*Bap re!* Loving the headline man! 'Murder probe mulled as senior government official dies'. Look at the big-shot journalist!" he said, eyeing Harsha up and down.

The big-shot journalist acknowledged this with a tired tilt of the head.

"*Wah*! There's even a sub-heading and all – 'Human rights advocate dies in the heart of TN government offices'. By Harsha Devnath and Sampath Kumar. Yeah baby! Who is this Sampath character?"

"He's a really good journalist who..." Harsha began, but stopped, smiling, as he saw Azhar's interest fade. He knew that his friend had an extremely limited attention span.

"What do you think of this headline, eh Paul? Full page spread!" Azhar said, giving the newspaper a dramatic flick and then placing it back on the table with exaggerated care.

"I did see it, made me think of mulled wine," Paul said, giving that odd barking laughter of his.

Harsha grinned. "Yeah, I hated that word 'mull' as well. But it's one of those that is useful for headlines because it's so short."

"*Arre*! Who gives a shit about this mull vull and all? The thing is – *you did it*," Azhar said, striding up to Harsha and punching him lightly on the shoulder. Harsha was touched by the undercurrent of pride in his friend's voice. "You crazy bugger, you actually managed to get your story done! You happy now?"

"I mean, it's an ongoing story, of course, and I still have

to pursue a few avenues, but yes, this is a good start."

"It's an *amazing* start, bugger! You need to stop and pat yourself on the back for this!" Azhar said.

Even Paul piped up, chewing his pizza as he spoke. "You know what, he is right, Harry. You don't give yourself enough credit."

Harsha smiled at both of them and nodded his head to signal his intention to pat himself on the back properly.

"And I know the best way to celebrate," Azhar said, throwing his arm around Harsha's neck. "Cocktails at Dynasty with these two hot girls we're going to meet tonight…"

Harsha eased himself out of Azhar's grip, laughing, and said: "Why is it always alcohol and women with you?"

"Because I love…"

"Nooooo…. Don't give me the 'I love women speech' again! I've heard it a million times over the last decade!" Harsha said, walking away from Azhar and barging into his room so he couldn't hear anymore.

"Yeah, bugger, while you're in there put on a decent shirt and some cologne! None of those pink monstrosities!" Azhar called out. He then turned to Paul, who was steadily munching through another slice of pizza, and said: "Sure you don't want to come with us, Paul?"

Paul shook his head, smiling. "I don't want to be a fifth wheel."

"What fifth wheel and all! We will find another girl for you! This place we're going – it's crazy, man, absolutely filled with chicks."

Paul looked utterly alarmed at this thought and shook his head firmly. Azhar looked in wonder at this odd creature who didn't want to go out and meet beautiful women.

Finally, he shook his head in mock despair before turning around to see Harsha emerge from his room wearing a deep red shirt tucked hastily into his jeans, a snakeskin-patterned belt visible in patches. "What the... we aren't going to shoot a Bollywood dance sequence, bugger! Go put on something decent!"

"Thought this was decent, didn't I?" Harsha muttered in an annoyed manner as he disappeared again into the room. Azhar turned and looked at Paul again, as though contemplating what he could possibly say to this pizza-eating, video game-playing recluse. Fortunately, Paul went first, saying: "These women you are meeting. Is one of them that horrible one that Harry said he would never go out with ever again?"

"What? He said that about Radhika? The cheek of the guy! She's the girl I'm dating! The least he can do is support me in my choices..."

"So it *is* her, then?"

"Oh, no – it's two completely different girls," Azhar admitted, grinning, prompting another barking laugh from Paul.

"Who are these women then? Tamil?"

"No, no, they're both Punjabi, from Delhi. One of them is a friend of my brother's. Super hot. The other one – I haven't met her, but don't tell Harry that. I gave him some *gyaan* about how amazing she is," Azhar said.

Paul laughed and took a long, loud sip of his Diet Coke. Sighing with satisfaction, he said: "Your secret is safe with me. But Harsha is a very odd chap – not sure what kind of woman would work for him."

"You're fucking telling me," Azhar said with heavy feeling.

Harsha came out in a plain black shirt, untucked over khaki trousers rolled up at the ankles above white trainers. Azhar looked him up and down approvingly. "That's better man! None of that B-grade film star nonsense. This is more like it. More *London*."

Harsha shook his head in amusement and then said: "Speaking of my story, I do need a favour from you…"

Whatever approval was on Azhar's face drained away and was replaced by panic. Harsha couldn't help but laugh slightly. "Don't worry!" he added hastily before Azhar could speak. "At this point, I just know you have contacts in the hospitality industry, and I was going to get you to ask around a little about human rights violations such as the transgender situation. I know that Gopu was looking closely at the sector."

"Oh, is that all!" Azhar thundered, throwing his hands up in the air. "You want me to go to all my hospitality contacts, developed over years not just by me, but also my father *and* my grandfather, and just ask them about any human rights abuses they may be guilty of?" He paced up and down the little space between the sofa and the entrance to Harsha's flat, waving his hands in disbelief. "You… You want me to burn all my bridges and basically start a massive scandal and you say it's a 'little favour'! Bloody hell, Harry, this is just typical…"

"Okay, okay!" Harsha said soothingly, holding his hands up in a placating manner. "You don't have to do anything, just be cool, man, I just thought… well look, never mind. You don't have to do anything just yet."

"Just yet!" Azhar said, his face going red again. "Bugger, I don't want to walk around knowing that you might suddenly drop some bombshell on me, or a sword or something, like that Greek fucker…"

"Alright, alright!" Harsha said, gurgling with suppressed laughter. "You don't have to do anything! Not a thing!"

Paul jut in unexpectedly and asked: "What Greek fucker?" Both of them ignored him.

"Good. Because I tell you, Harry, I've had enough of your Tintin shit!" Azhar said moodily. He kicked the back of the sofa lightly before quickly bending down and buffing his immaculate shoes with his palm.

"Ok buddy, no more Tintin stuff tonight," Harsha said, soothingly, putting one hand on Azhar's back. "Now let's go and meet these women. I'm looking forward to it, and I won't talk about transgender rights. I *promise.*"

Azhar reluctantly straightened up. He nodded towards the door and walked towards it, muttering inaudibly under his breath, though the phrase "Greek fucker" and "little favour" could be heard repeatedly.

Harsha waved goodbye to Paul and then made to follow Azhar out of the doorway.

"Harsha! Who is this Greek fucker?" Paul asked in agonised tones. "I have to know now!"

"Oh – I think he means Damocles," Harsha said, smiling faintly, and shut the door behind him, leaving Paul looking even more bewildered than before.

Azhar's mood only really revived when they were ushered out of the car by the doorman at The River hotel, where the bright lights of the establishment seemed to perk him up instantly.

He whistled as they walked down the corridor, which sparkled with lights from the great chandeliers and was suffused with gentle piano music. There was an intangible smell of opulence that Harsha found pleasant; he knew that

Azhar found it intoxicating.

"This is how a boutique hotel should look," Azhar said approvingly, looking benignly at the walls, which had some sort of tricky water display that made it seem like they were walking through a liquid corridor. "Elegant. But funky."

"Are you involved with this place?"

"Us? No, not at all! But dad knows the owner. Wealthy as fuck."

They walked over to one side, where a discreet corridor led to a sign marked "Dynasty".

"Here we are!"

A hostess and a door attendant stood by the entrance; the hostess picked up a clipboard as though to consult it – Harsha knew this was a standard tactic to keep out undesirables – and then, upon getting a closer look at the two men, lowered it again with a smile and waved them in. Azhar didn't give either of the staff a second glance but just walked through the entrance – being held open by the door attendant – with a slightly proprietary air. Harsha smiled at both of them and followed.

The inside of the bar was pretty standard fare as far as Harsha was concerned – a plush, low-lit bar playing the usual mixture of Top 40 pop hits and 90s nostalgia that wouldn't have been out of place in Shoreditch in London, but Azhar let out a sigh of pleasure. Clearly, he was seeing more layers to the place than Harsha was.

"Let's walk around and have a look," Azhar said loudly, leaning towards Harsha so he could be heard over the pounding music.

"Aren't the girls here already?" Harsha mouthed, knowing that Azhar probably would have planned to keep them waiting at least 10-15 minutes, if not more.

"Oh yeah, good point," Azhar said, as though this had only occurred to him. "Let's go say hi and *then* we can look around. Harsha shook his head in mock disbelief as they looked around to try and spot their dates, a little pointlessly in Harsha's case as he hadn't met them yet.

"Is that them?" he asked, pointing.

Azhar recoiled. "Dude! Why on earth do you think I would take you out with two aunty-*jis*?"

Harsha squinted through the low light of the room and looked again at the women in question. "They look alright to me," he said defensively, before they resumed their scanning of the room.

"There!" Azhar said and waved to a couple of girls who were nursing brightly-coloured cocktails and smiling benignly in their direction. As they walked up to them, Azhar hissed in Harsha's ear: "For God's sake, make an effort! Hi Simrat, hi Harleen," he boomed out, as he strode up to the two women and bestowed careless kisses on their cheeks.

Harsha stood there with deep misgiving. The two women were even more beautiful than he had anticipated. They were both in strappy, clingy dresses that made them look Delhi-sophisticated in a way that immediately made Harsha feel like a country yokel. He reminded himself of his five years in London and the brownie points that gave him, and tried to stand up a little straighter.

Both of them smiled in a friendly way when he was introduced, making him feel marginally better. "Harry here is a famous journalist, with *Southern Echo*. Front page story and everything," Azhar said, and Harsha suppressed a smile at the wingman role that Azhar was trying to play.

"Oh wow!" Simrat said. She had light brown, curly hair

that fell either side of a heart-shaped face and lustrous eyes. "What kind of stories do you write, Harsha?"

Remembering Azhar's strict instructions not to go down the transgender route, he just said: "A bit of everything really – culture, news. At the moment, we're reporting on a potential murder investigation into the death of a senior government official." He glanced at Azhar and received an approving nod that told him he had given just the right level of detail.

"That sounds really exciting," Harleen said, her eyes wide. "Tell us more!" she patted the seat next to her and Harsha felt a jolt of nerves. Why was this never easy? Harleen was perhaps not as obviously attractive as Azhar's date, but she had a model's high cheekbones accentuated by smooth straight hair that fell either side of her angular face, softened by a pair of bright, humorous eyes. Harsha's heart skipped a beat as she smiled charmingly at him at that moment.

"One sec, why don't we go get some more drinks?" Azhar asked happily. "What will you have?"

"Oh, this is a Tequila Sunrise."

"Long Island Iced Tea."

"Right, right," Azhar said, distractedly and muttered to Harsha as they walked towards the bar: "I hope you remember that, because I don't."

As they reached the bar and squeezed themselves between two occupied barstools, Harsha absent-mindedly excused himself to the woman sitting on the barstool next to him and did a double-take. He blanched and turned quickly away, staring at the row of drinks behind the bar.

It was Namritha.

"Harsha?" she asked, and he was forced to turn towards

her and put on an expression of surprise.

"Oh, Namritha! What a coincidence!" She was wearing a low cut red top, with matching lipstick, and was holding a book – *The Inordinate Lightness of Being* – as she sat at the bar. Definitely waiting for a date, Harsha surmised.

She gave him a little hug and a dazzling smile by way of greeting, and then said: "How *lovely* to see you here. And who is your friend?"

Harsha introduced Azhar. "Hello, Azhar!" she said with every evidence of delight, her eyes devouring the handsome young man. "Are you guys here just to have a drink and a catch-up? Boys' night out?"

"Er... we're here with..." Harsha gestured towards the table, where the two women were talking and laughing. Namritha's eyes widened. "My, my, Harsha. I had no idea you had such glamorous friends! Well, well. What a dark horse."

Azhar laughed loudly, though Harsha was sure he hadn't really followed the joke. To his total disgust, Azhar seemed quite taken with Namritha and chatted with her while Harsha ordered the drinks.

"Beer for you?" he asked Azhar.

"What? Oh yeah, yeah. And so Harsha tells me you're really senior there then? You must be very powerful indeed! Strong women are the backbone of..."

Harsha tuned out Azhar's risible flirtation and turned his focus back to the bartender, a young man with a sweet expression and an enthusiastic manner, to order the drinks.

When the drinks arrived a few minutes later, Namritha said: "Well, I'll leave you to your *glamorous* evening, Harsha. Lovely to catch up with you!" She picked up her book and smiled before flicking through its pages to find her spot.

As they walked back to the table, Azhar said: "That's your boss? She's hot, man!"

Harsha made a puking sound in response to this, but quickly straightened his face and put on his smile as they arrived at their table. He carefully placed the two cocktails down on the table and sat next to Harleen. He glanced over to the bar to see Namritha watching him with narrowed eyes from over her book and sighed. He had forgotten this downside to going out in Chennai – you would always be seen by someone you knew.

"One Long Island Iced Tea," he said, positioning a drink in front of Harleen. "Though I'm not sure this is quite how it's made – or at least, not how I remember it being made in London," he added modestly, cringing inside at this blatant bit of showing off.

"Oh! How is it made in London? You must tell us all about partying in London! It must be so awesome!" Harleen said.

Harsha glanced briefly at Azhar, then looked away quickly so he wouldn't be distracted by the man's idiotic grin, and proceeded to tell them all whatever he remembered about his limited experiences of going out in London.

12. Next steps

"*Enna man,* I know I told you to go do a serious story, but I didn't expect you to take over my job, *pa*," Kalyan said, grinning, as Harsha walked into work the next day.

Harsha dropped heavily into his seat, tossing his backpack into the space beneath his desk before swivelling his chair towards his neighbour. "I'm exhausted, Kals!" he said, ignoring the other man's opening remarks. "What a week!"

"Seriously man," Kalyan said, leaning forward and resting his elbows on his knees. "This is a fantastic story. I'm very pleased for you."

Harsha also leaned forward and said: "Thank you very much, Kalyan. For your encouragement and support."

"*Poya,* what support and all," Kalyan said, sitting up and going back to his desk. "But listen, one thing is that you should not stop here. You should keep going."

"Keep going where," Harsha asked, absentmindedly, as he booted up his computer and looked blearily at his screen. The previous night's activity hadn't gone by without exacting a toll on him.

"You must keep going on with your story, man!"

"Oh, yes? But what more is there to write? We got our main story out about the possible investigation. What else is there to write?"

At this, Kalyan turned away from his computer and wheeled his chair almost uncomfortably close to Harsha's and he looked very seriously at him. Harsha half turned, slightly alarmed, and looked at his older colleague apprehensively.

"Er... everything ok?"

"*Pa,* you must not ask 'what else is there to write'. You should be all over this story. Keep persisting. This front page is only the beginning, not the end. You have to *own* this story!"

Harsha turned back to the screen, his stomach churning slightly with nerves and partly from the previous night's excesses.

He was staring at the screen, where the word document version of his big story had just popped up, still open from the previous day, wondering how on earth he could follow up on it. Perhaps Sampath would know? He was about to send an email to the crime reporter when Nritya called over to him. "Come on, Harsha! Morning meeting!"

He sighed and made his usual resigned way to Namritha's room. Though this time, he was slightly aware that the subject of his ground-breaking, front page story might be a fairly dominant theme.

He was partly dreading this and partly looking forward to getting some praise for his journalistic work for once, so it was with mixed feelings that he walked into her room. Both embarrassment and pleasure went through him when he saw Namritha look up at him through her plastic-rimmed glasses with a dazzling smile.

"And here's the man of the moment!" she said. Everyone else turned to look at him as he sat down on his usual chair in the corner of her office, closest to the exit.

He coughed modestly and said: "Well, you know, it was nothing. It just happened that way, it was partly luck."

"Luck?" Namritha said, smiling at him coquettishly. "Oh, you make your own luck, you know!"

Harsha preened a little.

"What happened?" Nritya asked, unable to keep a little jealousy out of her voice. For some reason she seemed to consider herself Harsha's rival.

Namritha turned to the others and said. "This young man, yesterday I saw him and his friend – also quite a good-looking man – with these two *absolutely gorgeous* women at the new River hotel bar. You really are a dark horse, Harsha!" she said, turning to him again and smiling affectionately.

Harsha's mouth dropped open. He had been absolutely convinced that this was going to be about his front page story. Instead, she was talking about some bloody date she had seen him on. Was this for real? He realised she was expecting a response from him, so he mumbled something about just hanging out with friends, and then went quiet.

"Oh of course! Just friends!" Namritha said, and actually winked at him.

Harsha shook his head, sat back in his chair and didn't say much else for the rest of the meeting – during which absolutely no one mentioned his front page story. A front page story about a potential murder investigation, and all they cared about was who he was dating!

At the end of the meeting, he walked out of Namritha's

office and blinked.

"What the hell just happened?" he asked himself and marched off to the water cooler, still shaking his head all the way there.

He tried instead to focus on Kalyan's words as he stood in front of the weirdly industrial-looking device that dispensed cold water for *Southern Echo*'s weary hacks. It had been very gratifying to hear praise from the man he was rapidly coming to consider as his mentor in all matters journalism. But gratification changed to nervousness as he remembered Kalyan's advice about pushing for the next story. How on earth could he follow up on the great splash he had just had?

A shadow fell on the machine as someone stepped up to queue behind him for the water. Harsha felt a flash of mild irritation at this. Couldn't people just leave him to fill up his water bottle in peace?

It was one of those large metal bottles, and the trickle of water was quite slow. It was irritating and stressful to do this while someone stood passive aggressively close to him, awaiting their turn.

But then the person behind him spoke, saying: "Hi Harsha," in a decisive voice that instantly made him freeze.

"Oh, hello... er... Jaishree," Harsha stammered, still staring at the water dispensing device in front of him. How did one address the owner of the newspaper?

"Good story, today," she said briefly.

Harsha had a feeling this was very high praise coming from the owner, so he thanked her profusely and willed the trickle of water to intensify. He then made the executive decision to remove his bottle when it was only half full and moved aside awkwardly to make room for her.

"So what now, Harsha?" she asked as she picked up a plastic cup from beside the cooler and held it under the tap.

Harsha's heart sank. This was almost exactly what Kalyan had said to him. He remembered that strong feeling he had had that Jaishree was an intelligent woman and decided to go for complete honesty. "To be honest, Jaishree, I am not exactly sure."

Jaishree looked at him for a second and then leaned against the wall against which the water dispenser had been placed and said: "Harsha, one thing I can promise you – after our front page splash today, every single newspaper and news channel out there is going to be chasing this story. All of them are going to be pissed off that *Southern Echo* got this scoop and they are going to be determined to put us in our place."

She paused for a second to drink her cup of water in one gulp before holding it under the tap again.

"Today's scoop gives us a head start," she said as the water trickled out onto her cup. "But now we have to stay one step ahead of everyone else and keep pushing for the next story. The next scoop."

"Jaishree, I want to do it, I promise you!" Harsha exclaimed, bubbling over with determination to show how enthusiastic he was. "This is the kind of story I have been *desperate* to write about. Social, political, cultural — it has everything. I just don't know how to move it forward! I will keep contacting the police, but until there is a further development, what do I do?"

Jaishree stepped away from the water cooler and waved her fingers to get rid of a few droplets of water. She said: "Well, I'm not going to tell you how to do your job; I'm not a journalist myself. But I saw that article with the transgender person – Gita, was it? Good piece. I know it was never published, but maybe you could go back to her, try and update it a little, and see what you get out of it? And what about speaking to some of Gopinath's family and colleagues to get some ideas of what kind of enemies he might have made? Just a couple of ideas off the top of my head."

Harsha's head spun with pleasure to hear that the big boss had read his ill-fated piece, the publication of which had been blocked. His pleasure, however, was tempered severely by shame that he hadn't thought of these obvious ideas himself.

"I think Sampath was planning to speak to his family," he began but paused when Jaishree shook her head.

"I'm not sure that's the best idea. Sampath needs to work his police contacts and will have his hands full with contacting Gopinath's colleagues in the government. I think you should be the one to meet the family," she said.

Harsha's insides jangled. Meet the family of the man who had possibly been murdered? It sounded utterly dreadful. But there was a large part of him that rejoiced at the thought of doing some serious journalism. Already he had started picturing the story he would craft around their reactions. Did that make him a strange person?

A thought occurred to him. "Will Sampath be offended if I take that over? No offence, but I don't want to upset a senior journalist," he said apologetically.

Jaishree chuckled. "If I know Sampath, he will be delighted to get out of it. You already knew Gopinath, and I suspect you would be more comfortable than he would doing this," she said.

Harsha nodded. This made sense – he was from a middle class family, just like Gopinath. It stood to reason they may be more comfortable talking to him, even if that wasn't the most politically correct sentiment to express.

"Go have a word with Sampath to get an idea of what we want from the family interviews. We want a complete picture of the man before the next development hits, so that we can craft a story that really brings out the significance of this death," Jaishree said authoritatively, completely belying her assertion that she wasn't a journalist. "And meanwhile, get some fodder for a wider piece on Gopinath — the champion of the transgenders. That way you can get your transgender story in the newspaper with a fresh angle," she continued.

"I certainly will!" Harsha declared, clutching his water bottle and fizzing with enthusiasm. He had never had this type of clarity and guidance on his journalistic brief in his career so far, neither in England nor in India.

Jaishree nodded. "Good. Oh – and I need to have that word with Namritha about giving you a few weeks to focus on this. I'll go do that."

With that, she disappeared in the direction of Namritha's office and Harsha stood there, filled with fire and determination to do some more reporting. But first things first. He needed to talk to Sampath.

13. Family

Harsha walked under the beautiful canopy of trees on Boat Club Road, marvelling at the somnolence and quiet calm of this exclusive residential district hidden away in the heart of Chennai. Giant laburnum trees, *sarakondrai* in Tamil, flanked the quiet street, shedding golden petals onto the narrow pavements on either side.

But Harsha's insides were in turmoil.

He was about to perform that most dreaded of journalistic assignments — the death knock.

He closed his eyes and tried to picture Prof. Jonathan Clive's class on this subject back in the day when he was a journalism student at City University, London. "The thing to remember when you are visiting the family of someone who has died," Professor Clive had said, "Is that they *want* to talk. They want to tell you about their dead relative. Just be there and listen to them. Don't ask too many questions except to keep the conversation going."

This didn't still Harsha's pounding heart. It was all very well to want to do serious journalism. But now that it had come to it, the thought of asking Gopu's wife and daughter what they thought of his death made the bile rise in his throat. But it had to be done. Sampath was speaking to Gopu's government colleagues and working his police contacts, and Harsha had been tasked with speaking to the family as well as to Gopu's friends from the legal profession.

He reached the gate that bore the legend "Old no. 7, New No. 43" and sighed to himself. Would he ever get used to Chennai's unintelligible house number system?

He was saved from further peregrinations by the watchman of this particular house, who walked up and peered at him from between the iron bars of the gate, and gave him a cheerful smile. He looked all of 16 years old.

"*Kya chaahiye...* Hema madam?" he asked. Harsha nodded. Most people who worked as watchmen in Chennai seemed to come from Bihar or the North East of India — the poorer parts of the country. *What tough lives they must lead*, he thought to himself, and smiled as warmly as he could at the young chap. His Hindi was so rusty that he couldn't do much more than that.

Harsha walked down the massive driveway, breathing in the scent of neem and mango and looking around at the beautifully manicured garden. Birds cheeped softly and the breeze stirred the leaves, making a gentle rushing sound.

He suddenly realised he was on his own. The watchman had left him to his own devices. Harsha's nerves gave another lurch. By the time he reached the beautiful ornate front door, his heart was pounding again. He pressed the doorbell and stood there, contemplating the intricate flowers and leaves carved into the door.

The door opened surprisingly soon and Harsha was taken aback to find a young woman looking up at him, younger than he had expected. She had long, glossy black hair tucked behind her ears, a pair of sharp eyes and a rather determined-looking expression that reminded him strongly of Gopu.

"You must be from *Southern Echo*," she said. "Come in."

"Harsha," he said, smiling and shuffling forward. "I'm so sorry for your loss."

A shadow came over her face, and for a brief second Harsha caught a glimpse of the deep well of sorrow behind her expression before the woman smiled again, and said: "Thank you. I'm Neha."

Harsha shook the outstretched hand and then followed her nervously into a dimly lit, opulent living room. Divans and sofas abounded, loaded with embroidered cushions, their tassels tickling the colourful patterns of sofa covers. On one corner, a rather large woman was sitting in an attitude of grief, her eyes sodden with tears, a perfumed handkerchief in one hand and a steaming cup of tea in the other.

"Mrs Hema," Harsha said, nervously.

She looked up at him slowly and sorrowfully. "Please sit down. Some tea? Neha, please fetch some tea for the young man." The younger woman went away with alacrity.

Harsha sat delicately on the edge of an ornate chair and leaned forward with what he hoped was a comforting expression. "I am so sorry for your loss, Mrs Hema. I only met your husband once, and I thought he was a very good man."

"He was a *great* man," Hema said, heavily.

"Right," Harsha said, not knowing how to respond to this.

They sat in silence for a minute, one of the longest Harsha had experienced for a while. Finally, he asked: "Could you tell me a bit about Gopu as a person? What he did and what he achieved?"

Hema emerged from her handkerchief, looked bleakly at Harsha and then sighed before nodding.

"Where do I begin," she said, distractedly. "Well... He was a lawyer for many years before he became a civil servant. He was studying law when I met him. In those days it was not the prestigious profession it is now. My parents would have preferred a doctor or someone working in the Indian Administrative Service. But he was the son of a good friend of my father's so we met him as a favour," Hema said, as though by rote. "In those days, passing the I.A.S exam was one of the most prestigious things a young man could do. But I think my parents saw him as an investment."

Harsha did his best not to shake his head. Another arranged marriage. He just couldn't get his head round how normal this was considered.

"Of course, it was not guaranteed that he would be a success. But the minute I saw him — I knew he would. He had an air about him," Hema finished, somewhat enigmatically. "And he went on to have ten successful years as a lawyer. He became extremely well known. And in the middle of his job, he also managed to ace the I.A.S. exam — almost to prove a point."

"And... er... he joined the government after that?"

"The Slum Advisory Board. They have changed the name now to remove the word 'slum'. But he was in charge of building housing for poor people. He did a lot of good in that job. And in his career. He helped a lot of people," Hema said woodenly.

Was it Harsha's imagination, or was Hema talking in platitudes? He was struggling to keep his attention on what she was saying, so he silently turned on the recorder on his phone and settled back to just nodding and letting her words wash over him.

Soon, they were mercifully interrupted by Neha, who came in with two cups of tea and a plateful of biscuits. She nodded amiably to Harsha before placing the tray on the coffee table.

"Thank you so much, you shouldn't have," he said, but she just smiled again and sat down next to her mother on the sofa.

Harsha looked at them critically, and thought he could detect very little resemblance between them. Neha was more like her father in appearance.

"And what do you do, Neha?" he asked, politely.

"I work as a barrister," she said, surprising him a little. She looked incredibly young to be in court. But perhaps that was his own prejudice? "At the moment, I'm representing the Indian government, fighting patents."

"Oh?" Harsha asked, genuinely interested. "What sort of patents?"

"You know, Harsha, all these American companies keep patenting ancient Indian remedies and medicines," Neha said warmly.

"They do?" Harsha asked, smiling at the fire in her voice. He had missed this about India — when Indians took up a cause, they *really* took it up.

Neha pursed her lips and then said: "Did you see those neem trees outside this house? Well — they all belong to some American companies. *They patented the neem.* Can you believe that?"

Harsha put his notebook down and looked at her in disbelief.

"Come on. I don't believe that," he said finally.

"I am exaggerating slightly," she conceded, giving a wry smile. "But only slightly. They have patented many different applications of the neem tree that have been used in India for thousands of years. It is absolutely shocking."

Before Harsha could go any further into this conversation, Hema stepped in and said: "Aren't you here to talk about Gopu?"

He was surprised to hear an undercurrent of resentment in her voice, but the blood rose to his face, and he apologised. "I'm so sorry," he said hoarsely.

"Don't apologise," Neha said sourly. "Amma doesn't like me talking about my work."

"That is *not* true, Neha. I just think you should give it a break while you are here. If you must work all the time, at least don't talk about it in the few hours when you are not working," Hema said. She then turned to Harsha and gave him a painful smile. "She is just like her father."

Harsha watched Neha bite her lip and cringed inside. Some people may enjoy watching a domestic argument such as this one, but he wasn't one of them.

"It must have been a terrible shock to hear about Gopu's death," he said, gently turning the conversation.

Hema retreated behind her handkerchief but Neha just looked at him bleakly.

"So, so terrible," Hema sobbed. Neha didn't say anything.

Harsha let the silence continue for a few minutes and then asked the question that he most wanted to ask — but also dreaded asking the most. "Do you have any idea what happened?" he asked, gently.

The mother simply shook her head but Neha said: "You should ask those 1857 Society nutcases. I bet they will have a better idea."

At this, Hema looked up from her handkerchief and stared at her daughter in consternation. "Don't call them *nutcases*, Neha! They are not!"

"What do you think they are then? Do rational people threaten a man just for doing his job?"

"Threaten? What do you mean, threaten?"

"You've seen the letters. 'There will be consequences'. They say that again and again. How is that not a threat?"

Hema waved this aside as though it was an irrelevance.

"They just want Indians to be proud of who they are! What's wrong with that? They were just having a debate!" she said ponderously.

"A debate? They threatened to silence Appa!" Neha spat.

"No, no, no! You exaggerate," Hema said, smiling indulgently. Harsha screwed his eyes shut. There was only one way to react to such a patronising tone.

"How can you defend people who may be behind your husband's *murder*!" Neha yelled, jumping up, her eyes burning.

"We don't even know if it *was* a murder! Don't be a silly child!" Hema said thunderously.

Harsha stood up quickly, holding his hands up in a placatory gesture. "Neha, please... Can you, please, just sit down?"

She looked at him for a minute, and then brushed her eyes with the back of her hand and sat down. "I'm sorry," she said, unsteadily. Her mother put one hand on her shoulder, which she ignored.

Harsha tried to hold the question down, but simply could not. "What is this... 1857 Society?" he asked.

There was a slight pause, after which Hema muttered

something about the quality of journalists in this day and age, while Neha asked: "Where have you been, Harsha?"

"In England, actually. I recently returned," Harsha said as coldly as he could, though neither mother nor daughter showed any signs of remorse for their sharp words. They looked at each other and then Neha said: "On the face of it, they are just a sort of lobby group. In reality, they are this group of complete madmen who think violence is the answer to all of India's problems."

"Violence against whom?"

"Against anyone who isn't a patriot and who doesn't love India. That could be anyone — foreigners, women who wear mini skirts, environmentalists, anyone campaigning against discrimination or working to alleviate poverty and, of course, the oldest one of all…"

"Muslims," Harsha finished for her, his stomach clenching as he thought of Azhar, and his assertion that India was becoming a harder place for people of his religion.

"This is a massive exaggeration," Hema said, pouting slightly as she adjusted her sari. "They are just people who want to put some pride back in India. We are a very downtrodden country, and they want to lift us up again."

"But you can't deny that they hated Appa."

"They didn't *hate* him, they just disagreed with some of his views."

"They threatened to do him harm!"

"That is completely how you interpret it! Your father respected their point of view!"

Neha sighed. She turned to Harsha and forced herself to smile. "My father respected everyone's point of view. But that doesn't mean it was always reciprocated."

Hema came to herself with a start and turned to look at

Harsha. Her eyes narrowed as she saw him taking notes.

"Don't worry," Harsha said, hurriedly. "I'm just taking down the details of this 1857 Society. I suppose that's a reference to the Indian mutiny against the British in 1857?"

"Of course," Neha said, looking at him as though he was stupid. Harsha smiled mechanically. Sometimes as a journalist you had to ask the stupid questions.

"Do you know whom to contact there?"

Neha hesitated and then said. "Advaith something or the other. He is the one who had... the debate... with my father."

Harsha nodded his thanks and then said: "I think I have troubled you both enough. Thank you so much for your time." He couldn't resist picking up one of the biscuits — Marie tea biscuits, he noticed with a pang of nostalgia — before gathering all his things together and putting them in his backpack. Neha and Hema relaxed visibly, and Neha stood up to thank him.

Harsha slung the backpack over his shoulder and asked casually: "What on earth did this 1857 Society dislike about your father's work? It all seemed quite worthy to me."

Neha sighed again, and said: "All this work around transgenders. They seemed to think he was spoiling society by promoting them so much."

Harsha glanced at Hema before walking away from the room, and stopped short at her expression of anger. "Do you disagree, ma'am?" he asked.

"Oh? With what Neha just said? No. Those... transgenders were nothing but trouble from the beginning," Hema said, a vicious undertone to her voice. Harsha had a feeling she was about to call them *chakkas* before stopping herself. "What did they do once Gopu got them jobs in the government? They just left when they realised they would actually have to work hard. And then blamed *him*. Ungrateful bunch."

"Please, Amma," Neha pleaded.

Hema straightened with a start and then gave a sickly smile. "That's what I think anyway. But I might be wrong! You must do your own reporting on this, Mr Harsha."

She held out a hand and shook Harsha's limply before reclining on the sofa again.

Neha escorted Harsha to the doorway, looking slightly embarrassed. He thanked her again for her time, and he did so sincerely. Not only did he have plenty for his story, but they had even provided him with a promising lead, perhaps two. He pictured Azhar's expression of horror at the idea of Harsha embarking on another murder investigation and grinned to himself.

"Don't judge her too harshly," Neha said.

"Who?"

"My mother, silly! She is from another generation. She wasn't as progressive as my father — and she struggled with some of his choices," Neha said.

Harsha nodded, fully conscious of his own father's irritation with what he saw as his son's obsession with transgenders.

Neha hesitated and then held out a business card. "Please call me if you need anything at all. And let me know if you would like to meet to talk about anything further."

"Thank you very much," Harsha said. He walked a little way down the pathway and then turned around and said: "And I'm terribly sorry for your loss."

She nodded and stood by the doorway, watching him as he walked down the driveway out into the streets of Chennai.

14. Encounter

"Is there anything else you can tell me about him?" Harsha asked, politely, though he was flagging seriously at this point. He had done six interviews about Gopu this week, and though many of the stories had been touching, his mind could only process so much.

"Only this, sir. He was a very good man, and he was very good to everyone," the clerk sitting opposite him said, toying nervously with the end of her sari. "He had a very good sense of humour also and kept us all in good spirits at all times."

Good sense of humour – that was a constant theme with all those that Harsha spoke to, and he reflected briefly on what an underrated quality that was in a manager; the ability to make the daily job more pleasant. It was almost a superpower, as Gopu had said.

"Thank you, Ms Dharini," he said, and she bobbed her head in response. He stood up and left the lawyers' section of the High Court building, feeling the wave of warmth wash over him as he left the air-conditioned room and stepped out into the Chennai afternoon.

He felt wrung dry after a morning and afternoon filled with interviews, and mentally cursed Sampath again, though he was very sure that the man himself must be feeling a similar sense of exhaustion from talking to government employees and trying to milk his police sources. Harsha had tried Palanivel without success and had even sent him a message on Whatsapp, a bewildering new form of messaging that Harsha had only just caught up with. It was like banging your head on a wall.

He walked along the grand old corridor of the old colonial-era building, reflecting on his brief meeting with the man himself. Almost involuntarily, his stomach gave a little rumble, and he thought of that delicious *dosai* he had had the last time he was here. Could he go on his own and have one? Would he be allowed?

He glanced at his watch and then decided to chance it. He still had nearly 40 minutes until his next interview.

No one impeded his encroachment into the canteen, and he ordered a *dosai* and a coffee and sat contentedly in one corner of the room. He placed his books down on one side after giving the table a cursory wipe with a napkin.

He knew he really should have been writing down his notes while fresh in his mind, but he couldn't resist. He took out his phone and felt a little jolt of pleasure when he saw he had a new text from Harleen waiting in his inbox. He swiped up and opened it.

You're going to interview her alone? Is it safe? Be careful, ok? Don't want you to be beaten up or killed before our date :-)

Harsha looked down, smiling stupidly and happily at the words "our date". When was the last time he had even had a date? In London, dating as a concept was going through a weird transition from meeting "in real life" to meeting online. Since he loathed anything to do with technology, this had meant he either dated people he met through work or was single. In India, his job had left him no time for anything resembling a personal life.

Of course, there had been that weird incident with Maya at Pipal Resorts. They had nearly slept together – but had been interrupted by a gang of murderous goons.

"It could only happen to me," Harsha said out loud to himself, before thanking the waiter who had just come up with a plateful of *dosai* and chutneys. Before tucking in, he quickly sent a text back to Harleen.

I promise to be there as long as they're not life-threatening injuries :-) Even if they are, I'm sure a vodka tonic will sort them out. Can't wait!

He looked gloomily at his attempt at humour, but brightened at the prospect of seeing Harleen again. She was maybe a bit sophisticated for him, but her extremely sweet nature had made him feel protective and warm, and he was genuinely excited to meet her that night. He also had never dated a Punjabi woman before and found her lack of cynicism about life refreshing. It was so different from his own viewpoint these days.

He ate the rest of his *dosai* in a bit of a daze and it was only when the coffee arrived that he looked up to see that the waiter was saying something to him.

"Sorry, what?"

"Gopu was a very good man. Very generous," the waiter said, grimacing thoughtfully.

"Oh, yes of course... er... Dorai, is it?"

"Yes, sir," the waiter nodded, and Harsha was touched to see that the man looked genuinely grieved. Harsha sipped on his coffee and watched the man walk away and thought briefly about the impact a single person had on so many lives. And yet – what was another person among a billion Indians? Life was both meaningless and incredibly meaningful at the same time.

When he finished his tiffin and paid the bill, he said with sincerity: "Thank you, Dorai, that was outstanding."

He gathered his things and walked out onto the main road. He looked around amongst the smoke and noise of cars and car horns, and identified his way forward.

He had decided the day before to walk down to Burma Bazaar, where he was to meet his next interviewee. He had only once before been to the rambling old street full of so-called "grey market" shops, originally run by Burmese refugees in the 1970s, and remembered buying his first ever set of CDs and DVDs there. The Police's *Synchronicity*, Pink Floyd's *Dark Side of the Moon* – and possibly a couple of porn movies that were gathering dust somewhere, he thought to himself with a rueful grin.

Google Maps had told him it was about a 15-minute walk from the Madras High Court, so he started off at a smart pace down Parry's Corner, avoiding the main road and walking through some back alleys to save time.

As he progressed further into the old financial district of George Town, his heart started beating harder and harder. The contrast from the air-conditioned confines of the old colonial High Court building was stark – beggars with distorted limbs pawed at his trousers, shop wares spilled out onto the pavements and he had to step around some foul-smelling puddles more than once. Where had they come from, when it hadn't rained for weeks? Harsha thought it best not to think about it.

Once he stepped onto Burma Bazaar itself, the pounding

of his heart hit a crescendo. He vaguely remembered being affected by the squalor even back in the day. But now, with his experience of England and having gained more worldly wisdom and empathy, the experience was almost overwhelming.

He tried to create a little bubble in his own mind and ignore the yelling hawkers, the loud conversations around him and the dirt being kicked up by the many people crowding their way up and down the street. He resolutely made his way through this maelstrom of activity.

Finally, when he was well past the Chennai Beach station, he turned left into Sultan Street and then left again into the quaintly named Barrel Street – which made him think briefly and nostalgically of London – and took stock.

It was a particularly alien street to his mind, so far from the Neelankarai/Amethyst/Dynasty version of Chennai that he had been familiar with. It was a row of low block houses painted in different colours, though the paint was fading and peeling in many places. The road itself was more mud than tarmac, but scrupulously cleaned. One man in a *dhoti* and with a hostile expression was sitting in a foldable chair outside his house and fanning himself with an old towel, and eventually Harsha had to ask him where number 14 was, so bewildering were the house numbers.

The man started and stared at Harsha through gimlet eyes and said: "Why you want to go there?" in querulous tones.

"Do you know where it is?" Harsha asked, politely.

The man glared at Harsha as if offended, and then gestured towards a mouldering wall on one corner on which was embedded an unusual studded wooden door with an actual knocker. Harsha walked up curiously and then knocked on it, using the knocker, which was shaped like a gargoyle. What on earth was this weird place?

The door creaked open without warning, and a middle-aged woman in a sari peeped out and looked at him enquiringly.

"Er... this is Harsha here? To speak to Gita?" Harsha said nervously, licking his lips.

"Oho!" she said, and without any further remark, marched off into the interior of the house, leaving Harsha to shut the door behind him and scramble after her. Following her, his mouth dropped open as he entered a courtyard dominated by a *gulmohar* tree, its red flowers littering the concrete structure built around it for sitting. The rest of the building was crumbling and old, but the tree elevated the setting to a place of great beauty.

People walked in and out of the courtyard, one hanging a tattered set of clothes, another carrying dry rice in a vast container and so on, and Harsha realised that most of them were of indeterminate gender.

"What is this place?" he asked, more to himself than anything.

But the woman who had opened the door responded, saying simply: "It is The Sanctuary."

"And who pays for it?"

"A charitable endowment. It is all confidential."

"And it is for..."

"For people who are different," she said, smiling, and Harsha noticed that her jaw had a slightly masculine cast to it.

She seemed to guess his thoughts because she stepped back a little self-consciously, and then said: "Let me go fetch Gita. Oh wait! There she is. With Mithra."

Harsha followed her finger and saw Gita sitting on a chair under the *gulmohar* tree with two other women. She looked a very different figure from the one Harsha remembered from their first encounter, looking far more dignified and peaceful in a simple brown sari. Sitting next to her in another chair was an elderly woman with an air of command, also dressed in a simple sari. A third woman sat with her back to him.

"That's Mithra," said the woman who had let him in, a tone of respect entering her voice as she indicated the elderly woman. "She is our leader."

"And the other?" asked Harsha.

"Some social worker," the woman said dismissively before motioning Harsha to go towards the trio of women.

"Thank you," Harsha said and strode forward towards Gita.

Gita and Mithra looked up at him as he arrived, one of them apprehensively and the other calmly.

"Hi, Gita, sorry to interrupt," Harsha said. "Just wanted to let you know I'm here. Let me know when you're free to talk."

Gita stood up and shook hands with him and then motioned towards the elderly woman.

"This is Mithra – the head of The Sanctuary," she said reverentially.

"Don't you start calling it that as well!" the woman said, holding out one hand to Harsha without getting up. "This is the Aravanigal Society of Chennai — for some reason these silly young ones call it The Sanctuary."

Harsha shook hands with Mithra and felt the calluses beneath her grip.

"Pleasure," he said. Mithra had long, pure white hair

pulled into a neat bun, contrasting with the burnt dark brown of her skin. She had a handful of wrinkles and looked knowingly out at the world through a pair of round glasses. Harsha looked searchingly at her face to try and spot the telltale signs of a gender switch. There were none.

"Yes – I am an *aravani* too. Transgender," Mithra said, smiling. There was a humorous edge to her voice, but it also had a firmness running through it. This was no downtrodden person, beaten down by the injustices of life. This was someone who had been through the mill and had come out the other side stronger.

"Mithra – 'friend' in Sanskrit," Harsha said, choosing to focus on something different. It was interesting to think about how everyone who changed their gender then got to choose a new name. What name would he have chosen for himself in his adulthood?

The elderly woman smiled again. "I chose the name because I liked the sound of it. But now I try to live up to it by being a friend to the community," she said.

"Well, I look forward to speaking to you about your work, I'd be interested in learning more about this community," Harsha said.

There was a slight pause and then the third person in the group spoke.

"Hey, Harsha. Good to see you again," she said.

Harsha turned in surprise to see who this familiar voice belonged to. Bewilderment turned to shock as he realised who it was.

It was Maya.

15. Old flame

Maya. He had been in love with her for more than ten years, and though he had completely understood why she had needed to cut him off over the last two years, he couldn't help feeling infuriated that she just sat there looking at him in that knowing manner.

His eyes travelled of their own volition over her large, beautiful eyes, her resolute chin and the simple, dark red salwar kameez that clung to her slim, athletic frame. He pulled himself together and said: "Hi... er... how are you?"

"Very well, thank you, Harsha."

He turned to Gita and Mithra, smiled with an effort, and said: "Would you like me to come back later? Are you all busy?"

Gita looked hesitantly at Mithra and then said: "Is it ok if they stay with me while we talk?"

A pause. And then Harsha said: "I have no objection, but can I just clarify what everyone's role is here?"

Mithra was looking intently at him and at this point she said: "Gita is under the protection of ASoC now and I am here to make sure she is treated fairly by everyone," she said in firm tones that brooked no defiance.

Harsha nodded and then looked inquiringly at Maya.

"And you are... an adviser?" he asked as neutrally as he could manage.

"Nothing as formal as that!" Maya said, quickly. "I am just providing support."

"I see," Harsha said, trying to calm his thoughts and think through this rationally. How would he have reacted if he was Gita and a journalist wanted to interview him after a prominent murder that affected the community? Pretty bloody terrified.

"Well, I certainly want you to feel comfortable to talk to me, Gita, and if you feel you need these people to sit in with you, that's no problem. I completely understand."

He sat down on the edge of the parapet facing Gita and Mithra, but slightly angled so he could include Maya as well. He didn't want to appear like he was some forlorn, jilted lover. He took out his notebook, smiled reassuringly at his interviewee and began.

"Gita, the last time we spoke, we talked about your experience of transforming from a man to a woman. This time, as you know, I wanted to speak to you about your experience with Mr Gopinath," he said. He tried to push away the questions that kept popping into his head — why was Maya here? How was she involved with the transgender community? Why hadn't she contacted him?

Gita was saying something and he shook himself and tried to focus. This was much bigger than him and his idiotic love life.

"... and it was then that he actually started taking the issue seriously," Gita finished.

"Ah indeed! Very interesting," Harsha said. "And did you

consider at any point taking advantage of his programme to employ transgender people to government positions? Or were the positions too low?"

"As I was saying just now," Gita said, looking at him as though he was a bit stupid, "I would have taken the job if I hadn't already had commitments elsewhere. Or so I thought. At that hotel. Unfortunately, that didn't work out at all."

"Of course, sorry," Harsha said, a little flustered. He needed to focus. This was an important interview — they had already exhausted all avenues of reporting and he had to try and build a picture of what Gopu's work was like if they wanted to proceed any further on the story.

"And then you came here?" he asked, even though he knew well that he was the one who had given Gita the details of the organisation.

Gita looked at Mithra, who cleared her throat and said: "ASoC is an organisation that has many goals, but the main one is to find employment for *aravanis* - that is, for transgender people. I hear we must thank you for sending Gita to us. Well, she has been a godsend — I have made her the secretary of our organisation — she has very quickly become indispensable here."

Harsha took a deep breath and then asked Gita: "Were there any people who were opposed to the government programme? I mean, any groups or high-profile individuals who objected to it?"

Gita looked at him contemplatively, and Harsha tried not to imagine what she would have looked like when she was a man. It was all so confusing, even for a self-professed liberal such as himself.

"I think Mithra will be able to answer that better," she said finally.

Harsha politely turned to Mithra, who said in a matter-of-face voice: "There was nothing but opposition, Harsha. The member of parliament who brought forward the bill was not even convinced by it himself. The opposition party lambasted the government for bringing forward such 'frivolous' matters to the house when there was a water shortage to deal with."

She sighed, massaged one knee and then looked down at her wrinkled hand. "Outside parliament, newspapers either ignored it or wrote about it in joking terms," she continued, making Harsha jump guiltily for his profession. But hang on, that wasn't his fault. In fact he had wanted to write more about it even before the murder, he reminded himself. Once again, he pulled his attention back to Mithra's words and caught the tail end of her next comment.

"... there was the 1857 Society," she was saying.

"The 1857 Society?" Harsha asked sharply, thinking to himself that it couldn't be a coincidence that he was hearing this name twice in as many days. "What exactly…"

There was a sudden banging noise behind them that made all three of them jump and look around towards the door. Harsha saw the middle-aged woman who had first let him into the property hurrying towards them, a panicked look in her eyes.

"Mithra! Mithra! It's the police!"

These words had an electric effect on not just the three of them under the tree, but on all the other people who were milling about the place engaged in their own tasks. Almost everyone froze and turned to this woman, and a sort of collective panic seemed to run through the whole building. Harsha looked at the identical looks of dismay on each face and turned to Maya for the first time since his interview began, his eyebrows arched in query. She leaned forward and said quietly: "The police are not very popular here."

"I figured that out myself, funnily enough."

Her response was — perhaps fortunately — cut off by Gita, who gripped Mithra by the arm and said: "What will I do, Mithra? What... what will I do?"

Harsha was moved and saddened by the fear in her voice and he was forcibly reminded of Azhar's old resort manager Murugayya from a different age, who had been similarly terrified by the threat of police punishment.

Mithra herself was the only one who remained calm, putting one hand over Gita's and saying in a soothing voice: "Don't be ridiculous. Savitri! Go fetch some tea and some cups. We have several guests now," she said to the gatekeeper.

"Why would they jail you, Gita?" Maya asked gently.

"I... at the hotel... they said they would call the police... I..."

Savitri, the gatekeeper, hissed a warning and they all turned to the door again. Going by everyone's reaction, Harsha would have expected a police jeep or riot van to come roaring in, sirens blazing, and a number of stern police officers jumping out to descend upon the place. Instead, a solitary policewoman walked in, wheeling a rather battered bicycle through the large doorway and looking around curiously.

Harsha heard Maya's surprised intake of breath beside him, as he got up, dusted his trousers down and went forward to greet the woman.

"Constable Gautami," he said, extending his hand.

The policewoman looked at him, her mouth forming an almost comical expression of surprise. "You again? Why do you always pop up everywhere, when no one is expecting you?"

Harsha chuckled. "Funny. I was thinking almost the same thing."

"About me?"

"About women in general."

Gautami cocked an eyebrow at him and then, belatedly, took his hand and shook it, allowing herself a small smile.

"Well, Mr Devnath…"

"Harsha," he interjected.

"Well, Harsha, fun as it is to talk to you, I am here for work," she said, her eyes shifting from his face to that of Gita. Her eyes softened slightly when she saw how terrified Gita was.

At this point, Maya stood up, and said: "Hi, Gautami. I am so glad it is you."

This time, the policewoman allowed herself a fully-fledged smile and she shook Maya's hand warmly. "Always a pleasure, Maya," she said. "How is your little sister?"

"Oh very well! The little scamp, always making fun of how old I am. And she is getting more beautiful by the day and harder for my mother to manage!"

Harsha's eyebrows knit closer together as he listened to the two women chat. When on earth had they become so close?

Maya was now talking to Gita. "Gita, you have nothing to worry about. Constable Gautami is a personal friend of mine. You are in good hands."

Gita looked slightly mollified by Maya's reassurance, and the people around them gradually returned to whatever they had been doing. Mithra turned to Harsha and said: "Can you wait, Harsha? We would still like to speak to you."

"I only need ten minutes," Constable Gautami interjected briskly.

"Er... sure," Harsha said, wondering if Gita would be too shaken to continue talking to him after the police officer was done with her.

Gautami leaned her bicycle against the tree and took the chair recently vacated by Maya.

Maya herself walked a little away from the gathering, sighing. Harsha went to join her.

"It's best I leave them to it; Mithra is more than capable of taking care of matters," Maya said, and looked up uncertainly at Harsha, as though for his approval.

"Maya — what the hell are you doing here?" he asked, unable to contain himself any longer. "You seem to be involved in this whole thing somehow! And you seem to be on fantastic terms with that policewoman!"

Maya looked mischievously up at him. "You sound like you're not happy to see me, Harry?"

Harsha jumped at the playfulness in her voice; it transported him back to the days when he was a nervous, overweight teenager who was in love with the class beauty. He suddenly felt very aware of how tall she was — pretty much the same height as Harsha himself.

"Of course I'm happy to see you, Maya. Always," he said, tenderly, raising his hand with the vague idea of brushing a strand of hair away from her face before stopping, forcing his hand into a fist and dropping it back down by his side again.

There was a silence, and then Maya smiled a little wistfully at him and said: "I work for a charity called Helping Hands — it's a charity for human rights in Tamil Nadu. And I have been closely involved in trying to get crimes against transgender people taken seriously."

"Did you know Gopu?"

Maya shook her head. "Not at all. I know he was doing great work in transgender employment, but my work has been mostly with the police — which is how I know Gautami. I'm trying to educate them on transgender issues, and also trying to educate transgender people on their own rights, getting them access to some sort of representation. What are you smiling at, idiot?"

"It's nice to see you talk with so much passion. I knew you needed to come back to India," Harsha said, his smile broadening.

"Patronising asshole," Maya said, pinching him playfully on the arm.

For a brief and wonderful moment, it felt like they were all alone, just the two of them, before Harsha dragged himself back to the real world.

"How's your husband?"

Maya nodded to acknowledge his change of topic. "Very well," she said. "He is working for an IT company. In Tidel Park. And I get to work on my charity projects. I get paid a little stipend, enough for my expenses. We don't see each other much, as we are both so busy, but I think we are both happy to be back."

Harsha nodded. He took a deep breath and tried to ignore the aching in his heart. "Good for you. Genuinely, it sounds like you have improved your situation dramatically since last time. Glad it worked out."

She smiled and asked: "Are you happy here, Harry? I heard you were back in town, but... I... I thought it was best if..."

He briefly put his hand over hers and said: "I understand."

He thought briefly back to that period when they had nearly had an affair. Much as he had been in love with her, he was relieved that he hadn't slept with a married woman and didn't have that guilt to deal with.

"I am... learning to be happy, Maya," he said, and stopped for a second, and realised that the sentence he had just uttered summed it up perfectly.

"Aren't we all," she said, smiling, and he knew that she had understood him well.

He cleared his throat and tried to focus his thoughts on transgender issues and on Gopu's murder. "Do any of these people have any idea who may have done this to Gopu?"

Maya looked at him, her playful smile peeping out again. "You're not doing the Tintin thing again, are you, as Azhar would say?" she asked. Then, when he didn't say anything, playfulness turned to wonder, and she said: "Oh my god, you totally are! You're Tintin again!"

"For God's sake, Maya!" he said hastily. "I'm doing my job — as a crime reporter. An honorary crime reporter, just for this case, but still."

"Ha! Crime reporter! Tall story," she said, sounding for all the world like a petulant college student. "I bet your ass you get involved in the whole thing somehow before the end!"

Before he could reply, Mithra called out for Maya, and the pair of them turned to see Constable Gautami putting her notepad into a leather case. Gita looked over at them, looking a bit stressed but otherwise alright. Maya smiled and marched over, closely followed by Harsha.

She sat down next to Gita, and Harsha stood before them, all sitting under the tree in a semi-circle. He reflected on the odd set of women that suddenly seemed to have cropped up in his life. Add Harleen to the mix and you really had the whole spectrum.

Harleen! Harsha looked at his watch and groaned.

"What's the matter?" Maya asked him.

"I was supposed to be somewhere at 8pm. In Alwarpet, actually."

"That's ages away! You'll easily get there," she said.

"I was hoping to have a shower first. But I live in Neelankarai," he explained. "The other end of town."

"You seem perfectly clean," Maya said. "Is it that important that you shower?"

"I... never mind," he said, feeling oddly shy to tell Maya that he was going on a date. But the knowing look she gave him suggested she had guessed already. He transferred his attention to the policewoman as she got up and picked up her bicycle.

"Did you get what you want?" he asked, politely.

"Oh yes. It was interesting to talk about..." Gautami turned to Mithra again and said: "What was it again? The 1857 Society? Interesting. Well, goodbye and thanks."

Harsha had the oddest feeling that the policewoman was trying to tell him something with this little exchange, and he felt that familiar tingling sensation of being on the hunt. Suppressing his excitement, he walked a little with Gautami as she wheeled her bike towards the entrance.

"Inspector Palanivel is very busy these days, is he? Never picks up the phone," Harsha said, casually.

Gautami eyed him. "Yes, he is, Mr Devnath."

"Please, call me Harsha."

"Yes he is, Harsha. Now he not only has to do police work, but also deal with the politics. It's not easy."

"And you?"

"Oh me? It's pretty much the same. Chennai, Ramananpettai, it is all the same. Same crimes, same motivations."

They had reached the entrance so Harsha had decided it was time to end the pleasantries and said: "Can I just ask you if it is confirmed that it is a murder investigation?"

She stopped by the doorway, looked up at him and said: "Harsha, you are a good man. What you did last time in Arasur… it showed that you are a man of character and that you care about people."

Harsha felt unaccountably embarrassed by the words and her steady regard. Gautami hesitated and said: "Alright. I can confirm that it is a murder investigation. There was a single blow to his head…"

She stopped talking and smiled as Harsha scrambled to find a fresh page in his notebook to take down these details, pages flying everywhere.

"Blow to his head. Any idea what object was used?"

"A crystal award trophy. For his ten years in government or some such thing. It was put back on its pedestal — no fingerprints," Gautami said calmly, as though she wasn't just dictating the contents of *Southern Echo*'s front page splash for the next day.

Harsha furiously searched his brain for more questions.

"Anything else I should know?" he asked in the end, feeling a bit foolish.

Constable Gautami pursed her lips in thought and then shook her head.

Harsha nodded, looking down at his notes. He had learnt from Sampath by now that this was all that was needed for a story. The rest was just filler and context.

"Would it be alright if I called you sometime to get

updates on the case? Even details such as these are tremendously helpful," he said finally, feeling like there must be a dozen questions he didn't know to ask.

"Alright. Take my number. But don't call me after 7pm or my husband will think I am having an affair."

Harsha laughed weakly and took out his phone to take her number.

Just before she left the building, Constable Gautami turned and said: "Oh, one more thing."

In a flash, Harsha turned around and held his pen over his notepad, ready to take down anything important.

Gautami paused dramatically and then said: "He had a bookmark in his hand."

Harsha stared. "A bookmark?" he asked.

"Yes. A bookmark. Just a plain one. It took us a while to realise what it was."

"Why on earth would he be holding a bookmark?" Harsha asked, baffled.

Gautami shrugged her shoulders and finally left, the giant front door clanging shut behind her.

Harsha walked thoughtfully back towards the others. Gita seemed to be back to her normal calm self, possibly because Mithra and Maya had been giving her some solid reassurance. He was about to speak to her when Maya cut in and said: "Harry, I've been thinking. You can come to my place — I live near Alwarpet — and have a shower there before going to your next meeting."

The date! It had once again slipped his mind in the excitement of the juicy details that Constable Gautami had just given him. He briefly thought about cancelling it to work on his big story, but his brain rebelled against the thought of any more work that evening. The story could wait. But go to

Maya's place to prepare for a date with another woman? That was ridiculous.

"Seriously, Maya, no!" Harsha said, shaking his head. "What will Naveen think?"

"He won't mind one bit, and he works late anyway. You can even borrow one of his shirts — he has some lovely ones and he is your size. Especially since you stopped being fat," she said, grinning.

Harsha shook his head and said weakly: "Are you being serious?"

"Absolutely," she said with conviction, and gave him a brief smile. "That's settled then. And you can take your time with Gita here."

"Thanks, Maya," Harsha said, with mingled relief and exasperation.

He shook his head to clear it of the confusion induced by all these different women and turned to Gita and Mithra, who were sitting there placidly, waiting for him.

"Alright. Let's talk about the 1857 Society," he said.

16. Date

Harsha arrived at the date with his nerves in shreds. The evening traffic had put him on edge, clenching his fist and willing a water lorry ahead of his cab to move faster, or at least not take up the entire road. Every red signal added to his stress levels and he strode up in slightly panicked fashion to the Silk Road restaurant recommended to him by Azhar.

Thanks to Maya, at least he wasn't sweaty and hot anymore. He had showered in her beautiful apartment just off Greenways Road in a quiet but central part of Chennai, and donned some of her husband's Dolce & Gabbana aftershave and Ted Baker shirt. She had even found an old pair of his khaki trousers that fit him well. Harsha had looked in Maya's gilded mirror with its carved, golden leaves that ran around the frame and wondered to himself why he had never taken fashion seriously. Even these small, incremental changes made him look instantly so much better.

He walked through the delicately lit, open corridors that led up to the restaurant and admonished himself. This time two years ago, he had been fighting for his life in a raging river at midnight, trying to get away from some murderous goons, and yet he felt even more terrified now.

Before he had time to think too much more, he found Harleen sitting in a little cubby hole outside the entrance. She stood up and gave him a wave, and he blinked. The last time he had met her, she had been wearing a simple t-shirt and jeans (though she had still managed to look glamorous). This time, she was in a small, navy blue dress that started just below her bronzed shoulders and ended just above her knees, clinging to her slender frame in a way that was unostentatious and yet, he thought to himself, insanely sexy. Her hair was done up in a coiffure of some sort with a single white flower through it. He felt his heart pounding.

"Hi there," he said, suddenly not feeling quite so good looking despite the cologne and the shirt. On a whim, he decided on a European greeting and, placing one hand on her arm, kissed her lightly on either cheek, his lips barely making any contact. She was quite short — couldn't have been more than 5'3" — so he had to lean down to do so. She smelled of some exotic flower. Lilies? he wondered idly, and then thought of his grandmother's *Lily of the Valley* talcum powder and hastily repressed a chuckle.

"Good to see you again, Harsha," she said, still smiling heart-stoppingly at him and sending thoughts of his grandmother flying. "How is the intrepid journalist today?"

He laughed again and then said: "I may have massively oversold my job. But shall we go in?"

She nodded and they walked in together. Harsha briefly thought of guiding her by the arm or the small of her back but decided that was too creepy and put his hands firmly by his side as they spoke to the receptionist.

"Mr Harsha? Please, just give us a minute."

Harsha nodded and they stood awkwardly by the desk.

"How was your day," he asked, in a horrible, hearty voice that he barely recognised as his own.

"Not too bad, you know, just had to do a lot of paperwork for an upcoming case, you know, these companies..."

Harsha kept nodding, but tuned out her voice, because he had bigger things to worry about. Why was his table taking so long? He always suspected he was one of those people that didn't get served straight away. He didn't have the ease of command that Azhar did, for example. They would probably put him on a table next to the toilet, he thought gloomily. I mean, why not just take them to the table right away? He could see at least four or five tables were free. It was a total disaster.

"... and only then will it be filed with the registrar," she concluded, and looked at him expectantly.

Not for nothing had Harsha been a journalist for seven years. "That's pretty frustrating," he said, recognising the tone of voice, even if he had missed all of the content.

"What to do, *yaar*, that's how it works in India. Things move slowly. But at least they are moving."

A smiling waitress appeared at his elbow and said: "Mr Harsha, your table is ready."

Harsha jumped, startling both Harleen and the waitress in question.

"Lead the way," he said, trying to smile back.

Harleen looked at him a little oddly and the two of them followed the waitress, Harsha gloomily wondering if he had messed it up already.

The waitress led them to their table. Harsha did a double take — it was a little alcove, slightly separate from the rest of the restaurant and elevated above so you could look out onto the mostly candle-lit, elegant restaurant floor without being observed yourself.

The waitress was grinning at Harleen, whose mouth was wide open, as they walked up the little spiral stairway that led to this romantic little spot and, fortunately for Harsha, no one was observing him when they saw the two glasses of champagne on the table or Harleen would have seen it was as much of a surprise to him as it was to her.

Azhar, Harsha thought resignedly. Why had he got involved? All of this was so ridiculously over the top for such a down to earth, simple girl like Harleen. What would she think of Harsha?

He remembered himself and thanked the waitress profusely as she held the chair for Harleen to sit down. Over Harleen's elegantly coiffured hair, the waitress gave Harsha the briefest of winks. He nodded, jaw clenched. It wasn't her fault, after all!

"This. Is. Amazing!" Harleen said, beaming down at the champagne and the candles and then looking around at the restaurant from their little eyrie.

Harsha quickly revised his opinion — Azhar was a genius!

"Ummm ... glad you like it," he said, clearing his throat.

The waitress coughed — in a slightly mocking way, Harsha thought — and said: "I'll let you enjoy your champagne and fetch the menus in a few minutes."

Harleen turned away from admiring the view as the waitress left the alcove and looked at Harsha, her eyes shining. "Thank you so much! You shouldn't have done this!"

"Umm, you know... just wanted to... I mean, let's just enjoy the evening," Harsha finished lamely.

She smiled — she had a slight dimple on one cheek, he noticed — and picked up her champagne and sipped it delicately. "Delicious. So dry and toasty! High quality stuff," she said, nodding at him.

What Harsha knew about champagne would have barely filled a flute, so he sipped his drink — which tasted nice enough — without comment and said: "I've been..." he paused. Waiting for this? Counting down the hours? Desperate to see her again?

"... looking forward to this," he chose.

"Me too, Harsha," she said, pulling out that dazzling smile again.

He looked at her and his heart lifted before juddering to a nasty halt as a sudden memory of Maya's face and smile, dressed in her simple *salwar kameez*, infiltrated his mind. Was this really him? Sitting in a posh restaurant with a sophisticated lawyer? Or was he meant to be with Maya, in a simpler, more meaningful setting?

"Everything ok, Harsha?"

"Yes, of course! Tell me — what's it like being a criminal lawyer? Do you find yourself often fighting traumatic cases?"

She shrugged her elegant shoulders and said: "In my specialism of cyber crime, it can be anything from stolen mobile phones to more serious fraud, but generally fairly straightforward," she said. "But the more traumatic criminal cases that you are talking about; well, I tried that in my first year, and it really was not for me. I prefer this! Boring but safe."

Harsha laughed. "Sometimes too much excitement can be challenging."

"Exactly! But speaking of excitement — tell me how all your *investigation* was today?"

They were interrupted by the waitress, who brought them their menus and a bowl full of different coloured *pappads* and pickles to go with it.

"Just what I was thinking! This will go so well with champagne!" Harleen said, to Harsha's puzzlement. "Thank you, er..."

"Vijayalakshmi," the waitress said, smiling.

"Thank you, Vijayalakshmi!"

Harsha instantly liked the easy way in which Harleen interacted with the waitress. It reminded him a bit of Azhar, actually, the ability to be friendly with absolutely everyone. Maybe he shouldn't pigeonhole Harleen just yet as some posh, sophisticated woman, as his friends from London would have described it?

Harsha followed Harleen's example and took a sip of the champagne after biting into the pappad. He thought it tasted slightly better, but it all seemed a bit intangible to him.

"And so, Mr Detective, what did you get up to today? You have to give me the lowdown, no?"

"I'm not a detective," he said, hastily. "Just a journalist."

"But didn't you solve that mystery in Azhar's resort, he was telling us about it last time?"

Harsha nearly choked on his champagne, and then emerged, dripping slightly, and said, as he wiped his mouth: "Azhar is a big bullshitter. I played some role in that investigation, yes, but so did Azhar himself and ... another friend of mine."

Harsha thought of Maya for a second and his mind seemed flicker between her and Harleen sitting in front of him and he felt another wrench of the heart and an absurd surge of guilt that he was here with another woman. Or was he feeling guilty that he was here with Harleen and thinking about Maya?

Get over it! Get over her! He scolded himself, and wiped champagne off his shirt. Well, Maya's husband's shirt. *What a ridiculous mess this was.*

He tuned himself back into what Harleen was saying. "... but he is a loyal friend, even if I don't fully understand it," she finished.

"Azhar, you mean?"

She looked at him, wide-eyed. "Who did you think we were talking about?"

"Sorry," he said, sheepishly. "Just had a long day, brain not working properly."

She looked a little crestfallen, and he cursed himself and promised himself he would fully focus on Harleen and this evening from this point on.

"Shall we order some food?" he asked, as brightly as he could, and waved to catch Vijayalakshmi's attention, who smiled and nodded to show she had seen him and would come in due course.

"Azhar has been my closest friend for over a decade," Harsha said. "We lost touch while I was in England. But there's no one in the world who means more to me, other than my family. Well, perhaps even including my family," he added, thoughtfully, his mind briefly turning to some of the more objectionable of his cousins.

Harleen's crestfallen look disappeared at this and she smiled at him warmly, making his heart flutter slightly, and anchoring his mind firmly in the present. "I was..." he paused.

"Yes?" she asked.

"I ... sorry... you are... distractingly attractive," he said. "I lost track of what I was going to say."

Her smile grew broader and she said: "That's ok. I was just admiring your eyes, anyway."

He blinked at this, his heart pounding, and they looked at each other for a second.

"So! What will you guys have to eat?" Vijayalakshmi asked, making them both jump and look up at her in some confusion. The waitress looked from one to another and then smiled and said: "Shall I just give you a few more minutes?"

"Yes, please."

"Yes, please, thank you."

A couple of hours later, Harsha and Harleen sauntered out into a balmy Chennai evening, and were greeted by the faint "neek neek" of faraway car horns and the rushing of the sea breeze through the palm trees that lined the pavement.

Harsha could not remember an evening he had enjoyed more; he felt like he was floating on cloud nine. Already he was making roseate plans for the future: dating Harleen, getting married — would it have to be a Punjabi wedding? — and how they would pick names for their children.

"So are you working tomorrow?"

He shook his head to bring it back into the present.

"No, no — not officially anyway. Will type up my notes and so on but I'm looking forward to just hanging out with my flatmate," Harsha said as they made their slow way towards the car park.

"You boys and your Playstation," she said, laughing. "Is it Grand Theft Auto? My brother loves that game."

"Er... something like that," Harsha said. Then, feeling like he wasn't really portraying his more serious and artistic side, he also added: "I'm not just going to play on the Playstation though — I might just take my book down to the beach and read there for awhile."

"Oh!" Harleen said, turning to look at him enthusiastically. "What are you reading at the moment?"

Harsha was spared the pain of making up a book when she continued: "I'm just re-reading Nick Hornby's *High Fidelity*. It's one of my favourites."

Harsha felt a sudden stab in the pit of his stomach. Nick Hornby? Maybe they weren't so compatible after all.

"No," he said, shortly.

She turned to him in surprise again. "You're from London, an Arsenal fan, and you haven't read Nick Hornby?"

Harsha couldn't think of a way to say that his tastes were more literary than that without sounding like a snob, so he didn't say anything.

The lights flashed on a sleek black vehicle as Harleen pressed a button on her car keys and she walked up to it and put one proprietorial hand on its roof.

"You really should read Nick Hornby sometime. I really feel like he understands what relationships are *really* like," she said, pulling the door open.

Harsha thought it sounded dreadful, but he nodded. Right then, he would have agreed to pretty much anything. That said, their different tastes in books had stopped his imagination from running away with him. Perhaps he would need to get to know this Harleen better.

A sudden memory of discussing Chinua Achebe or Toni Morrison with Maya back in university, her eyes sparkling as she disagreed vehemently with a point he made, sprung up in his head and he thrust it hurriedly away.

"Sure you don't want a lift?"

"Absolutely sure," he said. "I'll be fine."

"Don't get accosted by any vengeful murderers on your

way back," she said playfully, and he laughed.

They stood slightly awkwardly there, and Harsha wondered whether he should kiss her or not. He looked down at her slightly parted lips and her slender and attractive frame and inched forward, undecided. As his mind raced with the possibilities, she nodded and then eased her way into the driver's seat and started the engine. She gave him another brief wave before the car pulled its way out of the car park. Harsha caught the make of the car in the street light — Skoda Felicia. An expensive car, certainly by Indian standards.

Wonderful as the evening had been, he couldn't help feeling they were from different worlds. Perhaps he shouldn't brainstorm their children's names just yet.

17. Plan of action

"What did I tell you? I *knew* you guys would get on!"

"Yes, but Azhar," Harsha said furiously into his phone. "I can't talk now!"

"And how about that champagne, eh? Proper vintage shit, man! Did she like it?"

"She did, but Azhar now is not a good..."

"And so? Did you take her home or not?"

"Azhar, no! I am not having this conversation right..."

"She's up all night to have fuuuun. He's up all night to get luckyyy..." Azhar warbled.

"I am hanging up now!"

Harsha hung up vigorously and then inadvertently dropped his phone on to his lap and then picked it up again, flustered, and then pressed the button as tightly as he could until the phone went blank, and then looked up apologetically at the sea of faces in front of him, and especially at the owner of *Southern Echo*, who was looking at him expressionlessly.

"Sorry," he said in a mortified whisper. "I thought it

might be... police contact... had to take it... idiotic friend... sorry," he stammered.

There was a silence for a second, and then Jaishree said, with a sardonic smile: "Are you sure you don't want to call him back? It sounded like an important matter."

"No no!" Harsha said, in a panic, not spotting the joke in his embarrassment.

There were a few chuckles around the table, and Harsha glanced at the others sitting around nervously.

"What it is to be young," said Mumtaz Hussain, the news editor.

There was Rahul Medappa, of course, the suave, keen-eyed editor of the paper, whom Harsha suspected to be a complete fraud, sitting at the head of the long table in the conference room.

Business editor Venugopal Acharya, or Venu as he was known, was blinking at Harsha through his glasses from Rahul's left. To Rahul's right, Mumtaz Hussain smiled briefly at him before going back to peruse her notes. Namritha was next to Mumtaz, smiling at Harsha in a predatory manner that made him nervously wonder what revenge she had in store for him. Probably a commission to write a full-length piece about teenage romance or the latest fashion boutique shop, he thought gloomily to himself. And finally, there was Jaishree, sitting discreetly opposite Mumtaz in the centre of the table — but very clearly the most powerful person in the room.

Then there was Sampath, of course, sitting next to Harsha, feeling the tip of his pencil and looking absently at the ceiling.

Rahul leaned forward with his customary zeal. "Why don't you give us a debrief of where you have got so far with the story?"

Harsha glanced briefly at Sampath — who looked away — and realised there was little choice left but to plough on through the Azhar call embarrassment.

Despite the chill of the air-conditioned room, he wiped a trickle of sweat from his forehead and said: "I had confirmation from a police source that they are conducting a murder investigation into Gopinath's death. And the murder weapon as well. Sampath confirmed this with his source, so we have written up a story."

Harsha had enjoyed writing the story with Sampath. His flair for words and Sampath's news sense had made for a potent combination and the final version of the story had filled Harsha with pride when he had read it.

"It is with the lawyers at the moment," Mumtaz said, cutting into his thoughts. "Jaishree will you have a final look after this meeting?"

The newspaper proprietor nodded without opening her eyes.

"I don't know about the rest of you, but I'd like to hear the whole story from the beginning," Venu said, smiling slightly as he looked at the two reporters. Everybody else went silent and looked expectantly at them.

Harsha once again ceded the floor to Sampath, but the crime reporter simply said: "Harsha is the one who first began to look at the transgender angle."

He was the cynosure of eyes once again. Harsha took a deep breath.

"My interest was first piqued when I met this transgender person called Gita..." he began.

The story took about ten minutes to deliver in detail between the two of them. But everyone listened in silence.

Rahul made a great show of taking notes — while Venu was also jotting down a few points. Namritha continued to glare resentfully at him and Jaishree seemed to be asleep. Certainly her eyes were closed and her impressive chin was resting on steepled fingers.

When Harsha finally came to the death knock, a few sympathetic nods and smiles sprung out among the journalists. They had all been there, in one form or another. At the mention of the 1857 Group, a few exclamations broke out: the first real interruption. Jaishree's eyes popped open and she turned to regard Harsha steadily.

"1857 Group? Are you sure?" Venu asked. "Very, very interesting."

"Oh yes — fascinating," Rahul interjected quickly, his polished accent and excitable manner contrasting with Venu's sturdy manner and guttural South Indian accent. "Er... Venu, just refresh us about this 18... er... 97 Group?"

Jaishree's eyes shut again, but Harsha thought he saw a little crease of annoyance form on her forehead. Mumtaz was rubbing her nose in embarrassment.

"The 1857 Group," Venu said implacably, with only a slight emphasis on the 'fifty', "Is a loyalist organisation which is trying to influence the politics of Tamil Nadu to make it more in line with pro-Hindu elements in the north of India."

"What do they want exactly?" Rahul asked casually, as though asking his question for the benefit of the group.

"Beyond what I just said? Eventually they want India to be a Hindu state — based on the Israel model," Venu said drily, smiling apologetically at Mumtaz, whose expression did not change. "But for the moment... Tamil Nadu has always had a bit of a separate identity from the big northern states and Delhi. The 1857 Group want to change that, and make us more patriotic, or so they call it."

"Who heads these nutcases?" Mumtaz asked.

"Advaith Mohapatra. Ex-politician, firebrand — very scary man."

Venu said it in a matter of fact way, but Harsha felt a chill go down his spine.

Namritha said: "But why would they bother with these ch... these transgenders? What has it got to do with them?"

Venu shook his head to show that he did not know, but Harsha gathered his courage and said: "According to Neha, they sent threatening notes to Gopinath. It looks like they saw him as a pseudo-liberal who was bringing disgrace to Hinduism and taking us away from traditional Indian values."

"Can we get hold of these letters," Jaishree asked, her eyes still closed.

Harsha jumped guiltily. He had been kicking himself for not having thought of this when he was speaking to Hema and Neha. "Er... yes, I will do my best," he said lamely.

This would mean he would have to get back in touch with Neha, which he was not at all in a hurry to do.

"Is there any other avenue we can explore?" Rahul asked briskly. Harsha wondered if he wanted to move on from the 1857 Group discussion as quickly as possible.

Sampath cleared his throat and the attention shifted from Harsha to him.

"Two things," Sampath said in his bored-sounding voice. "One, there is a lot of talk that this Gopinath may have been caught in a turf war between two sections of the transgender community."

Mumtaz frowned. "*Arre* Sampath, this is the transgender

community. Not some Italian mafia or something," she said.

"My sources in the police tell me they are looking into this angle," Sampath said in the same disinterested voice. "Also, I am told that one of the transgender people was actually in the building at the time. To collect her wages due, or something."

Eyes opened wide at this around the table, Harsha's included. This was new to him.

"Still — a very downtrodden community," Mumtaz maintained, mirroring Harsha's own thoughts.

"There is a lot of substance abuse in the transgender community," Venu said drily, coming unexpectedly to Sampath's aid. "And where there are drugs — there is violence. We can't rule this out."

Rahul turned importantly to Harsha. "Can you check this with your source as well?"

Harsha thought of the forbidding Detective Inspector Palanivel with some trepidation, but he nodded. He felt a deep sense that this transgender turf war was a blind alley. It was too easy to point to the most downtrodden community and blame them for all problems. But he reminded himself that he was a journalist, and therefore completely objective and open to all possibilities.

"Two," Sampath said, and all eyes turned back to him. "The new hydropower plant in Kovalam by the Boreas Vayu joint venture. There is some talk that they might have ordered this hit because Gopinath was holding back construction. With him out of the way, the project can go ahead."

The editors shifted in their seats and sat up straighter at this sensational revelation and began discussing it excitedly.

"Is this possible, Venu? A corporate hitman?" Mumtaz

asked.

Venu nodded thoughtfully. "This hydropower plant is a cash cow," he said in his thickly-accented English. "Power is worth more than gold in Tamil Nadu right now with all the shortages. Kalyan will know more."

"Absolute gold mine," Rahul said, nodding sagely. Venu didn't look at him, focusing on Mumtaz instead.

"But a *hitman*. It seems extreme," she said, pursing her lips.

Even Namritha made a contribution to the conversation. "But the Boreas Vayu JV is headed by Varun Dar, no? He is married to the former finance minister's niece!" she declared, looking shocked and excited.

Jaishree's eyes opened and everyone fell silent. She turned to look at Sampath and Harsha and eyed them beadily.

"This story is going beyond anything we had hoped for," she said finally, in her customary brisk tone. "Politics, culture, corporate interests, families — this may well be the most important story *Southern Echo* has written up to now."

A silence fell on the table. Harsha glanced at Sampath, who was looking as bored as ever. He swivelled round slightly to look at Namritha, who looked like she had swallowed something bitter. Harsha switched back to looking at Jaishree.

"You two have done *phenomenally* well to make sure we are the first on this story," she said, looking down at her hands. Her head then snapped up and directed her keen gaze first at Harsha and then at Sampath. "Now you must make sure we are the *best* on this story. For now I am inclined to let the two of your lead this coverage and not add to the confusion by involving others. But let us know what you need — you will get all the support you need from us in making *Southern Echo* the leading newspaper on this story," she said.

Rahul leaned forward and added some words that Harsha let wash over him. This was not only because Jaishree had just made clear that she was taking over the editorial responsibility from the chief editor, but also because he was reeling from the high praise from the newspaper's owner — while also feeling stressed about the responsibility she was placing on them. On him.

He looked up to see that Jaishree was still watching him.

"We will do our best, Jaishree," he said, finally, trying to ignore the swooping sensation in his stomach.

She nodded and gave him a rare smile.

18. 1857 Group

A few wisps of grass flew across the dry maidan of the cricket ground, baked by the lingering summer. Harsha scanned it, watching the dust and tufts of vegetation make their stumbling progress across the sparse outfield.

During the day, this would have made for an idyllic sight. A game of cricket would have almost certainly have been on, the sound of leather on willow echoing through the ground, the sun shining on the white uniforms of the players and the green expanse of the field, the umpires squinting from under the brims of their hats at the turf; a scene straight from Ruskin Bond's cricket stories.

But at night, it was unquestionably spooky. The ground stretched out on either side, bathed in the orange glow of the city lights, with a troubled ocean swaying fitfully on one side.

And this was without even considering the hundreds of people that had gathered in front of the pavilion. These people were also clothed in white, yet nothing like cricketers. They held wooden torches that flickered menacingly.

They stood facing a short man with greying hair combed

over to one side, a beatific smile on his face, a little microphone snaking its way towards his lips from behind his neck to capture his words.

He was in the middle of a speech that was terrifying Harsha to his very soul.

"There are some people who will tell you that Hinduism is a tolerant religion. That we are a kind people. That we show compassion to others," he said in a soft voice, smiling benignly towards his enraptured audience, holding them effortlessly. "And they are right. That is true."

The torches flickered in response and faces — men, women, young, old, poor, rich — stared seriously back at him.

The man stared intently into their upturned faces and continued: "But that does not mean that there isn't a time for ACTION!"

Harsha jumped at the sudden increase in volume, but he was the only one. The rest continued to watch silently.

"We are, and we always will be, a peaceful people. But when we are provoked — when our culture is put in danger — we must react quickly and strongly. Some false, self-proclaimed experts say that Hinduism has always preached tolerance and turning the other cheek. But this is not true! Do you remember the story of how Ravana set fire to Hanuman's tail?"

Harsha dredged up the memory of listening to his grandmother's stories from the Indian epic, the Ramayana, as she made him kesari on the old kerosine stove in her home in Kolkata. As he remembered it, the monkey god Hanuman had offended Ravana, the wicked king of Lanka, in some way. Ravana had ordered the Hanuman's tail to be set on fire as a punishment and warning. But the monkey god turned the tables on Ravana by using his flaming tail to set fire to the entire kingdom of Lanka.

This had seemed like a harmless enough story to Harsha until now; he had even laughed at how Ravana had got his comeuppance. He now watched as the myth took on a terrifying new layer of meaning in the words of the smiling man by the pavilion of Marina Cricket Ground.

"Hanuman was not satisfied with simply getting revenge on Ravana. He set fire to the entire city of Lanka, without mercy. And so we shall set fire to entire cities if that is what it takes. They hurt India and what it stands for — we BURN them to the ground!"

The entire crowd lifted their torches and roared their response, as the speaker listed out India's enemies on his fingers.

Harsha quailed in his corner of the maidan.

After the speech ended, Harsha gathered himself enough to go up to the speaker. The man was surrounded by a crowd of devotees, but some instinct must have alerted him to Harsha's presence, because he waved them aside impatiently and beckoned to Harsha.

"Mr Devnath? From the *Southern Echo*? I was told to expect you."

The man put his hands together and bowed in a traditional Indian greeting, two rows of his fans flanking him on either side, just as Harsha stepped forward and stuck out his hand. Harsha quickly withdrew his hand and bowed awkwardly as well.

"Mr Advaith Mohapatra?"

"Advaith will do," the man said, smiling warmly and simply. Harsha could barely reconcile this charming man with the one who had just given a highly inflammatory speech.

"Good to meet you, Advaith," Harsha said, as the man led him to a corner of the pavilion.

"Some tea?" Advaith asked, snapping his fingers to get the attention of one of the sari-clad women who seemed to be organising the event.

They sat on a pair of rickety plastic chairs and Harsha balanced his little notepad on his knee.

"How can I help?" Advaith asked, extending his arms to signal complete transparency and cooperation.

"Interesting speech," Harsha said, as much to give himself time to collect himself as anything.

Advaith laughed self-consciously. "Don't take it all too seriously. A lot of it is for effect. Though the gist of it is based on the best principles of the 1857 Society."

"So you don't want to take action against those who threaten India? And... er... burn them to the ground?"

Advaith laughed a tinkling laugh. "Only in a broad, ideological sense."

"Didn't you say you wanted to take action, though?"

"Oh yes, action. But action doesn't mean violence, per se."

"Then what, Advaith?"

Advaith spread his hands once more, encompassing the maidan. He continued to smile, but his eyes flashed with anger.

"It could mean any number of things," he said.

Harsha waited, but there was nothing more forthcoming from the other side, so he changed tack.

"Why the 1857 Society? What is special about that number?"

Advaith's brows contracted in a surprised frown.

"Surely even y..." he began before swallowing his words, and saying more politely: "Are you familiar with the 1857 Indian revolution against the British?"

Harsha was happy for Advaith to consider him ignorant of Indian history.

"Could you tell me more about it?" he asked.

The sari-clad assistant came up with a tray and two cups of tea in cheap plastic cups and silently served them both. Harsha absently took a sip of his cup and nearly gagged. It was extremely sweet; *rabri*, his grandmother would have called it contemptuously, referring to the Indian milk sweet.

"1857 was a great year in Indian history," Advaith said, cutting into Harsha's meandering thoughts. "It began with our brave soldiers, who took up arms against the British in Meerut, near Delhi. It inspired many other acts of rebellion throughout the country, first by other soldiers and then eventually by civilians as well."

The man sighed, smoothing his hair delicately, his eyes far away. "Many brave people emerged that year and the subsequent year. Many fought to overthrow the East India Company and its despicable rule of India. And many fought on the side of the British."

Harsha had no doubt whom Advaith's ire was most reserved for. Advaith shook his head and then sipped his tea, seeming to quite enjoy its sickly sweetness.

"It ended in Gwalior the following year. They defeated us. There's no two ways about that — they called in the army, they had superior firepower, and they had the help of traitors. And then — they smashed us. Have you read The Tears of the Rajas? You should. It was written by a Scotsman.

But it is very good. It tells us of the atrocities the British committed in this land."

Harsha licked his lips and asked the obvious question. "But ultimately, the 1857 Revolution failed, didn't it? The British ruled us for nearly a century afterwards."

"It was the beginning of the end," Advaith said calmly. "1947 would not have been possible without 1857. Today we attribute freedom to Gandhi. But we have forgotten the sacrifices of our brothers and sisters who came before."

Something about the way Advaith said 'Gandhi', with an undercurrent of contempt, prompted Harsha's next question.

"Isn't it true to say that Gandhi won us our freedom, though?"

Advaith shifted in his chair, which creaked under his slight weight, and looked carefully at Harsha.

"Tell me, Harsha — you spent a few years in England, didn't you?"

Harsha was impressed, and not a little flattered, that this man had done his research on him.

"Yes, I did," he said, simply.

"And how did you feel, working with the English? Working for them?"

Harsha scanned Advaith's face, looking for any signs of disapproval or judgement. What was the man getting at?

"I don't think I felt anything special," he said, finally. "I mean, it took a little getting used to, different cultures and all that, but on the whole I can't think of anything unusual."

"Did you not feel even a little bit... inferior?"

Light dawned on Harsha. "Because of my racial memory of being conquered, you mean?" he asked, smiling.

Advaith nodded, his eyes widening. "Exactly!" he said,

waggling his finger. "You are an intelligent young man. I like that. And did you?"

Harsha thought deeply and said: "Maybe a little."

Advaith nodded. "It is natural. They ruled us for two centuries with a paltry number of soldiers. Why wouldn't you feel inferior?"

The man then leaned forward and his face suddenly burned with intensity. "Now, imagine that we had thrown the British out with blood and fire — how would you have felt walking into that English office and speaking to your English boss? With your chin held high? Knowing that your ancestors had flung his ancestors back into the ocean?"

The harsh tone that came into the little man's voice was shocking. Harsha struggled to control his own voice.

"So, you think Gandhi was wrong?"

"Gandhi won us our freedom — but he traded our pride for it," Advaith said, leaning back in his chair, his composure snapping back comfortably.

"And you want Indians to... er... use blood and fire now to bring back that pride?"

"Oh no! I was not advocating anything!" Advaith declared airily. "This is just my opinion on our recent history. We just want to hold these matters up to light. That's our main aim."

"So you are historians, then?"

Advaith laughed. "Yes, you are an intelligent young man," he said, finally.

But he did not answer the question.

Harsha did not say anything either, at a loss for words.

Finally, Advaith sighed and leaned back in his chair, and said: "Harsha, come on. Why don't you ask the question that you are really here to ask."

Harsha's eyebrows rose. "What do you mean, sir?"

Advaith smiled in a slightly disappointed manner. "This government official. Gopinath. Don't you have any questions?"

Harsha hesitated, and then said: "Well, sir, we are told that you did send him some rather... strenuous letters. His daughter told us about them."

He didn't add that he was yet to see the letters in question. Neha had proved a little elusive.

"Sometimes, I let my passion get the better of me," Advaith said, sorrowfully. "Gopinath was a dedicated government official, the kind of person who helped rebuild the nation after three centuries of ruinous colonisation. I believe he acted with the best of intentions. But it is time for us to take the next step, to be bold and to assert ourselves on the world stage! That was the step that his generation was not able to take. And I wanted him to understand this. If I spoke too forcefully, I blame myself for this. I care too much," he ended virtuously.

Harsha looked down at his notes and said: "So when you said 'there will be consequences for you', you meant..."

Advaith looked at Harsha in a shocked manner. "My dear Harsha, there are consequences for all of our actions! That is karma. The very foundation of our religion!"

"But to say it repeatedly sounds a bit threatening..."

Advaith raised his hands in mock innocence. "Taken out of context, it sounds bad. But it didn't mean what you think."

"Was it written in a metaphorical sense?" Harsha asked sardonically.

"Exactly," Advaith said happily, as though Harsha had understood him very well.

Harsha looked into those watery eyes and once again

shuddered. This was a man with absolute iron conviction. No doubts whatsoever. There was nothing that Harsha could ask him that would shake him.

"I hope I can be in touch with you in the future if I have any more questions," Harsha said, finally.

Advaith leaned forward and clapped Harsha on the shoulder.

"Anytime at all, my friend," he said, sincerity ringing in his voice.

19. Suspects

Maya couldn't help feeling uneasy when she saw Gita's name flash on her mobile phone that morning. Usually it was a text in broken English asking for some help with a funding programme or assistance with a newly rehabilitated member of the community. This time, it was an actual phone call. She picked up the phone and said: "Everything ok, Gita?"

"Madam, please come at once. It is important," she heard Gita's voice say, and her heart gave a jolt. In a very short space of time, barely two months, Gita had become an important figure in the transgender community, organising various rescue and support operations and directing charitable funds to the right place. A call from her was not to be ignored — something serious was probably going on.

Maya took two minutes to pick up her jute bag and put on her sandals before heading out of her tiny office — she was the only one in at that hour — onto the street to hail an auto-rickshaw.

She flagged one down successfully. They set off with a roar and a puff of acrid smoke, and motored their way towards RK Salai, the auto-rickshaw bumping over a few potholes along the way. Maya clutched at the metal rail separating her from the driver and tried not to think of the gleaming cabs of Seattle and the butter-smoothness of American roads. *You chose this life*, she scolded herself.

She saw the auto-rickshaw driver glance at her curiously through the rear view mirror and sighed. The biggest challenge of coming back to India was what Junaina called The Male Gaze. It was that intangible sense, as a woman, of always being watched by men and never quite feeling safe. She missed being able to travel at night without feeling threatened, that was for sure.

But then, India was a more patriarchal society, no two ways about it. And did she want to avoid it as a result, or be part of the change? Her life here had a purpose — and part of that purpose came from her country's imperfections.

Also, on the other hand, there were things about India that were overwhelmingly positive. And high up on that list was the warmth of everyday human interaction. You just had to lean into it.

"Are you going via Mount Road?" she called out to the driver, as a way of starting a conversation.

"Too crowded at this hour, madam," the driver responded in a mellifluous voice. "We can go through Marina Beach road — much better."

She nodded and leaned back, trying not to wince with every bump.

"Do you have a business meeting, madam?"

"Something like that."

The gentle chat with the driver had cheered her up by the time they reached the entrance to the little transgender commune known simply as The Sanctuary. The auto-rickshaw made a jarring halt on the dirty, but quiet, side street just off Burma Bazaar.

"Here, madam?" the driver asked doubtfully, peering either side of the unlikely street.

"Yes," she said, scrambling and searching her bag for her purse.

After she had paid, he took out a magazine and sat cross legged on his seat with the air of a man making himself comfortable.

"I will wait here for you," he said, decisively.

"I don't know how long I will be," she said, exasperated and amused.

"I will wait," he said firmly.

She shook her head as she made her way towards the great iron gate. Why were men always trying to protect her? Yet, it would undoubtedly be useful to have her ride waiting for her outside, so she was not about to complain.

She rang the doorbell.

The gates of the old home creaked open and Savitri, the general factotum of the community, peered out at her and swung the gate open, smiling. Maya walked in confidently, nodding to her and glancing at the beautiful *gulmohar* tree that made up the main meeting place.

"Where is Gita?" she asked Savitri. Though she knew this was a troubled community with more than its share of troubles, she still thought Savitri's expression looked unusually grim.

Savitri nodded towards the area beneath the tree. "In the usual place."

"And Mithra?" Maya asked, as they made their way towards this spot.

"She is away in Mumbai on some work," Savitri said

grimly. Maya quickly marched towards the meeting point.

Gita was sitting in her usual peaceful spot under the tree facing two other people whom Maya did not know. But she could tell instantly why she had felt unsettled — these two did not really belong here. Most of the people in The Sanctuary had a purpose. Those who had been in bad places in their lives had already made their journey back towards some form of normality. Maya looked around to see them wandering around the courtyard peacefully.

But there was something defiant and angry about the way these two newcomers were sitting on the edge of their seats, gesticulating at Gita as they spoke.

As Maya neared them, she saw that the one closer to her was red with anger and the other was laughing oddly, a distant look in her eyes. Maya realised with a sinking heart that one or both looked to be under the influence of some illegal substance.

Gita glanced up at Maya's dismayed expression, smiled briefly, and caught hold of her hand and pulled Maya to her side. Maya gripped her hand gratefully in response.

"Who is this?" the red-faced transgender woman demanded angrily.

"Whoever she is, she is a pretty one," the other cackled.

Gita's grip on Maya's hand tightened.

"This is Maya," she said calmly. "She is a friend. This is Nangai and this is Jamuna," she said, turning to Maya and pointing towards the two transgender women in front of her.

Nangai, the red-faced one, shook her head in disgust. "When will you learn, Gita, that we *have* no friends. This woman is here to feed her own ego, to feel good, to..."

"I work for the Helping Hands charity," Maya said

quickly. "And we have done a lot of work with the transgender community."

"Maya is not just a friend to our community," Gita said softly. "She is also my friend."

Maya felt a lump rise in her throat.

"What type of friend," Jamuna asked, with a wink and a giggle.

Maya turned despairingly away from this strange duo. Up to now, her work with Helping Hands had been heartwarming, if challenging and at times frustrating. This dash of reality was shaking her foundations. She knew that many transgender women worked as sex workers, and had trouble with substance abuse. She just hadn't met any in those desperate circumstances. Until now. She had imagined sex workers — if that is indeed what they were — as figures of pity. But she found this couple terrifying.

"What do they want?" she whispered to Gita. Unfortunately, Nangai overheard this.

"None of your fucking business, is what we want," she said hotly. Maya looked fearfully at the woman and saw that a thick layer of cheap makeup had been applied on her face to hide a pockmarked and scarred complexion, and felt a surge of sympathy.

"They are here because they need our help," Gita said, calmly. "And since Mithra is away, I am doing my best to provide."

"Maybe, maybe not," Nangai muttered. Jamuna simply stared at them with glassy eyes.

"Yes, you do," Gita said firmly. "You don't want to be arrested by the police."

"Is that possible?" Maya asked urgently.

Gita nodded grimly. "It has happened before. We usually

don't have anyone to defend us, so we are an easy target."

"We didn't murder that man!" Jamuna yelled out suddenly, drawing all eyes to her. The difference in the tone was shocking. Gone was the inane giggling. Instead, she looked despairing and terrified for her very soul, and Maya's insides twisted.

Gita looked from Jamuna to Nangai, who grudgingly shook her head. "No we didn't — even though he bloody deserved it, the bastard."

"What are they talking about?" Maya asked Gita.

"Talk to my face, you fine madam! We are talking about that Gopinath asshole, of course!"

Maya turned, startled, to the red-faced woman. "Why would you? Of all people, he was trying to help you..."

"Ha! Like how you are trying to help us with your fine words? It's all bullshit. You are just trying to help yourself and your own conscience. And Gopinath was the same!"

Gita pulled up a chair beside her. Maya sat down and looked at the odd couple in front of them. Much as they terrified her, this attitude was alarming and she needed to know more.

"Why do you hate him so much? He was only trying to help," Gita said, mirroring Maya's own thoughts.

"Bah! Help! Help himself. He made himself look like a fucking humanitarian and threw us to the wolves!" Nangai declared.

"How so?" Maya asked, keenly. For a second, she thought Nangai was just going to insult her again, but instead she said: "We were a project for him. His way of displaying his credentials to the world. He put us in that government department where..." At this point, she seemed to choke with rage and frustration. She gathered herself and continued: "Where they treated us like rabid dogs. Like shit on the soles of their shoes!"

"But we are rabid dogs, Nangu," Jamuna said, chuckling, her manic giggle accentuating the pathos of her statement. "Just a pair of rabid bitches."

Nangai straightened her shoulders. "That may be, but I am not going to lie down to be trampled over. At least when we were whores, we had some freedom. It was a transaction. There was some fucking dignity to it."

Maya looked at her furious face and saw the vulnerability beneath, and her heart was filled with pity.

"But you... you did not hurt him?" Gita asked, hesitantly.

Nangai stood up militantly and Maya's train of thought was broken and replaced with alarm.

"I wish I had! But no — I did not," Nangai declared, folding her arms in front of her chest.

"Then what's the problem?" Gita asked, puzzled. "Why are you here?"

"That policeman is asking questions. And not in a polite way! And... We happened to be in the building when the incident occurred," Nangai said, her voice breaking.

Maya and Gita exchanged glances. This was not good.

"Why were you in the building?" Gita asked, gently.

"To collect what was due to us — our final paycheck. We didn't know that he would be murdered at the same time," Nangai said, as though Gopinath had got himself murdered just to spite them.

"But you weren't anywhere near him at the time, were you?"

"No," Nangai said, but she didn't look up at them. And Jamuna shook her head vigorously in a manner that instantly raised Maya's suspicions.

"That bloody policeman..." Nangai said again, her voice laced with fear.

Remembering Inspector Palanivel's robust manner of questioning suspects, Maya shivered slightly.

"And then there's that damned journalist as well. Also asking around."

"What? Harsha? Was that his name?" Maya asked, her heart sinking. Surely Harry couldn't be so lost to all compassion as to pick on these two poor souls?

But then Harsha was a journalist now — and journalists, well, Maya knew from experience that journalists would do anything for a story.

"I don't know his name," Nangai said shortly.

"He's a good-looking one though," Jamuna cackled. "Not bad to be caught by someone like that and held in his broad arms!"

Gita ignored this, instead taking a deep breath and asking: "How can we help?"

The two miserable people in front of them looked blankly at her. They clearly had no idea. Gita bit her lip, thinking.

"I can try and arrange for some legal help," Maya blurted out after a second's hesitation, and all three of them turned to look at her.

"You can?" Gita and Nangai asked at the same time, while Jamuna pursed her lips and looked at her in a calculating manner.

"I... that is, my organisation, knows some law firms that do pro bono work. It's worth at least trying."

Jamuna was the first to react. "Who would represent us?" she asked, laughing without any particular bitterness.

"You may be surprised," Maya said drily. "At least it's

worth asking."

Gita gripped her arm. "Thank you, Maya," she said, gratefully.

Maya looked up at Nangai, who was looking at her strangely.

"Thank you," she said as well, bowing her head slightly.

Somehow, Maya found the sudden humility more distressing than the anger.

20. Interlude

"How long has it been since we last came here, dude?" Azhar asked, leaning back and staring around at the beautiful garden that made up the outside portion of the sprawling Amethyst café in the heart of Chennai. "At least ten years!"

Harsha, who was sitting to Azhar's right, cast his mind back to university days when they would come to Amethyst and "study" together, consuming coffees and plates of chilli cheese toast by the dozen before heading off to some bar or the other in the evening.

There was a hum of chatter in the air as people took advantage of a pleasant October evening to sit outside, accompanied by the clink of cutlery and the sound of distant car horns.

"That's where we used to sit," Azhar said nostalgically, pointing at one particular table in the very centre of the garden. Harsha remembered that Azhar had always gravitated towards the centre, so he could be within sight of everyone.

"And that's where you used to smoke joints," Shane said from Harsha's other side, pointing towards a secluded corner behind a rose bush.

"Chuck it, man, been years since I smoked anything, let alone weed," Azhar said, leaning back and brushing some crumbs off his salmon pink shirt. "None of us smoke anymore. Even Harry bloody quit. How did you do it, Harry?"

Harsha nodded towards Junaina, who was sitting in brooding silence opposite Harsha. "I was inspired by Juni here. If she can quit, anyone can," he said.

Shane swallowed a mouthful of his toast and grinned at Harsha. "Did you also use the power of God, Harry?" he asked, dimpling.

Harsha chuckled. Shane knew well that he was a confirmed atheist.

"No — just Allen Carr's book. He's a quit smoking guru," he added for the group's benefit.

"Typical of Harry to turn to a book," Azhar said, smiling. "Probably more effective than..."

"Oy!" Junaina cut in testily. "If you are going to insult my religion..."

Shane put his hands up in mock innocence. "I was going to say, probably more effective than nicotine patches," he said, and winked at Harsha. "I would never insult your religion."

"Once bitten, twice shy, eh?" Harsha asked, smiling at Shane, who chuckled. Shane had been well-known in university for interspersing his conversation with a number of little aphorisms, and that saying had been one of his favourites.

"Giving me a taste of my own medicine," he said, and everyone groaned.

"Well, Harsha, we are all delighted that you quit

smoking," Azhar said in a statesmanlike manner. "Very hard to get a girl these days as a smoker. They've become bloody picky," he added gloomily.

"Be happy anyone picks you at all," Junaina said acerbically.

Ignoring this, Azhar said: "On that subject, dude..."

Harsha jumped guiltily. He had been dreading this.

"What happened to Harleen? Have you asked her out again yet?"

"Er... no."

"Why the fuck not?"

"Been busy with work and..."

"Rubbish! People find time when they are really into someone! And I thought you really were, last time we spoke! You were bubbling over talking about Harleen! What changed?" Azhar demanded, leaning forward aggressively.

"He saw Maya," Shane said, shrewdly, scrutinising his old university friend.

Harsha tried not to blush. He had forgotten how uncomfortably sharp Shane could be at times.

Azhar threw his hands up in the air, leaning back in his cane chair again.

"This shit again!" he said, and shut his eyes in exasperation.

"Dude," Junaina said, shaking her head. "Mads is one of my favourite people in the world. I get it. But she's married, you loser! You need to move on!"

"And you do that by sleeping with someone else," Azhar said briskly, opening his eyes and leaning forward earnestly. "If you don't want Harleen, then I know this other chick who..."

"Stop pimping women, you dick," Junaina said, slapping

the back of Azhar's hand lightly. "Harry needs to get himself right in the head first."

Harsha couldn't help smiling as Junaina and Azhar started bickering over what was the best solution to his romantic problems and glanced at Shane to see if he was deriving any amusement from this familiar sight as well.

But Shane was looking at him with some sympathy instead. "You know, Harry, they are both right," he said loudly, and the others stopped talking. "You do need to find a way to get over Maya."

Harsha didn't say anything, looking down at the dregs of his coffee instead. Yes, he could see what they meant. He needed to get over Maya. But how was he to do that? It was easier said than done.

He didn't believe in true love or soulmates or anything like that. Yet — why could he not let go of the thought of Maya's face, or the sound of her gurgling laughter? It had been two years since they had had that night of huge attraction for each other, and that connection that had seemed almost spiritual, like something out of Jane Austen.

Why had it not worked out between them? Was it just the fact that Maya was married?

Someone clearly had turned on the music, and it tinkled out softly from Amethyst's PA system. Harsha recognised Third Eye Blind's *The Background* as the song that came on. He laughed a little to himself — it was from his favourite breakup album. Was the universe conspiring against him?

"Not sure I can take this Maya shit for much longer," Azhar said in an irritated voice, cutting jarringly into Harsha's thoughts.

Shane turned to hush Azhar but Azhar waved him away. "No! I will not be quiet! Harry — you're 30 years old, bugger! This isn't the age for theatrics! It's all this bloody literature you have been studying! It's driven you crazy. Like…"

"Don't compare me to Don Quixote again, Azhar!" Harsha said crossly, putting his coffee cup down with an almighty clank.

"I was going to say like Anthony from *Anthony and Cleopatra*," Azhar said with dignity. "Let Rome in Tiber melt and all that shit."

Everyone turned to Azhar in astonishment at this unexpected display of erudition, and he blushed.

"Not that I believe in that 'thee thou' bollocks," he added under his breath.

"The Shakespearean scholar is right," Shane said, suppressing a smile. He leaned forward and put his hand on Harsha's shoulder. "You have to accept that this is over, Harry. Even if somehow you and Maya get together — it won't end well, my friend. She will be tortured by her broken marriage."

Harsha looked up at Shane's placid and benign face, hating him for being right. But eventually, he nodded. He gave a bitter laugh and said: "I fucking hate to hear that, Shane. But you are right, of course. As usual, you bastard."

Shane's grip on his shoulder tightened, and Harsha hastily swallowed a sob.

There was a brief silence while the group all kept silent out of respect for their fallen comrade. The happy chatter of the people around them washed over the group.

Finally, Harsha said with difficulty: "Give me a few weeks to get over this. I agree with you all — but I can't just turn it off like a tap."

Shane nodded. "Of course not."

Harsha glanced at Azhar. "Sorry about your friend Harleen, dude. I didn't mean to mess her around."

Azhar shifted in his seat, clearly uncomfortable with the seriousness of this conversation.

"How did you leave it?" he asked, finally.

"I just didn't call her, though I said I would," Harsha said, squeezing his eyes shut in embarrassment.

"Oh, dude. That's nothing! Leave it alone," Azhar said with some relief.

Shane said: "Maybe drop her a text and be honest about the situation."

Azhar shook his head decisively. "No way. That's the worst thing he can do."

Junaina, who had gone quiet as she usually did when Maya — who was her closest friend — was the topic of conversation, provided unexpected support for Azhar.

"Absolutely. Unless she texts Harsha, it will look ridiculous to send her chapter and verse about his complicated love life when they've only been on one date."

Harsha nodded miserably. He had forgotten this horrible side of dating — ending a romantic interest.

Azhar stood up. "Bloody waiters are never available. I'll go order at the counter. More chilli cheese toast and coffee?"

"Let me go this time," Harsha said, rising. "You've bought enough food for all of us."

He took their orders and wandered off in the direction of the main building, leaving the rest of them looking at each other knowingly.

"Poor Harry," Shane said finally.

"Come on, he'll get over it," Junaina said uncomfortably.

Azhar studied the dregs of his coffee moodily. "Will he, though? He's been pining over Maya for at least two years now. Maybe longer, for all we know. I've tried to introduce him to so many women — but nothing!"

"He needs closure," Shane said, wisely. "Right now, he still thinks it is possible to get back with Maya."

"And how the bloody hell will he get that?"

Shane hesitated, glancing at Junaina, and then said: "She needs to end it. She has left him hanging so far. But he deserves better than…"

"Hang on!" Junaina interrupted hotly. "What do you mean, she has left him hanging? She told him clearly that she was going back to her husband…"

"She said she was giving her husband a chance. Which means she could…"

"But she is married, for fuck's sake! Isn't it up to him to…"

"He deserves better than to be somebody's Plan B!" Shane said loudly, with uncharacteristic heat.

"Guys… guys…" Azhar said, weakly, looking around at customers near them, who were now staring at them in surprise.

"What's going on?" Harsha asked as he came back to the table, and Junaina and Shane looked away.

"Nothing dude! Come sit down," Azhar said hastily, unnecessarily adjusting his chair and dusting off the cushion on it.

Shane's grin came up again. "Nothing to worry about, Harry. Just a little kerfuffle."

Harsha laughed and plumped himself down on the chair.

"I bloody missed you guys," he said, smiling around at the group. "It was worth coming back to India just to be with you all."

Azhar leaned forward at this and said: "Harry —

Chennai is a better place with you in it." Harsha recognised that glazed look that was coming into Azhar's face that suggested he was about to say something emotional and groaned inwardly.

"You are a special guy, dude," Azhar said emotionally. "The way you are fighting for these transgenders. It's great, man. We are really proud of you."

Junaina cleared her throat at this and they looked up at her.

"I read your piece about transgenders yesterday, and that part about what that Mithra woman has been doing for years, and the things that she has seen... It... honestly, it made me cry, Harry," she said, quietly. She sighed, moved her coffee aimlessly further down the table and added: "I might have been a bit hasty in what I said about transgenders last time."

"You might have been a bit of a dick, you mean?" Azhar cut in.

"Shut up, fool," Junaina said cuttingly and turned to Harsha again. "The point is, while I still struggle with it — and I worry a little bit about what it all means for women — I can see that none of this is black and white. So, thank you."

Harsha looked down at his lap and bit his lip to keep from showing how moved he was by this. He often felt that journalism was a bit of a Sisyphean task. No matter how much work you put in, it seemed to get nowhere. It was nice to know what it looked like from the outside.

"I am so happy you feel that way, Juni, but sometimes you just get a great interviewee. Mithra — she is an extraordinary person," he said. "All the journalist has to do is listen and the story writes itself."

"Speaking of which," Shane said, taking a copy of

Southern Echo out of his backpack. "Nice front page spread."

He placed the paper on the table and Harsha glanced down at the headline: 'Murdered Civil Servant Killed With Single Blow To Head' with an "exclusive" tag plastered on one corner of the font. It did look impressive, he acknowledged to himself.

"Is this today's paper?" Azhar asked, looking up with mild interest.

"No — this went out earlier this week," Harsha said. "The broader piece on Gopu, Mithra and the transgender community went out yesterday — the one Juni is talking about."

"And what's next?" Azhar asked, crossing his legs and looking up at his friend.

"To be honest, I don't know — we are just waiting to hear from the police who the killer is," Harsha said, keeping his voice low so no one around them would hear. You could never be too careful.

"No Tintin stuff?" Shane asked, nudging him by the knee and smiling.

Harsha put his hands up defensively. "Not this time! This time we are just keeping in touch with our police contacts and we will try to be the first to report when they find out who did it. It should be any day now, and this story will be done."

"That'll be a relief for everyone," Azhar said fervently. Harsha grinned at him. His closest friend had borne the brunt of all of Harsha's stress over this story and the irritations of navigating the Southern Echo office politics.

"Let's talk about something else. I feel like I've taken up too much of your attention. How are the kids, Shane?" Harsha asked, folding his legs and pushing the newspaper away from him. He had had enough news for one day.

21. Interrogation

But the police investigation wasn't over in a few days. In fact, two weeks later, there was still no update on the case. Harsha felt like he was in limbo professionally and personally. He had been taken off the features desk to work on this particular story — but he had nothing to work on.

Sampath's police sources had dried up, Palanivel and Gautami were not responding to his texts and Jaishree was asking for daily reports on progress via Rahul.

Out of sheer desperation, Harsha went to the Thiruvanmiyur police station one morning. He was sick of looking at Rahul and Jaishree in the face and telling them on a regular basis that they were getting nowhere. So he embarked on another dreaded journalistic assignment — the doorstep. In other words, he was here uninvited, hoping to intercept the inspector and obtain an interview.

He kicked his heels and watched a calf lumber by, looking at him with its liquid, patient eyes. To his left was the towering structure of Marandeeshwaran Kovil — a 2,000 year old temple building with ornate stone sculptures climbing its steep slopes and a temple tank at its feet. The tank in front of the building was almost dry after a hot summer and with the monsoon yet to break. The calf wound its way through a few early risers hopefully towards the tiny pool of dampness at the bottom of the tank.

A few policemen and women slowly filtered into the red brick building, some of them glancing curiously at Harsha, but volunteering no comment.

He felt incredibly self conscious and wished he were anywhere else in the world — even at the local skateboarding rink taking pictures for Namritha's features section. But he sternly reminded himself that he was an intrepid journalist, scowled at his feet, and stayed put.

At ten to nine, a battered but clean Maruti Suzuki hatchback car pulled up to one of the allocated parking spots outside the station. Harsha recognised the familiar thin figure that stepped out of the car, and straightened. He had only seconds to admire the poise and swagger of Detective Inspector Palanivel before the man strode up to the station entrance.

Harsha stepped forward hastily.

"Inspector!" he said, half reproachful and half pleading.

Palanivel paused and looked at him, and his eyes expanded a little in surprise.

"Mr Devnath," he said, flatly.

Harsha paused. He knew this man well. They had worked together and got to know each other on a murder case two years before. Nonetheless, he still felt so intimidated by the other man's presence that he felt it impossible to deliver the admonitory speech he had been planning on his way to this spot.

"How are you?" he asked weakly instead.

Palanivel suppressed a smile. "Very well, Mr Devnath.

And you?"

"Look, inspector," Harsha said, abandoning his lame attempt at small talk. "I was hoping we could talk about the Gopinath case."

The police chief looked around warily.

"Not here," he said, curtly. He considered Harsha for a second and then cocked his head towards the entrance of the station and strode towards it.

Harsha scampered after him.

Harsha had only been to one police station before in his life. And that was in the sleepy, forgotten town of Ramananpettai near the border between the states of Tamil Nadu and Andhra Pradesh.

But he was struck by the similarities between that experience and this building in the heart of South India's largest metropolis.

Like the Ramananpettai station, the Thiruvanmiyur police building was dark, functional and intimidating. Wooden benches and cubby holes fringed the hallway and even the stone courtyard held an air of menace to it.

Policemen and women bustled around and there was a line of civilians sitting on one side — waiting for god knows what.

Some of the police officers looked at Harsha with deep suspicion, but moved out of the way, saluting Detective Inspector Palanivel smartly. He barely acknowledged them.

"Murugan, I want the Valmiki Nagar burglary report at my desk by the end of today," he said softly to one rotund policeman, who quailed visibly before nodding vigorously.

"Latha, where are the suspects? Have them processed immediately," he said to an incredibly young-looking policewoman, who bobbed her head in acquiescence and turned away to perform the task. "And send Gautami to my office as soon as she arrives," he called after her retreating figure.

They reached an unremarkable doorway that bore the legend: 'Dt. Insp. A. Palanivel'.

He pushed the door open and Harsha followed him into a tiny little office.

If anything, it was even smaller than Palanivel's office in Ramananpettai. But it had the same collection of his family pictures, commendations and newspaper articles, of which he had acquired even more since last time.

Palanivel sat down at his desk and motioned Harsha to the seat in front of him. He picked up a ballpoint pen and notepad.

"How is everything going, Mr Devnath?" he asked, cocking an eyebrow.

With a stab of intuition, Harsha realised that this was a test. If he had valuable information for the police, the inspector would give him something in return. He hesitated only for a second before plunging into an account of everything he knew. He had nothing to lose at this point.

Given that his visit to The Sanctuary was the most recent occurrence, Harsha started with this, though he withheld the conversation he had had with Constable Gautami. He wasn't sure how much the policewoman had told her boss, and didn't want her to get into trouble. The inspector took down notes in his battered notebook, but Harsha sensed that this was perfunctory — he wasn't saying anything that was new to the inspector.

He proceeded on to talk about his visit to the Gopinath household and briefly recounted his impressions of Hema and Neha. He then moved on to talk about the 1857 Society, and again, the inspector nodded, knowledgeably. Harsha remembered that Gita had told Constable Gautami about them as well.

That said, the inspector did sit up and listen more carefully when Harsha gave a brief and functional account of his terrifying visit to the 1857 Society rally. When he described the chilling conversation with Advaith, the inspector gave a low whistle.

"These are dangerous waters, Mr Devnath," he said, rapping his pen on the table, a faraway look in his eyes.

Harsha nodded gloomily. He was terrified of both the 1857 Society as well as the political currents that had swept it into his life.

The inspector waited, and when he realised Harsha had finished, he sighed and said: "Can we keep what I say next on background?"

"Of course," Harsha said, putting his pen down and closing his notebook with a snap. He felt a thrill of anticipation.

The inspector rubbed his eyes and then looked down at the desk. "We first looked at the family, which is the primary rule of all murder investigations. But the mother and the daughter both have alibis, and no obvious motive. So we moved on to look at various political opponents. He has many, but we narrowed down the possibilities to three."

He ticked them off his fingers. "One, he was killed by one of the transgender people that he offended somehow. Two, he was killed by someone at the 1857 Society as a warning. And three, it was a hit order by the Boreas Vayu energy firm. Do you know much about them?"

"My colleague Sampath has been looking into them,"

Harsha said, nodding. "It seems that Gopu was single-handedly holding back some of their energy projects — especially that hydropower dam in Kovalam. There's crores of rupees hanging on that, so I can see that as a powerful reason to take him out. But why kill him in his office? Surely it would have been easier somewhere else?"

"Maybe it was meant to be a message sent to anyone who opposes their interests?" The inspector sighed and leaned back. "The issue with the 1857 Society and Boreas Vayu is that they are both extremely powerful. So it becomes more challenging for us to investigate."

Harsha hesitated and then asked: "Do you think they are untouchable?"

"No one is untouchable, Mr Devnath," the inspector said, smiling. "But we may have to get creative at some point."

Harsha didn't say anything. The last example of the inspector's creativity had been bone-chilling and had nearly resulted in a man being lynched by a mob. But maybe that sort of cold ruthlessness was what was needed for someone like Advaith? He couldn't help but feel a sense of relish at the idea of Palanivel and Advaith locking horns. As long as he, Harsha, was the one to tell the tale.

"Do you think this Advaith character is capable of this?" Palanivel asked, intruding into his thoughts.

Harsha fought hard to suppress a blush. He was extremely flattered at being asked his opinion in this matter.

"Yes," he said, finally. "At least, I think it is more likely than the idea that the transgender community killed him out of revenge," he ended in a rush and looked down, embarrassed that he had let his objectivity slip.

The ball point pen was rapping the table again and Harsha looked up to see Palanivel looking at him carefully.

"Why don't you judge for yourself?" he asked finally. "We are about to interrogate two of these transgender people you mentioned who were in the building at the time of the murder. You can be a silent observer — I would appreciate your thoughts."

Harsha nearly fell off his chair in surprise at this offer. He controlled himself with an effort.

"Are you... is this serious?" he asked, not wanting to believe he would get such an exclusive insight into the investigation.

"Absolutely. Just don't report on it," Palanivel said drily as he stood up.

"Of course not!" Harsha said indignantly, standing up as well and waiting for the inspector to go past him towards the door.

He felt a surge of excitement and a stab of apprehension. He was familiar with Palanivel's robust methods of interrogation — Azhar's driver Selvam was still feeling the effects of it — but surely he would not do anything violent in the presence of a journalist?

As though reading his mind, the inspector pushed open a door that said "Interrogation Room 2" on its front and pointed towards a CCTV camera in one corner. "All recorded," he said, and looked down the corridor in irritation for a second before stepping into the room. "Where the hell is Gautami?" he muttered to himself.

Harsha sat down in one corner of the room where he had a good vantage point and was relatively out of view of the CCTV camera, and scanned the room. It was a simple room with a table and a few metal chairs strewn about. It was windowless, with two tube lights providing the illumination. It was nastily reminiscent of the interrogation rooms Harsha had seen on American TV programmes.

The inspector put his pad on the table and began his usual practice of rapping the metal surface of the table with his pen.

The door swung open, sounding unnaturally loud in the silence, and two of the most abject-looking people Harsha had ever seen in his life stumbled in. His experience with the community in recent weeks enabled him to recognise them both as transgender. They were dressed in worn-out saris and were giving off a powerful odour of sweat and fear.

They were followed by Constable Gautami, who gave Harsha a surprised look and a warm smile. The two suspects did not even notice him. Gautami ushered them both towards the chairs behind the table where they sat down and looked around apprehensively.

Gautami took her seat beside Palanivel, who muttered to her: "Is the camera on?"

She nodded and he turned to the two unfortunate persons.

"Names," he said abruptly, before looking at the first, larger woman.

"Er... Nangai... er... Kumaresan." She had a stubborn cast to her chin, Harsha thought, but looked utterly defeated in that moment.

Palanivel looked at the other, a smaller and slimmer woman, who gave him a coy smile that bravely hid her abject terror.

"Jamuna Mani, Mr Policeman," she trilled, batting her eyelashes at him.

Palanivel wrote this down.

Her studied flirtation made Harsha wonder if they had been sex workers at some point. Mithra had told him that many members of the transgender community were driven by poverty to this profession. He felt an additional stab of pity.

"Profession?" Inspector Palanivel asked, on cue.

They both looked at each other.

"We are currently looking for work," Nangai said.

Harsha wondered if the inspector would ask for more details, but he let this pass.

"How did you know Mr Gopinath?" he asked instead, going straight to the nub of the matter.

Silence from the two suspects.

The inspector's voice took on an air of menace.

"I said — how did you know Mr Gopinath?" the inspector thundered.

The pair of them jumped as though they had been slapped and then the first started babbling something about a charity event.

Harsha looked at the pair of them and thought he had never seen a more pitiable pair. They looked like the very dregs of humanity. Jamuna also seemed mentally disturbed — she kept giggling at odd times, completely incongruous with her expression of terror.

"And then he got you a job in the government office," Palanivel said, breaking into a rambling explanation unceremoniously.

"Yes," said Nangai.

"How did that go?"

"Badly."

"Why?"

"We were treated badly. Like vermin."

"But we are vermin, Nangu," Jamuna giggled. "Yes, yes we are."

Definitely mentally impaired. Possibly through extensive drug abuse? Or perhaps through years of working as a sex worker? Harsha felt another wrench in his heart. He had come to India to confront reality. But this was a particularly strong dose of it.

"Did that make you angry?"

Nangai's expression darkened. "It would have made a saint angry."

"Did you blame Mr Gopinath?"

Nangai struggled with her emotion. "No," she said finally, though her expression said the opposite.

Harsha glanced at Gautami, who was sitting there, expressionless. Didn't she feel any sympathy? She had championed the cause of downtrodden women in the past.

Both suspects were staring at Inspector Palanivel, transfixed, like snakes by a charmer.

"What were you doing in the government office on the day of the murder?"

There was a brief, agonised silence. Then Nangai licked her lips and said, carefully: "We came to get some paperwork done."

"Did you go to Mr Gopinath's office at any point?"

Both suspects shook their heads vigorously.

"No... no... *I* did not," Jamuna said, and then looked horrified as she realised that the emphasis on the "I" had given her companion away.

The inspector turned to Nangai. "Did you go to see Mr Gopinath in his office?"

Nangai shook her head again and attempted a nonchalant smile. "No, not at all. Why should I?"

Harsha closed his eyes briefly. Even with his lack of experience with interrogations, he could see that she was lying.

"Did you kill him?" Inspector Palanivel asked in a hoarse whisper, leaning forward menacingly.

At this crucial moment, the door behind them swung open with a huge, metallic squeak, making them all jump. A soft, firm voice rang out in the little room.

"You don't have to answer that!"

Everyone in the room turned to the door and the inspector swung around in his seat, the chair squeaking under him, an expression of fury on his face. A slim, shapely woman walked in, lighting up the room in a crisp, sky-blue shirt and a long black skirt that hugged her frame. She marched purposefully towards the suspects' side of the table.

"Who the hell are you?" barked Palanivel.

"I am their lawyer," the woman said, putting one arm on Jamuna's shoulder.

Harsha screwed his eyes shut and opened them again to make sure he was seeing right.

It was Harleen.

22. Lawyer

Harleen looked across at the two police officers, implacable in the face of the inspector's fury.

"I am Ms Nangai and Ms Jamuna's lawyer," she said, calmly, pulling one of the metal chairs up so that she could sit beside the two suspects. Both of them looked at her in bare-faced wonder, mirroring Harsha's own feelings.

They were an incongruous sight — the two transgender women, on the lowest rung of India's social ladder, and Harleen - beautiful and sophisticated, her perfect, straight hair falling around the perfect collar of her striking shirt, the top button undone to show a thin triangle of tanned skin. She looked absurdly young in this setting.

Constable Gautami was watching her with fascination, and Inspector Palanivel with open hostility.

"Look here, Ms..."

"Kaur."

"Look here, Ms Kaur. You can't just walk in here unannounced. I need to be given notice and you have to register with reception, fill out the requisite forms."

Red tape, the fallback option for scoundrels, Harsha

thought to himself.

Harleen's eyes widened and she assumed an expression of innocence.

"Oh, I'm sorry, inspector," she gushed. "I hadn't realised you were so obsessed with the formalities. Especially given that you have started an interrogation without offering these two people a lawyer?"

A silence fell over the room, during which the inspector turned stony-faced. He was no fool, and he must have realised that the power in the room had shifted.

"I beg your pardon, Ms Kaur," he said, politely. "The two suspects never asked for a lawyer."

"I believe you have to offer them one anyway?" Harleen asked gently, her fine brows lifting together.

The inspector bowed his head in acquiescence, as the tube light sputtered above him. "An oversight on my part," he said, smiling. An entirely humourless smile, but a smile nevertheless.

Harsha thought he saw Constable Gautami suppress a more genuine smile. He wondered if the policewoman was experiencing any mixed loyalties between the police and the sisterhood.

"Perhaps you thought having a journalist in the room would be sufficient?" Harleen asked, her eyes flicking towards Harsha.

Harsha immediately felt a burning sense of humiliation. Of course the inspector was using him to add a sheen of respectability to this interrogation as he tried to bully a confession out of Nangai and Jamuna! He should have known Palanivel wouldn't do him any favours and was pursuing his own Machiavellian agenda.

He forced his attention back to the conversation, where

the inspector was asking the two transgender women if they accepted "Ms Kaur" as their lawyer.

They both nodded their heads fervently, with the air of drowning people clutching at a life vest.

Harleen smiled briefly, but sincerely, at the two of them and then looked up at the inspector enquiringly.

Palanivel cleared his throat, looking uncharacteristically uncomfortable, and then said: "I was just... er... trying to establish if..."

Three pairs of eyes stared at him, two in apprehension, the third with composure.

"If... er... they harmed... in any way... Mr Gopinath," the inspector finished in a rush, scowling at his own clumsiness. This was obviously not the way in which he had wanted to frame such an obvious question. He had clearly planned on intimidating the two transgender women into getting the answer that he wanted.

Harleen turned to Nangai and Jamuna and said, quietly: "You don't have to answer that question."

She turned again to the inspector and gave him a bright smile. He grunted in a bad-tempered manner. *He knows she is completely in the right,* Harsha thought to himself.

The rest of the interview passed in a blur for Harsha, though he had a vague impression of the inspector asking a series of questions that were mostly batted away by Harleen. Only the most banal of questions were allowed to pass.

Finally, the inspector said shortly: "That will be all."

Gautami blinked in surprise.

"Then we will see you next time," Harleen said, standing up, dusting the front of her skirt.

"Wait," the inspector said as the two women stood up with Harleen. The pair of them cowered, but Harleen turned her guileless eyes in mock surprise towards the inspector, as though daring him to make the arrest.

A pause.

"You may go," the inspector said finally, with bad grace.

Gautami rubbed her nose, and Harsha wondered whether she was doing so to hide her surprise or another smile.

Harsha also stood up to follow the three people outside, though he paused by the inspector's chair and asked: "Can we talk later today?"

Palanivel looked up at him and seemed to shake off his bad mood.

"Yes," he said in his usual business-like manner. "Anytime between 4pm and 6pm."

Harsha nodded, then smiled at Constable Gautami before leaving the room.

He weaved his way past chattering policemen and women, ducking to avoid the tops of the low doorways, before finally emerging out onto a brightly sunlit street. The day's activity had kicked off, and a thronging scene of street stalls and pedestrians met his eyes. He turned this way and that, and then spotted Harleen standing with Nangai and Jamuna beside her sleek, black Skoda, which contrasted sharply with the inspector's battered Maruti Suzuki car. They were the centre of some attention — he couldn't tell if it was because of the transgender women or their glamorous counsel. Harleen herself looked utterly unconcerned by this attention; magnificently so, Harsha thought.

He hesitated, and then made his way up to the trio. Harleen seemed to be trying to convince her new clients to accept a lift from her to wherever it was they wanted to go, but they were shaking their heads in horror, unable to comprehend the thought of being driven anywhere in such a luxurious vehicle.

"Alright — I will call you this evening and we can talk further," Harleen was saying resignedly as Harsha reached them.

They took one frightened look at Harsha and then scuttled off into the throng of pedestrians.

Harsha was left facing Harleen.

"Hey... I... er..." Harsha said as an opening gambit, sidestepping a sari-clad worshipper who brushed past him, and leaning gently against Harleen's car. "Sorry," he said, moving away from the gleaming vehicle.

Harleen smiled and continued to look at him with her eyebrows raised. She seemed very good at that.

"I... I... Listen — I didn't mean to be the one enabling anything illegal back there," Harsha said, choosing to start with the easier of the two apologies. "That inspector — he is a clever bastard. I didn't even realise he was using me in any way."

Harleen nodded. "I believe you. You don't look like the kind of guy who would participate in a witch hunt," she said, folding her arms and looking him up and down in mock scrutiny.

Harsha winced. "Is that what you think that was?" he asked, frankly.

"I think he probably just needed enough to arrest them formally — most likely because he needs to show that the police are making progress. The chat is that they are under severe pressure to show some results in their investigation," she said, shrugging.

Harsha thought for a moment and then said: "Fair enough. And how... how on Earth did you end up working on this case? Is it black magic? All the women I know seem to turn up everywhere I go!"

She flushed slightly at this. "I don't know about that. I saw this case pop up on our file, and human rights have always been a passion of mine, so I put my hand up for it."

"But aren't you a cyber crime lawyer or something? You said you work mostly with multinational companies?"

She stuck her chin out defiantly. "I am. But just because we work with big companies doesn't mean we don't care. We do loads of pro bono work, I'll have you know!"

Harsha nodded, confused. Despite his extensive education and experience, he had imbibed some of his father's views on life. As an academic from the left-wing state of West Bengal, Devnath Senior basically viewed all wealthy people who worked for big corporate as borderline criminals. Harsha realised he needed to update his views a little.

"I didn't mean to give the impression that you don't care or something," he muttered.

"Hmph," was all she said in response.

The strangeness of the scene struck Harsha in that moment. Himself and Harleen, standing there while the hustle and bustle of Chennai revolved around them. All around the temple square and within the police station, other people were sorting out their own complex lives in similar fashion.

"And... and you had no idea that it was the case connected to the one I was reporting on?" he asked, hesitantly.

Harleen snorted. "Don't flatter yourself," she said, and opened the clasp of her handbag.

"Sorry, I didn't mean anything like that," Harsha said

hastily, looking down at his feet in mortification. Of course, she couldn't be *following him around* or something — that was absurd!

But because he had looked away, he missed the telltale blush on her face. It was perhaps to hide her confusion that Harleen buried her face into her handbag. She rifled through its contents, took out her iPhone, frowned into it and then dropped it back in and looked up at Harsha.

"Anything else I can help you with, Harsha?" she asked.

He rocked on the balls of his feet, preparing himself metaphorically for the plunge.

"I'm... I'm sorry I didn't call," he said, unable to look at her, instead focusing on a ragged stray dog that was picking at some rubbish from a nearby heap.

To his surprise, she laughed.

"It's not the first time I've been ghosted, nor will it be the last. Don't worry," she said kindly.

Harsha's head snapped up towards her in surprise. Is that what he had done? Ghosted this beautiful and sophisticated woman? He felt a mixture of shame, surprise and... a little pride as well. He was the one doing the ghosting, for once!

She was looking at him with that inscrutable smile on her face, so he said again: "I really am so sorry."

She shook her head. "Don't be. A text would have been nice, and I thought you were the kind of guy who would send a text, but we are all busy people. I understand," she said.

"It's not like that!" he protested, moving to one side as a cyclist narrowly avoided going over his feet. How was Harleen just standing there while the whole neighbourhood seemed keen to bump into him and run him over?

He took a deep breath and then said: "It felt...

presumptuous to text you and say that I wasn't going to ask you on another date and to explain the complex reasons behind that. I had no inkling that you would even be remotely interested. I would have explained the situation to you if you had got in touch. But I felt otherwise it was not my place to give you a long spiel about why I was not asking you on a second date."

It was the most honest answer he could think of, and he was relieved to see her think for a minute and then nod.

"That makes sense," she said.

"Can I just say that you are an incredibly attrac…"

"Oh please," she cut in impatiently. "I don't need to hear anything like that. It happens. I'm not taking it personally."

He subsided and went back to examining the stray dog. *It has sad eyes*, he thought to himself irrelevantly.

"How did you get here?"

Harsha started. "What?"

"I asked how you got here. Do you have a car? Or a bike?"

"Oh. No. Just by auto-rickshaw. But…"

"I'll drop you back to your office," she said briskly, and rummaged in her handbag for her keys. "Hop in."

She ignored his feeble protests, instead pressing the button that released the car door and motioning him towards the passenger seat.

Harsha took a deep breath and got into the car. What else was there to do?

23. Assessment

When Harsha got out of the sleek vehicle at the entrance to the glossy glass building of *Southern Echo*, he didn't really know what to say.

"Er... thank you for the ride... and... er..."

"We'll be in touch," Harleen said brightly, leaning towards him and smiling.

"Er... yes," Harsha said, nodding.

As she drove off, Harsha turned to see Ricardo looking at him speculatively, bike helmet tucked under one arm. It looked like he had just come back from some assignment. Probably some new male cosmetics salon or Harley Davidson sign exhibition, Harsha thought sardonically to himself.

"Walk of shame, eh?" Ricardo asked.

"What? No!" Harsha said, feeling irrationally infuriated by this tasteless question.

They fell into step together on the way to their section of the office. If Ricardo was interested in who Harleen was, he didn't show it, instead lazily strolling beside Harsha without volunteering any comment.

"How's work?" Harsha asked, politely.

Ricardo shrugged. "Decent. Attending a new version of *Les Miserable* today. Should be fun."

"Oh?" Harsha said, at a loss as to how to respond to this.

They took the lift up to the third floor together.

"How is your murder case?" Ricardo asked, as they emerged onto their floor and walked past the rows and rows of desks, nodding to the office boy, who grinned cheerfully back at both the journalists. There was a pleasant buzz from the journalists at this time just before lunch, with most back from assignments or not out just yet. More than one reporter was talking urgently into a phone while taking notes. Others were standing over the booth which contained rival newspapers, discussing some development or scoop.

Harsha sighed. "It's a bit stuck. We had one lead — or rather, the police had one lead, but I think it's a dead end."

Ricardo shrugged his shoulders. "Why don't you write that story? 'Police stumped by civil servant murder' etc?"

Harsha stopped short and stared at his companion, who paused a couple of steps ahead of Harsha and looked back quizzically.

"That's actually a really good idea," Harsha said.

Ricardo smiled briefly and muttered: "Not just a pretty face."

They resumed their walk to their corner at the end of the floor.

"But wouldn't a story like that alienate our police sources?" Harsha asked, frowning.

Ricardo shrugged again. "I've always found that people tend to respect you more once you've done a negative story about them. Sampath does it all the time — and it doesn't seem to have hurt his career. Speak of the devil…"

They had reached their desks at that moment and Harsha saw Sampath himself sitting in Harsha's chair, talking to Kalyan. When he spotted the two young men arriving, he jumped up and gave Harsha his usual bored grin.

"Here he is," he said, making Harsha's heart jump a little. What now? "Boss wants to talk," Sampath added, succinctly.

Harsha nodded goodbye to Ricardo and followed Sampath through the labyrinth of desks, a knot of worry in his chest. Much as he had wanted to do important stories, this constant interaction with senior people was doing his stress levels no favours.

Sampath led them towards Rahul's glossy office on one corner, but instead of heading into this beautiful glass room, he instead turned towards a completely normal-looking cubicle. Harsha followed him curiously into this cubicle and started. Jaishree was sitting here, her greying hair tied neatly into a bun. She was peering into a battered laptop, and around her, instead of awards, were cutouts and frames of newspaper articles.

This was the unassuming little office where the owner of Southern Echo sat.

Jaishree looked up, smiling briefly at the two of them, and motioned them towards chairs.

"What the latest? Anything new?" she asked, looking at Sampath, as they both awkwardly crowded into the cubicle and sat on swivel chairs set at varying heights.

Nine out of ten journalists would have had an answer ready for this type of question and could talk at length about leads and conversations which neatly disguised the fact that they had made no progress at all on their story. Sampath was the tenth.

He shook his head and looked at Harsha. Harsha took a deep breath and then briefly recounted the inspector's words about the three possible murderers of Gopu.

Jaishree did her trick of closing her eyes and resting her impressive chin on the tips of her fingers. When he finished, she looked up at him and then pursed her lips, thinking.

"So we have three suspects," she said, finally. "We were already on top of two of them. Any luck with this 1857 Society, Harsha?"

Harsha shook his head.

"They've clammed up since my last chat with Advaith. I also don't really have anything new to take to them. The police obviously believe they are suspicious, but I don't have any new information that would be helpful," he sighed.

Jaishree turned to Sampath.

"Nothing new on Boreas," he said, examining his fingers. "I have tried my best to get a contact within this company, but it's not my area of expertise. I hope it's ok I spoke to Kalyan..."

Here Sampath paused to get Jaishree's verdict.

"Of course. It is his patch," she said.

Sampath nodded and continued. "He says that he doesn't have any insiders either who can help. Because of his reporting around the opposition to the Kovalam dam project, the company are actually a little hostile towards him."

Jaishree snorted. "They become hostile if we don't report about them in glowing terms at all times. And some other newspapers do exactly that. Such is life. What about these two transgenders? What did you think of them, Harsha?"

Harsha gave them a brief account of the interrogation of Nangai and Jamuna, including the dramatic intervention by Harleen halfway through.

"I told the inspector I wouldn't report on it, though," he said apologetically.

"Hm... once the lawyer gets involved, it becomes a tricky business," Jaishree said, frowning. "Who is she?"

"Harleen Kaur — she works for Coleman & Woods — Indian division," Harsha said.

"Oh wow — wonder why she got involved in all this," Jaishree said, looking thoughtful.

A silence fell and then Harsha said, hesitantly: "I had a feeling that Nangai was about to admit something about being in Gopi's room. Before Ha... before the lawyer came in."

Jaishree pursed her lips. "So it could be her after all?"

Harsha shook his head. "Despite that, I still don't think she was involved. She was so terrified to be in that police station, I can't see that she would have dared to do something like this."

Sampath cleared his throat and said: "My police sources believe it is more likely to be either the Boreas Vayu hitman or the 1857 Society. Though I don't think they have got very far in proving it."

"What about those threatening letters that 1857 wrote to Gopu? Have you managed to get hold of them?" Jaishree asked, still looking at Harsha.

Harsha shook his head. "I have a meeting with Neha on Friday. She wants to have dinner with me," he said thoughtlessly.

Jaishree smiled briefly. "The hard work that we make you do, eh?" she said drily.

"Anyway, she said she will bring the letters along," Harsha added hurriedly.

Jaishree sighed and swivelled slightly to look at her open notebook. "Even if she does give you the letters, I'm not sure what we can or cannot publish. Bhuvi says we can't accuse them of murder, even by implication — the courts will have a field day over it," she said.

Bhuvneshwar was Southern Echo's resident lawyer, a man who understood Indian defamation law like no other. He had been poached from *The Hindustan Times* by Jaishree herself, or so Harsha had heard. Even at that stage, she must have been planning to kick up a fuss, he thought to himself.

He dragged himself back to the present as she turned to him again and addressed him.

"In the meantime, let's shake things up a little," she said, briskly.

She looked sharply at the two journalists one by one, and then continued: "Harsha — you haven't got anywhere with 1857. And Sampath — nothing more on Boreas Vayu. Ok — why don't you swap? Sampath — you have never met 1857 before. Why don't you join them — but as a devotee, and see what you can find? Have you gone undercover before?"

Sampath cleared his throat. "Yes, twice. That should not be a problem," he said in his usual monotone voice.

Jaishree turned her eyes towards Harsha. "And Harsha. Why don't you put on a nice shirt," her eyes flickering over the dull grey monstrosity he had on, before continuing: "And go meet the Boreas Vayu executives? There is some wind farm inauguration and press conference or some such thing due to happen tomorrow. You could go with Kalyan as part of the press pack. They are sick of Kalyan and his anti-business agenda, as they call it. Someone more middle class may reassure them."

"Am I to do a corporate puff piece?" Harsha asked, trying

not to sound annoyed.

"That's what they will think," Jaishree said calmly. "Just get to the press conference — you can feel free to ask some tough questions once you are there. Get Kalyan to give you some background information about them and set up your clearance. All clear? Good! Best of luck."

Jaishree turned back towards her laptop, which was clearly a dismissal. Sampath and Harsha stood up and eased their way out of the cubicle.

"Are you not scared, Sampath?" Harsha asked his laconic colleague. "I have never been undercover before, and I find this 1857 Society terrifying!"

Sampath grinned at him, his bristling moustache sticking up in all directions.

"Boss — you are the one who should be scared!" he declared.

"What? Why?" Harsha asked, grabbing the other's arm so they both stopped still in the corridor.

Sampath told him.

A few minutes later, Harsha raced up to his desk, startling the two women in his team. Kalyan eyed him from over his coffee.

"Kals," Harsha panted. "I need to know everything you know about this Boreas Vayu thing. *Everything.*"

Harsha sighed and leaned back in Namritha's chair. They had commandeered the features editor's office for the duration of the conversation so that they could talk privately.

"So... the Boreas Vayu company was essentially created last year? Out of thin air?" Harsha asked, putting his hand to his forehead. It had been a long day and his head was throbbing.

Kalyan shook his head vigorously.

"Ille pa, not that simple. Boreas is a Danish company that has been around for a long time. They have a series of new energy projects they want to run across Asia and especially India, but..."

"But a foreign company cannot just do business in India, it being a closed economy," Harsha finished for him.

"Exactly," Kalyan said, nodding. "So that's where Vayu comes in. It is a new company with influence and it teams with Boreas for a joint venture. That company is new."

"And it's led by the Prime Minister's nephew or whatever?"

"The ex-finance minister's niece's husband, Varun Dar, is the chief executive, yes," Kalyan said, smiling at Harsha's expression of confusion and distaste. "Vayu owns 51% of the company and Boreas owns 49% and does the dirty work. It's all completely legal and above board."

Harsha massaged his temples gently and looked around at the paraphernalia on Namritha's desk. All her office belongings seemed to be pink and fluffy. "And they are the ones you have been reporting on in the Kovalam hydropower project?" he asked, trying to keep his mind focused.

Kalyan nodded. "What is the use of renewable energy if you must make a group of people homeless and destroy a 2,000 year old ecosystem to do it?" he asked. "The hydropower dam will swamp that area. It will destroy the vegetation in that hill and the habitat of many animals and birds."

He sighed and leaned back in the chair that Harsha usually sat in when getting harangued by Namritha in their weekly meetings, his fingers crossed across his stomach.

"But they are ruthless, pa," he continued. "They will beg, borrow, steal, bribe and even kill to get what they need. One of the main environmentalists, Arun Joshi, a friend of mine, was found dead at home. Suspicious death but no evidence," he finished heavily.

Harsha's eyes gleamed as he swivelled in Namritha's chair and looked closely at Kalyan. "Sounds like somebody needs to take these fuckers down," he observed.

"It is precisely for that reason that you need to be careful," Kalyan said sharply. "I feel sure they killed Arun and they may have killed your Gopu as well. Though they do it rarely, it is possible."

"Tell me about this corporate hitman," Harsha said, pushing aside Namritha's vase of fake flowers and putting his arms on her polished and spotless desk.

"He is more of an enforcer than a hitman. His name is Mangal and he is ex-Indian army. I don't know much else about him," Kalyan said, chewing his lip thoughtfully. "Worked as a freelance security contractor for a few years and then joined Vayu last year when they began this venture. Here, I have a picture of him which I got from the military file."

"Should I fear for my life?" Harsha asked, smiling as he looked down at the picture of a bald, bullet-headed man with cold eyes.

Kalyan did not return the smile. "It probably won't come to that," he said, taking back his phone and putting it in his pocket. "The enforcer's job is to bully people and scare them off. Killing is an extreme option — and even then, he gives a warning first."

"A warning?" Harsha asked, still smiling. Here in

Southern Echo's gleaming offices, it was hard to be particularly worried about anything, particularly with the might of a national newspaper behind him. "Will I get a horse's head in my bedroom? Or the Black Spot?"

Kalyan raised his eyebrows, so Harsha added: "It's how pirates used to give each other warnings in *Treasure Island*."

The older man shook his head at his young companion's flippant tone.

"The enforcer's warning is usually a single cut on the cheek with a knife," he said, tracing his finger across the side of this face to demonstrate. "You will look even better with a scar on your face. Heroic," he ended solemnly. And then he showed his teeth.

Harsha was about to reply to this when he spotted Namritha coming towards her office. He scrambled from the seat as she pulled the door open.

"If you are quite done, I need to make a call," she bit out, smiling humourlessly at him. "But I don't want to disturb your important investigative work."

Harsha left silently and with whatever dignity he could muster, which wasn't much.

"Let's continue this outside," he muttered to Kalyan. "Over tea," he added, feeling the throbbing in his head intensify.

24. Meetings

Jamal Bhavan, a little udipi-style restaurant just off Burma Bazaar, had somehow become the meeting point for transgender people who lived in this part of the city. It was the one place where they could relax without feeling unwelcome or watched.

Occasionally, someone with traditional gender identities — Maya had to constantly refresh her terminology around this subject — would walk in and they either wouldn't even notice or they would soon leave if they did. For the most part, Chennai left this little restaurant to its own devices, and Jamal Bhavan did not bother Chennai's populace. Never had Maya seen any of the staff or regular patrons stare at anyone or go out of their way to make anyone feel out of place.

Yet, she couldn't help feeling slightly uneasy as she sat there in one corner table with Gita, an intruder in this haven.

Gita was, if anything, even more jittery than her, glancing at her watch and craning her neck to look at the entrance.

"When did you say she is coming?"

"At 4pm. Relax, it's not time yet. Two coffees, please," Maya said to the waiter who had swung by. He smiled and walked away. Maya noted that while he was dressed in male clothes — a white kurta and trousers — he had just a tinge of makeup and eyeliner on. There was such a spectrum when it came to gender identity, and she couldn't pretend she understood it all. She just knew she would fight with her every breath for these wonderful people (*and yet, were they not all on the same spectrum?*) who went through their lives with such strength and dignity.

The door of Jamal Bhavan swung open, letting in a blare of street noise and a gust of warm air. They looked up and Maya felt a rush of relief tinged with a stab of annoyance. The woman who walked in was beautiful and poised in a sophisticated North Indian sort of way, radiating an air of competence.

She immediately scolded herself for this. This had been Maya's idea, so she should be relieved that she had secured a lawyer who wasn't fresh out of university and green behind the ears.

The lawyer was slim, had straight, dark brown hair and bright, inquisitive eyes. She was semi-formally dressed in a shirt and trousers, looking even more out of place than Maya was in a sea of saris and *salwar kameez*. She scanned the restaurant confidently.

As her eyes fell on their table, Maya raised her hand and the woman smiled, showing a perfect, gleaming set of teeth, and walked up towards them.

She showed no signs of the discomfort about her surroundings that Maya was feeling, which Maya thought was unfair — if anything, this woman was far more out of place than she, Maya, was. She sat down as though she were in any high-end restaurant in New Delhi and held out her hand, first to Maya, and then to Gita.

"I'm Harleen. I will be representing Nangai and Jamuna. Hopefully they won't need me much," she said in a low, mellifluous voice. Up close, Maya could see that Harleen wasn't as beautiful as she appeared at first glance — she was a regular, pretty girl, who knew how to use makeup to make herself look exceptional. Maya felt a stab of contempt, followed by guilt. Why shouldn't Harleen, or any other woman, want to look more beautiful?

Gita looked entirely cowed by this smart lawyer — Maya felt another stab of irritation — and incapable of any speech.

So Maya said: "Nice to meet you, Harleen. Thank you so much for taking the case."

Harleen waved this away. "It is my pleasure," she said. "I spend most of my time poring over documents. This actually feels like I'm doing something meaningful."

That waiter came up and asked tentatively: "Coffee, madam? Sorry, I mean — we also have tea, chai and some herbal teas," he added, hesitantly.

Maya reflected wryly that she had never been offered herbal teas in this place.

"Oh no! I must have a cup of coffee. I love South Indian filter *kaapi*," Harleen said, bestowing her dazzling smile upon the waiter, who walked away looking immensely gratified by this order. He also ignored Maya, who was about to ask after her coffee — leaving her hanging with her hand raised up in the air.

"Shall I call him back?" Harleen asked.

"Never mind," Maya said quickly.

Gita still hadn't seemed to recover her wits, so Maya asked: "How are Nangai and Jamuna?"

"Scared but holding it together. I met them only briefly at the police station — where we managed to narrowly avoid an arrest," Harleen said soberly, as she took out a notebook and placed it on the table. "But the smallest hint that they were involved in this crime in any way would mean that they will be in deep shit. The police will make sure of that."

Maya's heart gave a jolt and she exchanged a troubled look with Gita. The situation sounded very serious.

Maya said: "I know the inspector in charge of this investigation. He is a tough bastard but a fair one. And his deputy — Constable Gautami — I believe she is a good person."

Harleen shook her head. "They are under serious pressure to show progress. They might just lock Nangai and Jamuna up while they look for the more likely criminals. But what if they then don't find another murderer? That's what concerns me."

"But surely they have to prove that they did it? Not just keep suspects in prison indefinitely?"

"If they put these two in front of a jury — I don't like their chances. And if that happens, it could become even more political. This government has actually made some strides in upholding transgender rights. This incident could make them look very bad and any efforts to improve the lives of the transgender community could be seriously undermined."

Maya and Gita stared at Harleen, aghast. This was far worse than anything they had expected. It wasn't just the lives of Nangai and Jamuna at stake, but the welfare of the entire community, it would seem. Maya could well imagine relatives of hers, even her mother, harrumphing over their newspapers about those feckless so-called transgenders and how they didn't deserve any help whatsoever.

The waiter came by again and brought over a steaming cup of coffee in an ornate, porcelain cup. He placed it in front of Harleen and received a grateful smile in response.

Harleen blew delicately on the surface of the cup to cool the coffee, before saying: "There is an additional complication — though it could prove to be a point in our favour — I'm not sure yet."

The two of them looked bleakly at the lawyer as she sipped her coffee and smacked her lips appreciatively. She continued: "This journalist, Harsha Devnath, was present during the questioning of Nangai and Jamuna. I don't think he means ill, but…"

"What?" Maya barked, and several heads in surrounding tables turned to look at them in surprise. Maya looked around and leaned forward and said in a softer tone: "What? *Harsha* was there?"

Harleen nodded. "I believe he is well-connected with the police in charge of this case. But I suspect the inspector was using him as a buffer against any criticism of his questioning of suspects."

Maya shook her head in exasperation. "What an idiot! Allowing himself to be manipulated like that," she said.

Harleen's eyes narrowed and she scanned Maya's face. "You know Harsha, then?"

Maya controlled herself and said briefly: "Yes. I went to college with him."

Their eyes met and Maya thought the other woman read a lot more in her expression than she had intended to give away.

"I see," Harleen said, finally.

Maya felt unreasonably irritated by this mundane statement.

"Why do you ask? Do you know him?" she asked, trying to arrange her face into an expression of polite enquiry.

"I was introduced to him by a common friend..."

"Azhar," Maya finished in exasperation.

"Yes, that's right. Do you have a problem with that?" Harleen asked icily, her fine eyebrows rising.

Maya pulled herself together. What business of hers was it who Harsha and Azhar hung out with, or partied with or even slept with? For a brief second, she imagined Harleen and Harsha kissing and felt a sharp and ugly stab of jealousy.

"Is everything ok, Maya?" Gita asked, placing one hand on her arm, her voice laced with concern.

"Y... yes," Maya said with an effort, and turned to look at her friend. Why was she getting distracted? *There are far more important matters afoot than this rubbish*, she said to herself, fiercely ignoring the catch in her throat.

"So... Nangai and Jamuna," she said, looking steadily at Harleen.

"Yes," Harleen said, blinking and picking up her notebook, looking unusually flustered herself. It was the first time Maya had seen the other woman's composure disturbed. When Harleen looked up again, though, she looked as calm as ever, and she trained her eyes on Gita this time.

"So, I need to know whether you can vouch for them," she said in crisp tones.

Gita looked taken aback. "Vouch for them? In what way?"

Harleen sighed. "In some ways, Madras judges are old-fashioned. I need to know if you will be prepared to say before a court of law that you believe them to be of sound and excellent character. It may actually help," she said.

"I mean, I... know them a little, but... I don't... well," Gita stammered.

"I see," Harleen said. She turned to Maya, who looked down at the table.

"I don't really know them either," she admitted.

There was a silence in which only the ambient sounds around them could be heard; the clinking of cutlery, the soft chatter at a nearby table, the door of the restaurant opening.

"Do you see what we are up against?" Harleen said finally. "On one side we have the police, the media and the state. On the other side, two former sex workers and substance abusers whom nobody will speak up for — not even their closest associates."

"I will speak for them," said a voice and all three of them turned to look up to see who had spoken.

It was Mithra, standing by their table like an ancient prophetess, the sunlight shining in through the glass front of the restaurant and illuminating her simple, white sari, the purity of which was only outshone by the whiteness of her hair.

"Mithra!" Gita and Maya said together in wondrous tones, their chairs scraping as they involuntarily stood up to greet their leader in these matters. She must have quietly slipped in through the doorway while they were talking intently. Maya wondered how much of their conversation she had heard.

Mithra briefly clasped both of their hands and then pulled up a chair.

The waiter scampered up and greeted Mithra respectfully.

"The usual?" he asked. Mithra nodded, giving him a warm smile as she sat down between Maya and Gita, directly opposite Harleen.

"It seems that quite a lot has happened while I was in Mumbai," Mithra said drily. "That said, I have spoken to Nangai this morning, and she has brought me up to date. I happen to know her and Jamuna very well. And I will vouch for them. What else do you need? Funds? I can arrange for that."

Harleen shook her head. "Coleman & Woods has taken on this case *pro bono*, so we don't need funds. But I do need to know who you are and what your interest in this matter is," she said firmly.

An amused expression came over Mithra's face. "I am Mithra — the head of the Aravanigal Society of Chennai. As for my interest in this matter... My dear child, I have been supporting people like Nangai and Jamuna for over thirty years. I have spent more time in court than you ever will in your entire career as a lawyer. The question really is, what is your interest in this matter?" she asked.

Harleen blinked, losing her composure once again. Maya smiled to herself, pleased to see this confident young woman taken down a peg.

"My interest? I am their lawyer," Harleen said, frowning to try and figure out the older woman's meaning.

The waiter arrived with a tumbler and *davara* full of hot turmeric milk and placed it in front of Mithra.

"Thank you, Suresh," Mithra said composedly, picking up the tumbler and pouring some of the fragrant, steaming liquid into the *davara* so that the steam rose in billllows. "What I mean is — what is your interest in representing them? I need to know this isn't a box-ticking exercise, or even worse, an ego trip."

Harleen went red. "Ma'am, I can assure you that is not the case. You can look up my credentials — I am not a graduate trainee, I have a strong track record in my area."

"I didn't ask about your qualifications. I asked about your intentions," Mithra said calmly, still pouring the milk from one receptacle to the other to cool it.

"My intention is to do the best for my clients," Harleen said stiffly. "And I could do with all of your help in this matter."

Mithra picked up the tumbler and sipped her milk, looking carefully at Harleen from over the brim of the vessel.

"You will get it," she said finally. "Come by our office tomorrow — any time after 10 am. Gita can give you the address."

"I know where it is," Harleen said. "I will be there at 10.15 sharp."

She gathered her things, put them in her designer handbag and stood up.

"Thank you for the excellent coffee," she said to the waiter, who returned the compliment with a pleased smile and a little bow.

All the eyes in the restaurant followed Harleen as she moved her elegant frame through the little restaurant and out of the door into Chennai's teeming streets.

"She is a bit annoying, but I was told she is an excellent lawyer," Maya said apologetically to Mithra.

"I like her," Gita said unexpectedly. "She seems to care."

Mithra nodded. "I like her too," she said. "Well done, Maya."

Maya didn't know whether to feel gratified or annoyed.

25. Wind farm

The minute he got on the minibus and squeezed himself onto the only available seat, Harsha started to feel sick, and cursed himself a hundred times for not having equipped himself with tablets for motion sickness.

Well, at least you don't smoke anymore, he thought to himself, remembering the thorough awfulness of having to light up a cigarette to feed the addiction on a queasy stomach.

"Which paper?" asked the man next to him, a rotund and amiable looking chap with a pencil moustache, gold-rimmed glasses, greying hair and twinkling, brown eyes.

"Southern Echo," Harsha responded, adjusting in his seat so he could better see this man.

"Vignesh from *The Hindu*," said the man, holding out his hand and giving Harsha a firm handshake. "So you're the new kid on the block," he added.

Harsha smiled dutifully. *The Hindu* was Tamil Nadu's traditional newspaper, known well for its dependability and somewhat left-wing views. It once was the runaway market leader for English language news in the state, challenged only by *The Indian Express*, but many pretenders had arrived on these shores now: *The Times of India, Deccan Chronicle*, and now, of course, *Southern Echo*. It was remarkable how the newspaper industry in India kept growing, Harsha thought to himself, at a time when it was in severe decline in England and most other parts of the world.

He exchanged some small talk with Vignesh about these matters as the bus wound its way through the sporadic traffic on Old Mahabalipuram Road. In sharp contrast to the 2,000 year old stone edifices that made up the temple city of Mahabalipuram, where this road ended, they were in the so-called "IT corridor" now, where technology outsourcing companies had set up their glossy offices and campuses.

Glass buildings abounded on either side of the road, visible through waving palm trees and interspersed with tea stalls and the occasional stray dog or cow, serving as reminders that they were still in Chennai and not in some futuristic city from the West Coast in the U.S.

"What do you know about Boreas Vayu?" Harsha asked during a break in the conversation. A journalist from The Hindu could be a valuable source of information, and Vignesh came across as extremely knowledgeable.

A smile spread across Vignesh's face.

"The censored version or the uncensored version?" he asked, his eyes twinkling.

"The uncensored, please!"

"Maybe later," Vignesh said, nodding towards the blond, blue-eyed corporate communications officer, who was sitting a few seats ahead of them, talking unctuously to a rather snooty-looking woman in a patchwork *salwar kameez*.

"Right — censored then."

Vignesh paused and then said, as though by rote: "Boreas is a global player in renewable energy. They focus on emerging markets — South East Asia, Africa, Latin America, and now India. India is a big market for them because we import so much energy and want to reduce dependence on Russian oil and gas.

"At the same time, there is a big clamour for renewable energy — not just because of the environment, but also because there is a lot of Western investor money looking for so-called 'green investments' — huge amounts of cash waiting to be deployed in this space. When I say 'billions', I mean hundreds of billions," Vignesh said, taking off his glasses and wiping them on his shirt. "The Norwegian wealth fund alone is investing billions in this space, as they want to diversify away from oil."

The bus swooped around a corner, but for once, Harsha did not heed any sign of motion sickness. He was instead drinking in every word Vignesh was saying. It was incredible what geopolitical forces swept around one little wind farm on the outskirts of Chennai.

"Boreas is in an ideal spot to benefit from this; because they are an emerging markets player — they know how to... get things done in places like India," Vignesh said, smiling.

Harsha smiled. He knew exactly what the man from *The Hindu* meant.

"And what about Vayu?" he asked.

"I don't know if you are aware that for any foreign company to operate in India, they need to have an Indian partner?"

Harsha nodded. He knew that no foreign company could own more than 49% of an Indian enterprise — possibly a hangover from British colonialism via the East India Company, which made India suspicious of any foreign companies who wanted to operate in India. And perhaps rightly so, he thought to himself.

"So this creates... opportunities for some people," Vignesh said, and Harsha definitely caught something unsaid in his words. "Vayu did not exist until a few years ago, when these renewable contracts were first being awarded. Now they are a multi-billion dollar company," Vignesh continued.

"Owned by the ex-finance minister's relative?"

Vignesh put a finger up to his lips.

"Later, later," he said.

Harsha shivered slightly. Corruption in India used to be low-level stuff — police officers taking 100 rupees as a bribe when you were caught speeding, that sort of thing. In this new liberalised economy, it seemed India had not only imported the technology and competence from the West — which Harsha believed was a good thing overall — but also the institutionalised corruption, taking the sums involved to stratospheric levels.

But on the other hand, did it matter if some politicians were taking a kickback, if it was bringing renewable energy investment into India? These were the sorts of complex questions that Harsha hadn't expected to be confronted with on this story.

The minibus swung into a side road onto what felt like a dirt track, judging by the bumps and potholes. Harsha caught his breath — in the distance, he could see a field of huge wind turbines turning majestically in the sea breeze.

"How is Southern Echo?" asked Vignesh, who seemed unimpressed by this sight. "And this Jaishree woman? Any good?"

Harsha answered mechanically, his mind on the wind turbines up ahead. How would he go about his assignment today? It seemed foolhardy and idiotic in the cold light of day. Now Azhar can truly compare me with Don Quixote, Harsha thought to himself wryly.

They arrived at their destination a few minutes later and the blond corporate communications officer turned to address them all, telling them in clipped tones where the press area would be and what food would be served. Most of the press contingent brightened at the mention of food.

Harsha thought the man was talking in quite a patronising tone to these Indian hacks, not even bothering to introduce himself, but no one else seemed to notice. Well, perhaps apart from Vignesh, who was staring at the man with narrowed eyes. Harsha noticed that the Danish executive avoided looking at Vignesh as well.

When the blond man finally stopped talking — Harsha hadn't listened to any of the guff about the company — they finally got out of the minibus and Harsha took great gulps of blessed fresh air, noticing the slightly salty tang to the breeze that was propelling the slow rotations of the wind turbine blades.

He was expecting to be greeted by the company executives — but oddly enough, they looked occupied, sitting in a semicircle just outside some complex looking control panel, large enough to fill Harsha's bedroom.

"Those are Jens Landström and Christian Plenov, the chief executive and chief financial officers of Boreas," said the corporate communications officer, pointing at two of the figures seated in front of the mechanism. "And that one is Varun Dar, CEO of Vayu."

"What are they doing?" someone asked.

"I believe it is a — how do you call it — a puja before they inaugurate the farm," said the blond one.

They were now close enough to see the priest, holding a copper vessel with some leaves sticking out of it, muttering some prayers and asking each of the three executives in turn to repeat something he said. He occasionally sprinkled some of the water from the vessel into each of their outstretched hands.

Close up, they could see that there was already holy ash and kumkum applied to the foreheads of the three young men. They were each staring intently at the priest as he prayed for the safety and success of the wind energy venture.

Harsha shook his head. No scene could possibly be more Indian than this. Would it happen anywhere else in the world? Certainly not in England. He gave grudging kudos to the two Danish executives for going with it and respecting the local customs. Though from what little he could see of their faces from behind, they seemed to be completely transfixed by the experience.

"Refreshments are ser..." the corporate communications drone began, but he barely had time to finish the sentence before the journalists stampeded towards a makeshift table laden with food, and inspected its contents.

Journalists, like soldiers, marched on their stomachs, as Harsha knew well.

He watched Vignesh pick up a cracker with a pâté spread over it and peer at it suspiciously. It was probably some half-hearted attempt to introduce Danish cuisine to Indians. Harsha wasn't sure it would be all that successful.

He snorted at the expression on the older journalist's face when he bit into said cracker.

Tiring slightly of this mild entertainment, Harsha then turned and began to walk towards the wind turbines, his shoes sinking a little into the fine beach sand. Up close, he thought they looked quite beautiful, with pristine white blades turning lazily in the sunshine.

"Excuse me?" Harsha turned to see the Danish communications man had walked up to him and was addressing him. "I am Lars from Boreas. Refreshments are over there," he said, pointing towards the table as though Harsha was an idiot.

"I don't want any," Harsha said coldly and turned towards the wind turbines again.

"You will get opportunities to talk to the CEO at a later stage," the man said sharply, walking slightly in front of Harsha to partially block his way. "Just go back where you are supposed to be."

The rudeness startled Harsha. He hadn't been spoken to like this in years — not since his brief stint as a waiter while studying in London, and certainly not as a journalist. Anger, yes, but downright rudeness, as though he was a second-rate human, was very unusual.

"I don't want to talk to your CEO — I just want to see the turbines up close," Harsha said impatiently, aware that he sounded a bit like a child, but not willing to concede anything to this rude foreigner.

"You are not allowed to go there. Go back or you will be thrown out," Lars said, the icy stare turning into a threatening scowl.

"Not allowed to go there? By whom?" Harsha asked, genuinely angry now.

"By me," Lars said, shortly.

It was the contempt that riled Harsha up more than the words.

"I don't know about Denmark," he said as bitingly as he could, "But India is a free country."

He brushed past the other man and walked towards the wind turbines rapidly, the blood pounding in his head.

What an asshole, he thought to himself.

But suddenly, another man loomed in front of him, barring his way. This one was not very tall — certainly not compared to Lars, the corporate communications officer — but his bullet-head and sharp eyes gave him a more dangerous air. He had on a loose-checked shirt that couldn't hide the bulging muscles beneath, and looked entirely incongruous in this setting. The sunshine shone off his bald pate.

He said nothing but just looked at Harsha in a calculating manner, as though assessing a threat. Harsha met his gaze and couldn't quite repress a shudder — there was nothing in those black eyes, no life, no emotion.

Lars appeared at his shoulder again.

"Go back to the other journalists or we will take legal action against your newspaper for harassment and against you personally for trespass," he said, calmly.

But it wasn't these devastating words that quietened Harsha. With a grinding of gears in his brain, he had suddenly remembered who the bullet-headed man was — it was Kalyan's enforcer.

Harsha had just made the acquaintance of a hired killer.

26. Press conference

The shock had worn off by the time the journalists, fed and watered, had sat down for the press conference. This was to be held in front of an impromptu, raised stage, where the three executives sat like kings holding court over the press pack, who were on plastic chairs below. Behind them, the blades of the wind turbines turned serenely.

"They are so young!" Harsha breathed, looking up at the three leaders of the enterprise, finding it hard to believe that they were in control of this remarkable project. They were, at most, in their mid-thirties.

"Oh yes. If you have the right ideas and the right backing, age doesn't matter," Vignesh said beside him.

Jens Landström was tall and sharp-featured, and could have walked off a Hollywood movie set. He was certainly attracting some attention from the female contingent of the press pack, and even eliciting a few giggles. Thomas was shorter, rounder-shouldered and wearing a pair of round glasses, giving him a secretarial air. Varun Dar was just as good-looking as Jens, his muscular arms straining against his tight, white shirt.

The blond corp comms officer sat in one corner of the stage and introduced himself as Lars Andersen. He was to direct proceedings.

Harsha struggled to keep his attention on the pompous presentation about how Boreas-Vayu was going to save India from a bleak future of power outages and climate catastrophe, only paying attention whenever he saw Vignesh take notes. He then dutifully took a few notes himself on the megawatt output and whatnot. He would decipher these later. If he could write an interview with Salman Rushdie from a few drunken notes, he could handle this.

He glanced at Lars and caught his eye. The man didn't even have the decency to look triumphant or smug. Bullying some insignificant Indian journalist was all in a day's work for him, apparently.

But there was worse to come — the journalist questions.

Harsha listened open-mouthed as journalist after journalist asked the most banal questions, often bordering on the sycophantic.

"How do you feel about the crucial role you are playing in the war against the climate crisis?" the snooty-looking journalist in the salwar kameez asked in gushing tones.

"How important do you think your Indian operations are in the context of your global operations," asked another chap in a pink shirt, giving the executives an open goal to talk about how much they valued India and Indians.

A third asked about Danish-Indian business relations, and the three executives gravely said they hoped that this enterprise would be the start of a new era in diplomacy between the two countries and peoples.

Vignesh was the only objective one, but even he only

asked complex questions about wattage and the national electricity grid.

Lars glanced at his watch, looking even more bored than ever, a slightly contemptuous smile on his face.

Anger at his fellow journalists added to the humiliation and shock Harsha had already been feeling.

He raised his hand.

Lars spotted Harsha's raised hand and paused. Then he nodded in a regal manner towards him, a minister permitting a lowly subject to speak to the kings. This did nothing to improve Harsha's mood.

Fuelled by anger at Lars, the chief executives, his fellow journalists and some deeper resentment that he couldn't quite put his finger on, Harsha asked: "A question for Mr Dar. Mr Dar, given your close relationship with the government through your wife, is there not a conflict of interest given that your relative was instrumental in handing out these contracts and permits to energy companies?"

A deathly silence fell over the group, the slow creak of the wind turbines the only sound.

Lars was the first to react. "You don't have to answer that question!" he barked to the executives, reminding Harsha forcibly of Harleen talking to Nangai and Jamuna — though in her case she was protecting the extremely vulnerable rather than the extremely powerful.

"You decline to comment on the matter?" Harsha asked, smiling.

Lars hesitated. He knew that it would look bad for the company if they offered no response at all.

"It's alright," Varun said quietly to the man.

He looked at Harsha and a flash of anger momentarily

touched his eyes before he smiled carefully.

"I can assure you that this project only emerged well after my wife's uncle left his post, so there was no question of conflict of interest," he said politely.

Harsha winced. It was a good answer — one that could never be proven wrong, even if it was a complete fabrication.

"Besides," Varun continued, speaking with a New Delhi polish-bordering-on-arrogance that Harsha couldn't help envying, "While the central government does offer broad guidance on energy policy in India, the ultimate decision on this project was down to the Tamil Nadu government — which I don't need to remind you, was allied to the opposition party at the time. In other words, there is no conflict of interest."

It was a masterly response that should and would have stumped Harsha. Some of his fellow journalists were even looking embarrassed.

"If I may add..." said Jens, and Varun nodded gracefully. Jens turned his blue eyes onto the audience and said: "We are in the business of progress. And when you make progress, there are always those who look to pull you down."

Some of the journalists nodded in an understanding manner and the woman who had asked the first question gave Harsha a disgusted look.

"And there are always journalists who look for sensationalism over facts," Jens continued, raising his voice slightly. "But we are confident that the way we operate is beyond reproach and that our reputation for the best corporate governance in the world is beyond question," he said, speaking in polished English with only traces of his native Danish accent.

Not once did he look at Harsha through this pompous

little speech, so Harsha really enjoyed asking his next question.

"Aren't you the subject of two bribery investigations in Zambia and in Indonesia?" he asked, his voice carrying clearly over the crowd. "And hasn't the MSCI put you on review for exclusion from its sustainability indexes?" *Whatever that means,* he added to himself in his head.

A real shock went through the group this time. Though the snooty-looking journalist gave him another annoyed look, Harsha was gratified to see that some of the others were now alert, pens poised over their notepads to take notes on Jens's response, whatever it might be.

Lars said something sharply to his boss in Danish, and Jens closed his mouth with a snap.

"Another decline to comment?" Harsha asked, showing his teeth to the corporate communications officer.

"We cannot discuss an ongoing investigation! It would be a breach of the law!" the man protested in a strained voice. "We will be happy to answer any other questions."

"I do have one more, then," Harsha said calmly.

A buzz broke out on the group and a few people glanced at Harsha again.

Lars seemed to have lost the will to speak, so Harsha ploughed on.

"What is the latest on your Kovalam hydropower project? Have you managed to convince the government that the protesters are wrong and that the displacement of locals and disruption to wildlife are acceptable?" he asked.

Jens was red with rage by now, which showed up beautifully against his pale skin, but he collected himself at this and said stiffly: "We are confident that the Tamil Nadu government will make the right decision for the people of this state."

The hitherto silent CFO, Christian, leaned forward with a nod to Jens and then said in turn: "The Kovalam hydropower project will provide as many as 2,000 new jobs, create a new eco-city in that vicinity and will provide several megawatts of electricity per day for this great state."

Even Vignesh was taking notes at this barrage of statistics.

Christian turned to Harsha and smiled, far more composed than his compatriot. "We believe that the government will see, as we do, that the benefits of this, both in the short term, and long-term, are immense, and will give us permission to proceed rapidly."

"Especially now that M. L. Gopinath is dead?" Harsha asked, and there were audible gasps in the press audience.

"I don't know who that is," Jens said, contemptuously.

Lars stood up. "That is all we have time for, ladies and gentlemen," he said weakly.

Harsha almost felt sorry for him.

There was a great scraping of chairs as everyone stood up, and a release of tension in the air. The three Danes huddled together in conversation.

Varun stood a little separately, staring expressionlessly at Harsha. Harsha met his gaze as blandly as he could, but could not quite repress an internal shiver. He had just made a very powerful enemy.

The snooty-looking woman was also glaring at Harsha. She shook her head and stalked away, saying loudly to a fellow journalist: "Some people just stand in the way of economic progress."

"Ignore her." Harsha turned to see Vignesh standing next to him, stretching as he spoke. "Some journalists are just corporate cheerleaders. She is one of them."

"Thank you, Vignesh," Harsha said, shaking the older man's hand. "And sorry for stealing all your intel for my questions."

Vignesh straightened at this and shook his head. "Don't apologise! You actually had the guts to ask the questions that some of us had in our minds."

He eyed Harsha up and down and said: "You will go far, Harsha from *Southern Echo*. Unless…"

"Unless?" Harsha prompted.

Vignesh laughed and said: "Unless someone has you silenced first."

Harsha felt a chill go down his spine and looked around furtively. But the enforcer was nowhere to be seen.

27. Letters

If Harsha hadn't had a sudden, nostalgic hankering for parathas that evening, he would never have taken Neha to the *Paratha World* restaurant and events could have turned out very differently.

As it was, he always looked back on that night as one of the most inexplicable, bizarre episodes in his career to date.

He was apprehensive when he got off the auto-rickshaw at the little building where that restaurant used to be located in his youth.

Would it be anything like how he remembered it?

His parents used to take him there when he was growing up, when his father had a spell of nostalgia for his North Indian cuisine, and they would sit on the rickety plastic chairs, Harsha swinging his legs in anticipation of the delicious treat ahead of them. He would speculate loudly on whether he was going to have it stuffed with *aloo* or *methi* or just have it plain to dip into the delicious spicy chutneys that came in little *katoris*. The benign-looking owner would pinch his cheeks and make an extra one for him shaped like a bunny rabbit or a dog, depending on the day.

His mouth watered as he made his way up the driveway, just as it had all those years ago, and he felt a tug for his gentle parents. It had been such a long time since he had seen them — he really must make the trip up to Kolkata to see them again.

He felt another pang as he walked into *Paratha World*, which thankfully still existed. The tables and chairs had got an upgrade from plastic to wood, but otherwise the place looked absolutely the same — pictures of different parts of the Indian countryside adorning the walls, a counter on one side presided over by a woman (was it the same one?) who gave him a motherly smile.

Only one other couple sat in the corner, holding hands and oblivious to the world around them.

Harsha sat down on the table furthest from them, close to the entrance. A young, smiling waiter came up with a laminated sheet that represented the menu. Harsha took it and said: "Thank you. I'm waiting for someone."

He smiled at the man's familiar head bob and looked towards the doorway.

He didn't have long to wait. At 9pm on the dot, a Ford Escort came to a smooth halt outside and Neha stepped out, saying something cheerful to her driver before stepping up towards the entrance.

Harsha stared as she swung the glass door open and walked in. She was wearing a sparkly blue dress that ended a few inches above her knees, and her hair straddled her shoulders in neat, straight lines; a complete transformation from their first meeting.

"How quaint!" she exclaimed, looking around.

The waiter and the owner gaped at her open-mouthed, and even the loved-up couple broke apart to stare at this glamorous sight.

Harsha stood up and looked ruefully down at his plain white T-shirt and khaki trousers and said: "Uh... sorry, maybe I should have warned you this isn't a posh restaurant," he said, as he leaned forward and brushed her cheek with his own by way of greeting.

"Oh, this?" she asked, making a face as she indicated her dress. "I'm going out afterwards. You should come!"

Harsha smiled weakly. "I'm afraid I'm still working," he said. He had enough trouble in his romantic life without getting involved with the daughter of a murder victim.

Neha pouted but did not insist.

The smiling waiter came up with another menu and withdrew discreetly.

"What do you recommend?" Neha asked, smiling up at him and batting her eyelashes slightly.

Harsha was not a naturally intuitive person. But years of working as a journalist — and one intense experience reporting on a murder case — had taught him some sensitivity in reading people. He saw the deep trauma behind the façade.

"Are you ok, Neha?" he asked, gently.

She blinked and said: "Oh yes. Life moves on, you know? My mother taught me that," she said, a trace of bitterness entering her voice.

Harsha said nothing.

"Do you know she is already going on holiday tomorrow? To Greece. 'To see the history', she says. Always wanted to study history, but my father wouldn't allow her, she claims," Neha ended with a snort. "As though he were even capable of such a thing."

"Was he?" Harsha asked, to keep her talking.

"Oh yes! He never asked her to do anything. He was a very busy man and needed some upkeep and support. But he always encouraged her to occupy herself in her free time," Neha finished uncomfortably. Harsha thought that maybe she was only now realising that it wasn't so straightforward.

He couldn't help saying, as gently as he could: "Women of that generation often have unfulfilled ambitions, and a lot of frustration."

There was an uncomfortable silence, and then Neha nodded. "I do get it. Yes, I know she would have loved to have done something more with her life. But to talk of my father as though he was some tyrant! He *wasn't!* He was the gentlest of souls," she said.

Harsha didn't say anything. He knew that tyrants came in all shapes and forms. You didn't have to be a fire-breathing dragon to be able to manipulate someone into giving you exactly what you needed. In a patriarchal society, someone like Hema would have had no chance. A bit of emotional blackmail here and there, and she would no doubt have felt completely trapped in her role as a homemaker, while her husband got all the plaudits.

"I mean, you met him — he wasn't like that, was he?" Neha asked pleadingly.

Fortunately, the waiter came up at this point and asked for their orders.

"One *aloo paratha* and some watermelon juice," Harsha said.

The waiter did his head bob and then turned to Neha.

"Oh, the same," she said impatiently and turned back to Harsha.

"I asked her — is this the time to go on holiday? And you

know what she said?"

Harsha shook his head.

"Appa wouldn't take her. He was always too busy." She looked out at the little passage by the restaurant where cars could pass and sighed.

Harsha continued to maintain his silence. He hadn't considered the possibility that someone could feel a sense of freedom once their spouse had died. In a conservative society like India — it must feel like the shackles had been removed, especially for a woman.

Neha was shaking her head. "She just didn't get it. She was so traditional. She didn't understand what he was trying to do."

If Neha had been one of his friends, he would have told her to be kinder to her mother and to try and see it from her mother's point of view. But he was a journalist. So he just said: "Maybe she was worried that he was fighting too many battles? Making enemies?"

Neha snorted. "Anyone in public life worth their salt makes enemies," she said, contemptuously. "Speaking of which…"

She rummaged in her bag and pulled out a plastic folder filled with letters and handed it over the table.

"Amazing!" Harsha said, grasping the folder and holding it in his hands as though it were a great treasure. He couldn't help glancing at the top letter, which began: 'Mr Gopinath, are you aware that your actions have created a situation where people cannot feel safe in their homes? You have brought this great country…'

"Who the hell still writes letters in this day and age?" Neha asked, contemptuously, cutting into his reading. "Though of course, there are some emails in there as well, which I have printed out for you at the bottom. Do you know how hard it is to access someone's email after they have d... passed, Harsha?"

Harsha shook his head. "Thank you so much for this," he said fervently, giving the folder a little shake. "It could be really, really helpful. I don't know how much of this we can publish, but..."

His voice trailed off as he lost himself in reading the top letter and Neha looked piercingly at him.

"Have you been to see these 1857 fuckers?" she asked.

The waiter came up just at that point with their food laden on a massive tray and jumped at her use of profanity.

"Thank you," Harsha said, giving him a brief smile before turning back to Neha, trying to ignore the glorious smell rising from the plates and resisting the urge to tuck in straightaway.

"Yes, I did," he said and gave her a brief account of his encounter with Advaith on the maidan.

She tore strips off her paratha and put them in her mouth, oblivious to their extreme heat, and chewed absentmindedly, her eyes fixed on him.

"And?" she asked, when he finished speaking.

"Er... that's it," he admitted.

"I meant — did he do it? Or was he involved in any way?" she asked breathlessly, scaring him slightly with the intensity of her gaze.

Harsha shook his head. "That's not my job, Neha. I'm not a detective. Or even an investigative journalist. That's a job for Pa... for the police."

She shook her head impatiently. "But they don't even know how to look into this Advaith guy. They are clueless! I tried to tell them — they didn't even give me a chance."

"Well, I did tell them. And the inspector in charge is good. Very good. He will take it seriously," Harsha said as reassuringly as he could.

"Well, that's something anyway," Neha said and fell to staring at her plate.

Harsha felt safe to pay some attention to his food, finally, and tore a piece of his *paratha* and dipped it in the coriander chutney, his mouth watering. He chewed it slowly and mindfully, and felt a sudden, sharp stab of nostalgia. To his embarrassment, he felt tears sting his eyes without warning.

What is wrong with you? He scolded himself.

"Where are you from, Harsha?" Neha asked, smiling at him now, as though determined to forget her own troubles for a moment.

Harsha swallowed and said: "My father is from Bengal. My mother is from here. I was born in Kolkata but then I grew up here."

"I wouldn't have had you down for a Bengali," Neha said, smiling. "You don't talk much, for example."

Harsha smiled and tore another piece of the *paratha*. It was an irritating stereotype that Bengalis talked too much. Though he had to admit, when he thought of his family, that there was at least some truth to that. Somehow he had always been more of a listener. Maybe that's what made him a good journalist.

"Where are your parents now?"

"They are back in Kolkata. They moved there when I went to England," he said shortly. He felt strongly that it wasn't a good idea to talk too much about his family to Neha or anybody else connected with this case.

They talked in general terms through the rest of the meal and Harsha found himself relaxing a little bit. It was very comfortable to sit there and talk about life in Chennai, and what it had been like growing up in the city in the nineties and noughties. The lovelorn couple left, a couple of others came and went, and they still chatted.

They were well into their third *paratha* when the smiling waiter came up and said: "Sorry, but we are closing in ten minutes."

Neha gave a start and looked at her slim watch. "I was supposed to be there twenty minutes ago! The girls will be waiting."

"Just go and I will pick this up," Harsha said.

Neha hesitated and then said: "I had a really good time, Harsha. It was so nice to get away from everything. Are you sure you don't want to come?"

Harha had a brief vision of going out with a group of attractive women in a crowded bar. It was tempting, but he had a lot of work to do, and he instinctively knew it would not be a good idea to get involved in Neha's life.

"Seriously, I'm ok," he said, signalling to the waiter for the bill.

"Perhaps I can give you a ride somewhere? To be on the safe side."

"Oh, I'll be fine! This is Chennai," Harsha said, smiling.

She nodded and then reached into her bag and took a book out, hesitated, and then handed it to Harsha.

He took it casually and looked at it and felt the hackles rise on the back of his neck.

It was a copy of *I Am Vidya* — the novel Gopu had told Harsha about when they met all those days ago.

"Appa was reading this book when he... when he... Well, he really loved it. And I want you to have it," Neha said, blinking and then surreptitiously wiping a tear away.

"Neha, this is... I don't know what to say," Harsha said, his eyes scanning the book cover. An image of a transgender woman looked back at him, her intense eyes seeming to burn into his soul. Above that was a large yellowing blotch.

Neha sniffed loudly and then said: "Sorry it's not very clean, he must have spilled tea or something on it. But it was his own copy."

"That's ok," Harsha said, quickly. "Are you sure you want me to have it?"

Neha sighed as she stood up. "I think that's best. My mother cannot be trusted around any of these books about transgenders. That's why he usually left them in the office. I actually found this book in the bin at home! I just happened to find it by chance when I was throwing something else away. She is really..." She choked her words back and slung her handbag over her shoulder. She put on a smile and then said: "Sure you don't want to come?"

"I just have so much to do," Harsha explained carefully, standing up and giving her a brief hug. "You take care of yourself, Neha, and let me know if I can help with anything."

After she left, Harsha sat back down and looked down at the copy of Gopu's book, thinking of the old man that he had met, and felt a stab of sadness and confusion. Could he reconcile that lovely gentleman with a domestic tyrant? He was learning rapidly that there were too many complex layers to human beings to be able to bracket anyone in any one single category.

The waiter came up with the bill. Harsha paid it and took one last look around the restaurant that meant so much to him before going out into the night.

28. Flight

Harsha walked out of *Paratha World* and headed down 6th Main Road in R.A. Puram, looking around for an auto-rickshaw. The street was entirely deserted apart from a lone stray dog that was picking hopefully at a pile of garbage on one side of the road.

The streetlamps shed a dappled orange light on the pavements, and the line of tamarind trees that fringed the road on either side cast shadows on the tarmac, waving slightly in the breeze.

Harsha shivered slightly despite the balmy night air. It was later than he expected — nearly midnight, how had that happened? — and he had forgotten how this sleepy town turned a bit spooky at night. It wasn't a twenty-four hour city like London or even Mumbai.

He walked a little further towards the direction of the main road — Greenways Road, if he remembered correctly. As he approached it, he saw an auto-rickshaw speed past.

"Auto! Auto!" he yelled out, but the man motored on, ignoring him.

He sighed as the roaring of the engine faded into the

distance.

And just as the sound faded almost to nothing, he thought he heard footsteps behind him. He spun around and looked sharply back the way he had come. There was nothing there, just trees on either side leaning into the road, stretching their branches protectively over the road.

"What's wrong with you!" he scolded himself. "This is *Chennai.*"

He had a choice either to go right towards Chamiers Road, which would almost certainly be busier, or left towards Adyar Bridge. That was a longer walk, but there would almost certainly be some form of public transport available at some point. He also had that somewhat irrational dislike of walking further away from home, even if it made more sense to go to a busier part of town.

He went left.

He regretted this decision about five minutes in. Not a single shop was open, nor a single light on any store front or house.

He walked rapidly, trying to shake the impression that his footsteps had an echo. He looked behind him once or twice, but saw nothing but shadows.

The tree branches waved above him, tossing the orange street light around the potholed streets, sudden rushes of wind through the leaves the only sound. He even longed for the "neek neek" of car horns that were usually audible in Chennai's streets.

He turned around again — and jumped, his heart pounding horribly. There had been a definite, unmistakable shadow of a person walking behind him, though it was only briefly visible as he walked further down a bend in the road.

Involuntarily, Vignesh's words flitted through his mind.

"You are a journalist to watch. If you are not silenced first."

Harsha cursed himself a hundred times over for not arranging transport. For not getting his driving licence and buying himself a car like a normal person. For not going out with Neha and her friends. He could be sipping cocktails in a trendy bar with beautiful women right now instead of playing hide and seek with some shadowy figure.

He turned again and saw that the shadow had become longer as the man had drawn nearer. Much nearer.

He turned and stepped up the pace, his breath coming in short, sharp bursts. He was nearing a left turn, just past a small roadside temple. His heart pounding horribly, he gave a small, fervent prayer to whatever deity was in the temple to keep him safe, adding an apology for his atheistic views as an afterthought.

On an impulse, he decided to turn left to try and lose this person behind him. He briefly saw the road sign that read 'Crescent Avenue' — why did that have a familiar ring to it?

He ploughed on at a rapid pace.

If the street before had had plenty of trees, it was nothing to this one. Any hints of moonlight or starlight were completely blocked by the thick canopy of trees, with only the occasional street lamp providing a dim impression of the road; just enough for Harsha to navigate with.

He turned again and saw, to his horror, that his follower had also turned into the road.

It was time to put pride aside. Harsha pulled out his phone and started to call Azhar.

"Come on, you dick, pick up! Pick up!" he grunted into the phone, which rang morosely back at him.

There was no answer. Whom else could he call? Paul

would be asleep. Shane? He had children — he must be asleep as well. His parents in Kolkata? That would be crazy, surely.

The footsteps echoed behind him and Harsha gave up any sign of pretence that he wasn't in a sticky situation. With fumbling hands, he found the keypad. It was time to call the police.

But what was the number? Harsha strode as quickly as he could while staring at his mobile phone and coming to the ridiculous and horrible realisation that he did not know.

Was it 911? No! That was the U.S. Was it 999? That was Britain. But this was once a British colony — maybe that was valid for India as well. He tried that and heard in Tamil: 'This number does not exist.'

"Fuck!" Harsha yelled at his phone.

He glanced behind him, seeing the street lamp light shine off his follower's bald pate in a sinister fashion and briefly light up the man's intent eyes. His heart leapt into his mouth. He turned back to his phone and hurriedly scrolled through his contacts to find Inspector Palanivel's number.

He hesitated very briefly before pressing the green button to dial the number.

"Come on," he pleaded as the phone began to ring.

And to his huge relief and joy, he heard the staccato tones of Detective Inspector Palanivel's voice.

"Mr Devnath?"

Harsha could have sobbed with relief.

"Yes... I... Sir, I'm being followed by someone! Please do something!"

To his tremendous relief, there was no hesitation in the inspector's voice.

"Where are you?" the man asked.

"In Crescent..."

Harsha felt a vice-like grip grab his shoulder and spin him around. His mobile phone clattered to the floor and his pursuer kicked it aside before reaching for him with both hands.

Harsha scrambled to keep his balance. He threw a wild punch and found that his fist was being gently propelled aside with ease, a small grin appearing on his assailant's face. With a shock, Harsha recognised Mangal, the enforcer from Boreas Vayu. So it was them after all!

He lashed out with his foot instead. It was unscientific and probably would have looked ridiculous to an observer, if there had been one, but by some stroke of luck, he caught the man on the knee. The enforcer grunted. Harsha tore himself from the man's grasp, turned and ran down the street, feeling suddenly better. He had just remembered where he had last seen Crescent Avenue — it was the street where Maya lived.

Harsha's mind raced as he ran, breathing in great gulps. It was an apartment complex called Ceebos or Ceebros or something. And the number? 72, he thought, though the classic old number/new number confusion might lead him to entirely the wrong place.

Even if he got there, would the watchman even let him in? He didn't know, but the thought of another human being on his side, even if it was an underpaid, badly-trained and badly-slept security official, was very appealing.

He continued to pound away, staring at the apartment complexes on either side of the palm fronds, trying to see something familiar, and suddenly, without warning, his assailant was on him again, this time catching him by the throat and slamming him against a compound wall.

Harsha felt a whooshing sensation in his chest. *So this is what it feels like to get the wind knocked out of you,* he thought wildly to himself. Once again, he threw a punch, which again, was parried, though this time there was no smile on the other man's face. Instead, he reached for Harsha's throat with one hand and pulled something out of his pocket with the other. It gleamed in the faint light of the street lamp. It was a blade.

Harsha's terror was extreme but he could do nothing against this killer but flail against him.

The man released his throat and pushed against his chest, pinning him to the wall with incredible strength. Harsha could barely move.

Is this how it ends? Harsha asked himself. After a night eating *parathas*. He would never see Maya... Azhar... his parents, ever again.

A rush of emotion filled his heart at the thought of eating *parathas* with his mother and father and as if from nowhere, a conversation with an old Scottish colleague in London surfaced in his brain.

"When in a brawl... if you're losing... give them the old Glasgow kiss. They won't see it coming!"

Almost without thought, he snapped his head forward and smacked it as hard as he could against the other man's forehead.

The two skulls came together with a dull crack and Harsha blinked, stars floating into his sight. He felt like his head must have split in two.

But the other man's reaction was even more dramatic — he stumbled and fell on his backside onto the pavement and sat there stupidly.

Harsha stumbled forward, blinking to disperse the sudden, sharp dizziness that came over him and clutched his throat where the other man's fingers had mercilessly choked him. He found, miraculously, that his legs did not give way, so without further delay, he set off on a trot down the road.

Maya's house, he thought himself hazily, and his feet took him to the front gate of the quiet little apartment complex that was his sanctuary.

He rattled the gate, not daring to look around to see if the killer was following him.

He spotted the watchman sitting on a chair behind the gate to one side, fast asleep. Harsha hesitated for a second and then decided not to waste time waking the man up. Instead he clambered over the gate as best he could and collapsed on the other side and stumbled towards the apartment entrance.

The watchman gave a little snort and a snore. Shaking his head, Harsha had a sudden awful thought — what if the apartment was locked?

He tried the door fearfully, and, wonder of wonders, it opened!

He ran into the foyer and pressed the button to call the lift several times. He waited agonisingly for it to reach the ground floor, listening to the creaks and the clanks that old elevators made. As soon as the doors slid open — achingly slowly — he squeezed himself in and pressed the button for the third floor forcefully. The device made its slow and lumbering progress upwards.

Fuelled by fear, he stepped out of the lift when it finally reached the third floor, walked up to Maya's apartment and rang the doorbell loudly and repeatedly.

Then he paused and waited. Surely she would be at home? What a cruel twist of fate it would be if she was away!

And then — he could have cried with relief — he heard a sound from the other side of the door and a voice asked urgently: "Who is it? What do you want?"

It was Maya's husband.

29. Naveen

Harsha stared at the wooden door in front of him. He was trying to get into the apartment of his childhood sweetheart to hide from a killer. The only thing between him and safety was her husband. *What the actual fuck!*

"I'm... I'm... Harsha... Maya's friend!"

"*Harsha?*" the man asked sharply, his voice muffled by the doorway but still transmitting shock and anger.

"Please! Please let me in and I will explain! I've been attacked!"

There was a pause and then, mercifully, the door opened.

Over the last several years, Harsha had pictured Maya's husband as a typical programmer — well-to-do, smug, perhaps with large glasses; the kind of chap who would stride confidently through the corridor of a glossy building in a Silicon Valley office. And while he was too fair-minded and self-reflective to look down on such a person — he could hardly lecture anyone on smugness, anyway — he thought that such a person would be wildly unsuitable for Maya.

Instead, what he saw was Naveen.

Naveen was tall, taller than Harsha himself, gaunt,

clean-shaven and with dark circles under his eyes that somehow made him more of a romantic and appealing figure. His tight expression hardened and his somewhat thin lips curled in a sneer as he took Harsha in. Despite this, Harsha couldn't help admiring the look of the man.

"The famous Harsha," Naveen said in an unpleasant tone. "You've got guts, coming here."

"Listen... I... I'm sorry, I had no choice!"

"Did you not?"

"I've been chased and attacked!" Harsha said, feeling his head, which was throbbing alarmingly.

Naveen's eyes narrowed. "Who by? The mafia? The CIA?"

"I... I... don't know... I think he is a hired killer," Harsha said, clutching at the door frame as another spell of dizziness overcame him.

He had intended to soften the thunderous expression in this man's eyes, but, if anything, it hardened even more.

"You are being chased by a killer and you brought him *here*? Where *Maya* is?" Naveen asked, contemptuously.

Harsha hung his head. He hadn't thought about Maya's safety. He had been in pure fight-or-flight mode — concerned for nothing but his own skin. He pushed himself to an erect position, ready to leave. Naveen was right. He had to keep Maya safe.

"He did exactly the right thing!" a familiar voice said, ringing out behind Naveen. Harsha blinked and saw Maya emerge from one of the rooms, lacing up a faded green dressing gown as she strode up to the two men. She managed to look beautiful even in this, Harsha thought through his haze.

"But Maya..."

"I should leave..."

"All you bloody men, looking to protect me all the time," she muttered to herself. "You are going nowhere, Harsha. Naveen, let him in. He is clearly in a bad way."

Naveen hesitated and then, to Harsha's surprise, stepped aside rather meekly. Harsha gratefully stumbled into the house. The sound of the door closing on the terrifying world outside was like balm to a wound, and he let out a deep breath. He hadn't even realised he had been holding it until that point.

Harsha looked around, blinking. Maya's flat was looking a bit blurred.

"I... Maya..."

Two pairs of hands grasped him by either arm. He hadn't even realised he had collapsed.

"Get him to the sofa — he needs to lie down," Maya said decisively.

"No!" Harsha said, urgently. "Need... need to throw up. Bathroom!"

He was guided to the bathroom where he vomited violently into the toilet bowl, feeling his head pounding against his temple again.

"What's happened to him? Is he ok?"

"Let's ask questions later."

That was his Maya. Cool and authoritative in a crisis. He felt her small hands supporting him as he sank onto the floor and heard the flush of the toilet above him. He was too dizzy and sick to feel any shame.

"Harry? Let's get you back to the sofa."

"No," he said petulantly. "Like it here."

And indeed, the cool bathroom floor tiles felt incredibly soothing and comfortable after the terror of the sultry night air.

"Come on, Harry."

Again, two pairs of hands grabbed him and helped him back up. In what felt like a long and gruelling journey, he slowly and steadily made his way to the sofa before gratefully collapsing onto it.

"Should we call the hospital? Or the police?" he heard Naveen ask, and felt oddly ashamed that there was genuine concern in the other man's voice.

"Both, I think. The hospital first, maybe."

"No. The police first," Naveen said, firmly. It was the first time he had made a decision since Harsha had come in.

There was a pause and then Maya said: "Whatever you think is best."

There was a brief silence in which the only sound was the three of them breathing and Naveen fumbling with his phone.

"Hello? Police? Yes, yes this is an emergency... A friend of ours has been attacked on the street... Yes, yes... We are in Crescent Avenue, R.A. Puram... What? Already here? How?"

Harsha opened his eyes and stared at Naveen, and saw that he was looking equally baffled.

Naveen listened for a few seconds and then said: "I see. Well, if you need to come see us we are on the third floor, Number 7... Er..." He hesitated when he saw Maya's expression. "We may be taking him to the hospital. Can you get a witness statement there? Yes, thank you, one of us will be here."

He hung up the phone and said brusquely to Harsha: "The police are outside. They are investigating the scene on the street, they say."

"How did they get here so quickly?" Maya asked.

Naveen nodded towards Harsha. "Sounds like you called some inspector? He ordered them to come here apparently."

"But how did…"

"Never mind all that, Harry," Maya said impatiently. "It's time to get you to the hospital. Naveen?"

"I may have to deal with the police outside."

Maya nodded. "I'll call the nearest hospital."

"I would go straight for Apollo," Naveen said. "If he has to stay there he will be more comfortable."

Maya considered and then nodded. "Apollo it is."

Harsha chuckled suddenly. "My mum used to work there. Maybe she will take care of me," he said, laughing more and more.

Naveen and Maya exchanged glances.

"What the actual fuck?" Naveen muttered.

"He is fine — just delirious. I will call Apollo," Maya said in her reassuring voice.

Those were the last words Harsha heard before he passed out.

30. Hospital

When Harsha woke ten minutes later, he was jerked to wakefulness by the fact that Naveen was sitting on a chair by his head. Maya was nowhere to be seen.

Naveen blinked and pulled his chair up closer.

"Are you ok?" he asked and handed Harsha a steel tumbler full of water.

Harsha winced and sat up a little on the sofa. His mouth felt utterly disgusting and his head still spun slightly. But otherwise, he felt actually fine.

He forced himself to drink the water in one gulp and then looked blearily at the other man.

"Maya?" he asked.

"Talking to the doctor. Trying to get you an ambulance to get you to the hospital right away."

"Oh God!" Harsha groaned. "Must I?"

"Yes — you are clearly fucked up," came the frank response.

Harsha chuckled gently. Naveen was nothing like he had expected.

Naveen pulled his chair still closer, looking uncomfortable. Harsha noticed that he was wearing an Indian Terrain T-shirt, and liked him for it.

"Listen," Naveen said. "I'm sorry about earlier. I should have just let you into the house, of course. But I let my anger get to me. I'm sorry."

Harsha's eyes widened and he turned his neck to scan the other man's face. Was the husband of the woman he was in love with actually apologising to him?

"Mate, I'm surprised you didn't slam the door on me or knock me back down the stairs," he reassured him.

Naveen laughed at this. "The thought did occur to me," he admitted. He then sighed and added: "Life is complicated. Before I met you today, I always had you down as some sort of smooth player. But now I see that you're just a normal guy. No horns growing out of your head. I don't know what to think any more."

Harsha was astonished by this parallel to his own thoughts, minus the horns of course.

"Reality has a weird way of surprising you," he croaked and tipped the last few drops of water into his mouth.

Naveen leaned forward and refilled his glass from a large plastic jug.

"Thank you," Harsha said, sipping the water. "And what now?"

"We wait for Maya," Naveen said, his gaunt eyes dropping to the carpet.

They sat silently for a few minutes, Harsha trying to process the events of this mad night. Somehow, meeting Naveen felt even more momentous than the attempt on his life.

Maya came in and Harsha saw that she had quickly

changed into jeans and a loose checked shirt.

"Ambulance will arrive in five minutes. Naveen, can you get us a bottle of water?" she asked.

Harsha tried to sit up. "I feel ok now. No need for that," he said briskly.

Maya ignored this and took the bottle from her husband, briefly squeezing his hand in gratitude. "You understand?" she asked him, concern etched on her face.

He nodded, smiling reassuringly. "I'll deal with the police," he said.

She smiled at him warmly.

"You don't need to come with me, Maya!" Harsha declared, alarmed that he was being a burden or putting a strain on their marriage.

"I definitely do," Maya said firmly.

Naveen and Maya bundled Harsha into the ambulance — a rickety white Maruti van — assisted by some friendly and incredibly young-looking paramedics, and it clattered its way through Chennai's potholed byways.

"You need to be in perfect health to ride on this ambulance," Harsha said grumpily.

Maya gave one of her gurgling laughs and put her hand on his shoulder reassuringly.

The hospital itself was clean and friendly, but to Harsha it seemed a nightmare of stretchers and paperwork. Fortunately, Maya was there to take care of it all, which she did with brutal efficiency and calm.

"Please don't tell my mother," Harsha pleaded with her as they wheeled him down a corridor. "They all know her here."

"Why not?"

"She..." How could he explain? His mother had worked

as a doctor for years and had seen every possible ailment and complication. Ironically, that also made her the worst person to have around when unwell — she lost her cool completely and always imagined the worst when a family member was involved.

Finally, he was installed in a comfortable room and he was able to look up at Maya and thank her properly.

"You can go home now, I don't want to trouble you any further," he said.

"Helping a friend is never any trouble," she said, sitting in a comfortable-looking chair by his bed and sipping a coffee. "I want to hear what the doctor says. I have my book. You just go to sleep."

He considered this advice gravely, and decided it was good. He closed his eyes.

Harsha awoke with a jerk in what felt like hours later. Maya had her nose buried in a tattered copy of Emily Bronte's *Wuthering Heights*, one side of her face visible in the light of the bedside lamp that she had dragged over by her chair.

"Mads?" he asked, surprised to hear his voice sound so tired.

She jumped, dropped her book and leaned forward, looking concerned.

"How are you feeling, Harry?" she asked, smiling.

"Absolutely bloody fine!" he said crossly. "Why am I here, Mads? I'm ok!"

"Er... your mother said..."

"Bah!" Harsha turned his head away from her. "I told you not to call her! She is a massive hypochondriac!"

Maya looked sternly at Harsha. "She thinks you may have concussion and is getting the doctor to check you for it."

"And who is going to pay for this room and everything? I'm a journalist, you know — not exactly rolling in it."

"I've arranged all that. I've spoken to your office — the medical insurance will take care of all that," Maya said calmly.

Harsha threw his hands up in frustration, as though Maya had offended him by resolving this difficulty for him, and looked around to try and think about something else. He noticed the outline of a man wearing a peaked cap visible through the frosted glass of the entrance to the room.

"Who is that?" he asked, though he thought he knew the answer already.

"The police have assigned someone to watch over you in case there is another attack," Maya said.

"Oh. My. God. This is ridiculous!" Harsha declared. "How on earth could he get through an entire hospital? This isn't some American mafia film..."

"It is the right thing to do, Harry. Better safe than sorry," Maya said firmly, but not without a little smile at Harsha's frustrated response. "And plus they managed to find your phone on the street last night. It's there beside you."

He glanced at his battered phone on his bedside table, but didn't pick it up.

"At least tell me my mother isn't coming here to watch over me as well?" he asked.

"Er... well, I think she is coming, actually," Maya admitted, not looking at him.

"Ma-ya!" Harsha sank backwards onto the cushion.

"Most people like seeing their mothers!"

"Not my mother when you're unwell," Harsha said.

The door of the room swung open and a doctor walked in, her badge bouncing against the front of her white coat.

"And how is our patient?" she asked breezily.

She was a tall, striking-looking woman with hair falling neatly into a ponytail which hung by one side of her face.

"Marvellous," Harsha muttered grumpily.

"He is just sulking, but otherwise fine," Maya grinned, standing up and shaking hands with the doctor, who smiled back at her. "I'm Maya," she added.

"I am Dr. Lavanya. I have been expressly asked by Dr Ramya Devnath — who is my absolute hero by the way — to take care of her son," she said jovially, winking at Harsha. "And it's not every day I have to get through a police cordon to get to my patient, so you are a VIP around here. Expect the full works."

Harsha was so lost for words that the doctor turned instead to Maya.

"Are you his wife? Girlfriend?" she asked.

There was an awkward moment but Maya put paid to this by quietly saying: "Just a friend."

The doctor did not ask any more questions, instead coming forward and beginning to examine Harsha.

He cheered up a little after realising she was rather attractive and about his age.

"Hmm..." she said, as she thumbed his eyes wide open and peered into them carefully.

"What?" Maya and Harsha asked together.

"Any pain here?" she asked, ignoring this and tapping the side of Harsha's forehead.

She continued to examine him for another few minutes and then stood back.

"I don't see any lasting damage. Did you experience any dizziness or nausea at any point?"

"No!" Harsha said at the same time Maya said "Yes!"

Harsha scowled at Maya. "A little," he admitted grudgingly.

"He threw up into my toilet," Maya said drily.

The doctor sat down on the edge of his bed. "That does suggest a concussion. Bad luck, Harsha. I will order a CT scan for you later today, as soon as possible. Hopefully it is only a mild one. If that's all fine, then you'll be good to go."

She patted Harsha's hand, smiled at Maya and then bustled out of the room, a whirlwind of energy.

"I like her," Maya said.

"Yeah, she's delightful," Harsha said, putting as much sarcasm as he could into his voice. He then looked at Maya and his expression turned serious. "Never mind that, Maya — why are you still here? Does Naveen…"

"I wanted to hear the diagnosis," Maya said calmly, and sat down again, picking her copy of *Wuthering Heights* back up from the ground.

"Oh well, you can leave now if you want," he said.

"You seem to be in an awful hurry for me to leave," Maya said, pouting slightly as she pulled her feet up to sit cross-legged on the chair. She caught Harsha's expression and quickly added: "I'm just waiting for Azhar to relieve me."

"Oh my god — I'm fine, Maya! Honestly…"

Maya hesitated and then snapped her mouth shut again. There was a moment's silence in which they just heard the soft beeping of the heart rate monitor.

"Maya, I…"

"Shut up for a second, Harry. I'm just… thinking," she said, rubbing her forehead.

He leaned back in his bed. "Thinking about what, Maya?" he asked wearily.

"How to say this."

He waited.

Finally, she sighed and said: "Harry, I've been unfair to you. I feel like I sort of led you on. The truth is..."

"You are going to stay with Naveen," he finished for her.

She stared at him dumbly. Finally, she nodded.

He leaned back on his pillow, trying to hide the stab of sadness that he felt.

"I saw the two of you interact. You... you work as a couple. And you care about each other," he said. "Also, I..."

"You what?" she asked, before she could stop herself.

"Also, I like him," Harsha said with a laugh — though Maya could hear the undercurrent of bitterness in that laugh.

She looked at him, blinking back tears.

"I'm so glad, Harsha. He really is..." she began, but then cut off when he raised his hand to stop her.

"I like him, but I don't really want to hear an encomium," he said shortly, and closed his eyes.

She nodded understandingly and took a deep breath. She still needed to finish saying something that had been on her mind for a while now.

"I feel I really led you on and kept you hanging for too long. I'm so, so sorry Harry," she said, her voice breaking slightly. "It was really unforgivable of me."

He opened his eyes, and somewhat to her surprise, gave her a cheeky grin that reminded her startlingly of their university days together.

"Stop talking shit," he said. "If you really feel bad, find me some breakfast before you leave."

When Azhar came into the room, he found Harsha sitting up in his bed and his head buried in Maya's copy of *Wuthering Heights*.

"Ho!" Azhar said, stopping short. Harsha looked up, smiling, and put his book down beside him on the bed, after carefully placing a bookmark in his spot.

Azhar strode up to the bed.

"I come here expecting you to be at death's door and you're bloody reading a book as though you're studying for an exam or something. How are you, bugger?" Azhar asked brusquely, placing one hand on the edge of the bed.

"Absolutely fine!" Harsha said in a put-upon voice. "I mean, thanks a million for coming and all, but…"

"Sh. Be quiet. I know the full situation. I am here to take you back when the CT scan comes through," Azhar said, his grip tightening on the bed.

"I've already had the test, numbnuts," Harsha said, gesturing to a sheet of paper beside him. "But I have to wait for the doctor to look at the result."

Azhar sat down, resting one ankle on the other leg, the smooth skin of his knee showing through an artful tear in his jeans.

"Heard there was some drama with Maya?" he said casually, though he observed his friend closely through his half-closed eyes.

Harsha swallowed painfully and said: "Yes."

Azhar looked at him for a second and then wisely changed the subject.

"Police are on the hunt for your hitman. Inspector whatshisname personally appeared at the crime scene last night, apparently," he said.

Harsha nodded. "He is coming here shortly. If the doctor permits."

"What doctor schmoctor and all," Azhar said comfortably. "You look absolutely fine to me."

"Yes! Thank you, Azhar. Finally someone speaks sense," Harsha said, ignoring the fact that the room was swimming slightly for him.

"Spoke to Harleen," Azhar said casually.

"Oh yeah?"

Azhar leaned back, smiling slightly at Harsha's feigned casual tone.

"Said she would text you," he said.

Harsha saw Azhar's mischievous grin peep out, and sat up.

"What did you tell her?" he asked, resignedly.

"Me? Nothing," Azhar said, putting on an expression of great innocence that filled Harsha with foreboding. Harsha grabbed his phone from the bedside table and found that he had three messages from Harleen on Whatsapp.

"Ah — she texted me this morning," he said.

"And you didn't reply?" Azhar asked, looking at Harsha as though he was mad.

"I'm still getting used to this Whatsapp thing," Harsha said defensively. "Hey, I'm supposed to be unwell, idiot!"

Azhar shook his head in despair. "Anyway, what did she say?"

Harsha opened the messages and, after a second's hesitation, read them out loud: "'Really sorry to hear that you're hurt'. 'Let me know what the doctor says'. 'Let's catch up when you're feeling better.'"

Azhar gave a silent fist pump. Harsha felt a surge of happiness flow through his body, but he frowned when he looked up. He wasn't going to let Azhar off the hook so easily.

"What shit did you fill her up with?" he asked sternly.

Azhar flicked some dust off the knees of his jeans.

"Just told her your story. All the mad shit with Maya

and so on," he said smoothly.

"You did not!"

"Yep. Told her you really like her but were still getting over the Maya situation. To give you a bit of time," Azhar said matter-of-factly, as though he were telling Harsha what groceries he had bought that morning.

"You told her I like..."

"Someone had to," Azhar said calmly, leaning back in his chair.

"Why? You don't know that I like her!"

"Oh, give me a break! I may not be good at all this literature stuff," Azhar said, gesturing towards the copy of *Wuthering Heights*. "But I know *you*. I'm your oldest friend — remember?"

Harsha laughed. It had just occurred to him that even though he was away from the stifling influence and interference of his actual family, he seemed to have acquired a makeshift one — in the unexpected shape of people like Maya and Azhar.

"By the way, I'm not asking you to marry her or anything," Azhar said in a plaintive voice. "Just get to know her for fuck's sake. What's the problem? You don't like hanging out with beautiful, intelligent women or what?"

"Yes, dad. Whatever you say," Harsha said with heavy sarcasm.

Before Azhar could reply to this, the door swung open and Dr Lavanya bustled in, brisk and business-like.

"How are you feeling, Harsha?" she asked in her bracing tone.

"Fine, doctor!" Harsha said as brightly as he could, his eyes on the chart in her hand.

She sat on the edge of his bed and smiled down at him.

Azhar, who had been examining his fingernails carefully, noticed her and then jumped theatrically in his seat.

At the same time, Dr Lavanya noticed Azhar and was momentarily distracted, looking at this newcomer with wide eyes. Subtly, Azhar broadened his shoulders and smiled.

"My report, doctor?" Harsha asked meaningfully.

"Oh! Yes," the doctor said, looking flustered. "Er... yes — you have concussion."

"Ok? And?"

She seemed to realise that she had delivered the prognosis in a somewhat blunt fashion, because she blushed and said: "Sorry. I meant to say you have a moderate concussion. I believe you will be fine but we will keep you here for another day to be safe, and then you will have to live a somewhat restricted life for a while, I'm afraid — especially in the next few weeks. And you will need to come back at the end of the month for another scan."

She stopped talking and smiled at Harsha's groan of frustration and despondent expression.

"It could have been worse — believe me!" she ended.

Harsha covered his eyes with his hand, striking an attitude of despair at the idea of having to come back to the hospital.

"What restrictions?" he asked weakly, eyes still covered.

"For one month — no exercise," the doctor said firmly.

Harsha took his hand away from his face and looked at her hopefully. This had got off to a good start.

"No alcohol for a month," she continued.

"Holy shit," Azhar interjected.

"And no coffee," the doctor finished.

Harsha gave an even louder groan at the last pronouncement and collapsed backwards onto the bed.

"Once a day, you can have a cup of tea if it isn't too strong," the doctor continued, soothingly.

"One whole month?" Azhar asked, aghast.

"It could have been a lot worse!" she reminded the horrified pair. "You could have been murdered, I am told! That's why I have to show my badge to that policeman in my own hospital," she added drily.

"So sorry for the inconvenience," Azhar said obsequiously, but Harsha was too busy contemplating a whole month without alcohol and coffee to notice.

"On that subject," Dr Lavanya began, eyeing Harsha. "I have another guest, waiting to see you."

Harsha snapped out of his gloom at this and looked at her in intense alarm. "Not my mother?" he asked, his voice cracking.

She shook her head. "Not Dr Ramya, unfortunately. This is Detective Inspector Palanivel. You must be even more important than I thought! He has been waiting outside for half an hour to speak to you."

Harsha sat up at this.

"Are you serious? Why didn't you let him come in?" he asked, incensed at the idea of the inspector sitting in a waiting room.

Her eyebrows climbed up towards her neatly tied hair and her expression reminded him that she was the doctor, and therefore the one in charge.

"I wanted to complete my examination first," she said, haughtily. "Now sit up and take your shirt off."

Harsha self-consciously did as he was told, looking up to see Azhar grinning, enjoying his discomfiture.

He really shouldn't have to bare his torso for such a young woman, he thought to himself. And then he remembered all the women who had to deal with male doctors and felt slightly ashamed.

She sped through the examination efficiently, which was mostly painless apart from when she dug her fingers sharply into the area just under his armpits. She finished by looking deeply into his eyes while clasping his head firmly with her hands.

Finally, she nodded and said: "Alright. I will send the inspector up. But you will have to leave while he is here," she said apologetically to Azhar. "Only one guest at a time."

Azhar hauled himself obediently to his feet.

"I'll go get a co… a drink," he said, glancing at Harsha. "Maybe you would like to join me, doctor?"

Harsha shook his head as Dr Lavanya looked flustered, her composure slipping slightly.

"Uh… sure. Just for ten minutes," she said.

"You are incorrigible, Azhar!" Harsha muttered to himself as the two of them left the room.

He watched the glass pane of the doorway intently, where the silhouette of the police officer charged with guarding his door could be seen.

Finally, he saw the officer straighten in a salute and trivial matters fled his head.

The inspector was here.

31. Inspector

Inspector Palanivel was in full uniform when he walked into the hospital room, looking oddly out of place in that sanitised environment, despite his trim and immaculate appearance.

"Mr Devnath," he muttered, unslinging his backpack and dropping it by the bed before taking the seat Azhar had recently vacated, looking slightly uncomfortable there.

Harsha sat up as straight as he could and nodded respectfully. He was still a little awed by his old acquaintance and quite flattered that the man had taken the trouble to visit him in hospital. He looked closely at the policeman and thought he looked quite tired, despite being as well-groomed as ever.

"So, Mr Devnath. Another exciting midnight adventure for you?" Palanivel asked caustically.

Harsha swallowed, his head beginning to throb slightly again.

"I'm sorry I called you. I didn't know what else to do," he said, apologetically.

"Try dialling 100 next time an attacker is after you. Which I expect will be within another month or so, when you write your next story," the inspector said, smiling slightly.

Harsha looked at him in surprise. The man had actually cracked a joke. Maybe he was human, after all?

"But you were right to call me. Seriously, in an emergency like this, do not hesitate," the inspector continued, his expression turning sombre again.

Harsha squirmed with guilt.

"Uh... sorry about my last article," he said.

"About how the police are hopelessly stumped over the Gopinath case? Ha!" the inspector said, leaning back and rubbing his eyes with his knuckles. "Maybe it is not the worst thing in the world. The killer thinks he has got away with it. Unfortunately — he may be right."

Harsha stared at the inspector.

"You mean... you don't think it was this killer whom I was having my 'midnight adventure' with? Mangal or whatever his name is?"

The inspector frowned. "To be honest, Mr Devnath..."

"Call me Harsha."

The inspector inclined his head in acknowledgement.

"To be honest, Harsha, I am not even sure he meant to kill you," he said.

A silence fell over the room, apart from the beeping of some mysterious medical device.

Finally, Harsha said in an exasperated voice: "Inspector, I am here in this damned hospital room because..."

"I think he was meant to scare you. And maybe he got a bit carried away..."

"A bit carried away!"

"But to kill you? In the middle of a residential street in Chennai? With a knife? That's not how hitmen operate," the inspector finished.

Another silence fell in which Harsha felt unreasonably annoyed that the inspector was taking away his status as a survivor of attempted murder.

"It didn't feel like he was just trying to warn me — he was flashing that knife bloody close to my face," he muttered mutinously.

"But that is exactly how these corporate enforcers send a warning — a single cut to the face," the inspector said darkly, motioning with his finger across his own chiselled cheekbone. "I was just reading about a case of a journalist in Orissa who was investigating a company pumping effluents into the river, very, very similar to this."

Harsha felt slightly mollified that he had at the very least been at threat of facial disfigurement.

"I am told you had... an interesting site visit with Boreas Vayu," the inspector said, smiling again.

Kalyan, you old gossip, Harsha thought to himself. Or maybe it was Sampath who had told his police contacts?

"Are you going to question him, though?" Harsha asked.

The inspector shook his head. "No one knows where he is. The company claims he worked there as a security contractor via a third party company, and they knew very little about him."

"They are saying he was a *security guard*?"

"We can't prove otherwise."

"But he is ex-military!"

"Many security guards are."

"Well, at the very least, you can't rule him out, anyway — that company has a strong motive for the murder," Harsha said.

The ends of the inspector's lips dropped in a grimace, and

Harsha's heart fell.

"We looked deeply into the angle of whether or not Gopinath was standing in the way of the Kovalam hydropower project," Palanivel said. "The truth is, they were going to get permission to go ahead anyway. It was all signed and sealed, more or less. There really was no reason for them to eliminate Gopinath."

Harsha shook his head. "So, back to square one," he said bitterly.

"Isn't that what you wrote? 'Police stumped on Gopinath case'? At least it's true." There was no smile on Palanivel's face this time.

"Well, you used me to interrogate those poor transgender women, so call it even," Harsha retorted with spirit.

The inspector sighed. "Fair enough," he said.

The two men sat there despondently, weltering in the knowledge that all their efforts and adventures resulted in the square root of zero. They had got absolutely nowhere.

The inspector sighed. He stood up, turned around to pick up the backpack he had brought, and held it out towards Harsha.

"Anyway, here is your backpack. You dropped it in Crescent Avenue," he said.

"Thank you," Harsha said automatically, receiving the bag.

As the inspector turned to leave, he suddenly remembered his duty as a journalist and asked: "Do you have any other line of pursuit, inspector?"

"Absolutely none," the inspector sighed, dusting off the front of his trousers and walking towards the door. "All we have is a dead man and a missing book. I'd better leave for now, Mr... Harsha. Hope you get better soon."

Harsha felt a prickle of wonder and fear go all the way up his spine. For a second he didn't realise why, or what had prompted it.

"Inspector!" he said sharply, sitting up suddenly.

Palanivel froze in his tracks at the sudden note of urgency in Harsha's voice. He turned and frowned at the younger man.

"What is it?"

Harsha brushed his eyes, trying to focus and think clearly.

"Say what you said again?"

"Said when?"

"Just now! Just... say it again," Harsha implored.

Palanivel thought for a second and then said: "All we have is a dead man and a missing book? That one?"

Harsha's face wore a strained look as he combed through his mind to try and discover why he had felt like he had seen a chink of light, that sudden sense of understanding, which was now eluding him.

"The... bookmark..." he said, staring unseeingly at the door. "He had a bookmark in his hand when he died."

"Yes, yes he did," the inspector said, frowning as he tried to understand what Harsha was getting at.

"So if he had a bookmark — there must have been a book."

"There was none in his hand or around his desk. All the books in the room were neatly stacked on the shelf," the inspector volunteered.

"So it must be... oh my god, it must have been that!"

"Are you alright? Should I call the doctor?" the inspector asked, frowning, as he watched Harsha rip open the zip of his backpack and rummage inside.

"Sit down, inspector," Harsha said excitedly, as he pulled a book out. The inspector obediently sat back down on the chair and looked warily at him.

Harsha pulled out the stained paperback copy of *I Am Vidya* with trembling hands and then held it out for the inspector to see.

"What is this?"

"This is it!"

"This is what?" the inspector asked, looking baffled.

"The book, man! The missing book!"

The inspector's eyes widened in shock and he sat down again, staring reverentially at the book in Harsha's hand. Later, Harsha would feel flattered that the man's initial instinct was to believe him implicitly.

"But... how?" Palanivel asked in a hushed whisper.

"I visited Gopu before he was murdered. That was the book he said he was reading. It didn't occur to me until today that there was a missing book — bloody stupid of me! A bookmark in his hand — of course there was a missing book!" Harsha declared.

The inspector waved this away, some of his scepticism returning.

"Alright. But what makes you think it is this book?" he asked.

"This is the book that was in his office! He said he could lend it to me afterwards. It was in his office!" Harsha said, waving his book back and forth, unable to believe the inspector wasn't getting it.

"Ok, but how is it that you have it?"

"Neha, his daughter, gave it to me. She brought it from her house!"

The inspector tutted, now looking annoyed. "So he just took it home! Big deal!"

"No! I really don't think so. Look at this cover — it is stained — it is stained with blood! His blood!" Harsha now held the book by the corner furthest away from the stain, as he realised what it must mean.

The inspector's expression grew interested again. He leaned forward and finally took the book from Harsha's outstretched hand. He looked at it interminably and then held it up near his nose and sniffed it.

"Ok," he said, his voice tense and tight. "Let's assume this is the missing book, and this is Gopinath's blood. How did it end up in their house?"

"Oh — his wife must have taken it home after she killed him," Harsha said without thinking. But he instantly knew that he believed that this was what had happened.

The two of them looked at each other as the words rang out in the quiet hospital room. It felt, once Harsha had said it, that they had crossed some sort of Rubicon.

The inspector stood up again and started pacing the room.

"But she had an alibi," he said, half to himself, frowning in thought.

"What was the alibi?" Harsha asked.

The inspector came back to the side of the bed and sat down on the chair, still frowning.

"Their watchman said she had been at home all that day," he said finally.

"Inspector..." Harsha began.

"I know! I know! It's not a watertight alibi. But at the time, we thought she had no motive, so we accepted it," he said, wincing as he realised that this had probably been a mistake.

"Right, I can see how that might happen," Harsha said generously. "Let's focus instead on how she might have done it and why the book ended up in their home."

Palanivel nodded and said: "Let's think this through... she kills him... his blood... or her blood... is on the book... She puts it in her bag, doesn't know what to do... throws it in the trash at home..." He suddenly pumped his fist into the palm of his other hand. "I should have known — it's always the spouse! First rule of murder investigations!"

Harsha shook his head. "Inspector, I am the fool here. Bookmark in hand, missing book. How could I not have made the connection?"

The inspector sighed.

"But what's the motive? Why would she do it?" he asked, more to himself than to Harsha.

"It could be any number of reasons that we don't know about," Harsha said, soberly. "But I do think they were ideologically in very different places. And... it sounded like she felt very trapped in that marriage."

Palanivel nodded soberly. "We got that impression too."

Harsha took a deep breath and let the air out slowly through puffed-out cheeks. "This is insane," he said. "*Insane.*"

"Alright. Let's not get too excited," the inspector said, his face going back to the stone-faced expression he usually wore as he held the book up to the light so that the stain was clearly visible. "I will get this tested and then we will see."

"Can you get a DNA sample from this?"

"We can try!"

"So if there isn't..."

"We will find another way," the inspector said calmly. "Now we actually have a lead. I can work the case. However long it takes, I can…"

Harsha sat up and held his hand up to stop the inspector speaking, his face contorted in shocked remembrance.

"What is it?" the inspector asked sharply.

Harsha pulled himself up the bed, the pillow tumbling to the floor.

"Hema — Gopu's wife — she is going to Greece today! The daughter told me!" he exclaimed.

"To *Greece*? Why?" the inspector asked blankly.

Harsha laughed bitterly. "To see the history. Can you stop her somehow?"

The inspector thought for a moment, his finger pinching his thin lips, and then shook his head. "Only by arresting her — and we have no evidence without that DNA test. Not enough for an arrest."

Harsha's face fell and his shoulders slumped.

"She has outsmarted us," he said wearily. "What are the chances she actually comes back to India?"

The inspector stood up. It was the way he stood up, with a tremendous air of purpose and finality, that suggested some major event was about to unfold.

"If that is the case, then we have no time to lose," he said decisively. "Mr Devnath, it is time to… get creative."

Harsha felt a jolt of mingled excitement and dread rise in him. He had seen the inspector bluff without any aces in his hand, so to speak, once before.

"Are you going to her house now?" he asked, urgently.

"Yes! We will have to try and get a confession out of her," the inspector said, turning and marching towards the door purposefully.

"Can I come?" Harsha asked eagerly after him.

The inspector paused with his hand on the door handle.

He turned and looked at Harsha.

"I can't say no — it's thanks to you that we have this lead — but the doctor has to release you first," he said, frowning slightly at Harsha.

Harsha was already throwing off his bedsheets and clambering out of bed.

"I'm a journalist, inspector," he said haughtily. "So I know better than anyone — patients are not *released*, they are *discharged*."

"What does that mean?"

"It means, Detective Inspector Palanivel, I am absolutely coming with you," Harsha declared, and then looked down at his bare legs and boxer shorts. "Er… once I find where my trousers are."

32. Confrontation

"So, how are you going to get her to confess?" Harsha asked over the blaring of the police siren. "Assuming she is guilty," he added, conscientiously.

Yet, somehow, he was convinced that Hema was guilty. Everything he remembered about Gopu's wife made him think that she was eminently capable of this. The bottled up rage. The straight-laced views. Or was that Harsha's own prejudices speaking there, as a somewhat left-leaning, liberal person?

"*Assuming* she is guilty, my main job is to keep her in the country. Anything else is a bonus," the inspector yelled back.

The Toyota Qualis police car sped along, its siren screaming for Chennai's crawling traffic to part, weaving its way through gaps as though it was a bicycle. Harsha glanced at Gautami, who was sitting opposite and looking intently at him. The third police officer, a man of roughly Harsha's own age who had been introduced to him as Senthil, simply sat in the car with a blank expression.

"Did she say when her mother is flying out?" the inspector barked.

Harsha shook his head. He only knew that it was that morning. The Qualis sped around a corner, startling a fruit vendor, who was pushing a three-wheeled cart laden with guavas.

They were off the main road now, and the driver turned off the siren as they eased into the select neighbourhood of Boat Club Road. The sudden silence was soothing to the ears.

Harsha felt a jangle of nerves.

"Gautami — you take the questioning," Palanivel said quietly, to Harsha's surprise. "I'll step in with Plan B if that doesn't work."

Constable Gautami simply nodded, but Harsha couldn't help himself.

"What's Plan B?" he asked.

The inspector looked out of the window.

"We are here," he said.

The watchman looked at them with hostility and said: "*Kya chaahiye?*"

This created some confusion among the police officers, but there was no mistaking the tone of voice.

"Is Mrs Hema still in the house?" Inspector Palanivel asked in his staccato manner.

There was a collective intake of breath as four people waited for the response.

"Why do you ask?" the watchman asked, querulously. As much as Harsha was on tenterhooks, he couldn't help but admire the man's courage.

"Because we are the police," Palanivel said icily. "And we feel like being polite today."

The watchman hesitated and then, looking at Palanivel's intimidating profile, nodded briefly. Harsha's shoulders slumped in relief.

"I would like to see her, please," Palanivel said calmly.

It took a bit more to-ing and fro-ing, but eventually the four of them were allowed to march down the driveway. It was a strange group that walked through that beautiful garden, with just the sound of their shoes on the pavement and birdsong echoing through the trees.

Hema was waiting by the doorway, clad in a faded red sari and sensible black shoes, an odd combination that suggested she was preparing to do some walking. As Harsha got near, he recoiled. She looked like some sort of avenging angel, a sickly cast to her pale face, a rictus of a grin, humourless and forced, plastered against it as she scanned the quartet of people in front of her.

"How can I help you?" she asked in her thickly-accented English.

Constable Gautami stepped forward, smiling warmly.

"Some new evidence has come up in the unfortunate case of your husband, ma'am, so we wanted to clear one or two things with you. It won't take long," she said in flawless English. "May we come in?"

Hema glanced at the Ford Escort parked near the doorway. Harsha saw that the boot was open and piled with luggage.

"Ok," Hema said, finally. "I have only about 20 minutes. I am travelling on an important matter today."

She disappeared into the house. Harsha and the police officers followed silently, Gautami in the lead. They trooped into the living room that Harsha remembered so well from his first interview with Hema and Neha.

Palanivel and the other policeman sat uncomfortably on the plush chairs while Hema planted herself on the gilded sofa.

Hema put her hands on her lap primly, smiling humourlessly at them all.

"What do you want?" she asked, sounding a touch impatient. There was no offer of coffee or tea this time.

Constable Gautami sat on the edge of her chair and leaned forward, her hands placed together and her chin resting on the tips of her fingers.

"Ma'am, we have had some new evidence come forward and we wanted to run it by you," she said, speaking English in a slightly sing-song tone.

"And what is this evidence?"

"It is... a book," Gautami said.

Inspector Palanivel was leaning back casually, but Harsha had the impression he was observing Hema closely. The other constable, Senthil, who had come along with them, simply stared at his fingernails as though this matter had nothing to do with him.

A little flicker of the eyes, and then Hema asked: "What book?"

Gautami opened her backpack and pulled out the copy of *I am Vidya*, encased in a plastic cover, the brown stain on its cover still visible.

"Ma'am, we believe that this book is key to the whole murder," Gautami continued, waving the evidence back and forth to make her point. "We believe that it was at the scene of the crime, and that there is blood from your husband on its cover. We have already had some samples from the cover tested for analysis, both DNA and fingerprints. We are waiting for the results. It is just a matter of time," she added, almost apologetically.

All of this was delivered in the gentlest of voices. Harsha

could feel himself being lulled by the calmness and understanding in the policewoman's tone.

Gautami then leaned forward and said earnestly: "It was given to us by your daughter — she said that she found it in this house. So whoever brought it here either killed your husband or was there when he died — we have good reason to believe it is his blood on the cover. I think it would be best if we heard your side of the story, ma'am."

"My side?" Hema asked, blankly, her hands clasped firmly in her lap, gripping the folds of her sari.

"Yes, ma'am." Gautami edged forward in her chair. "Where were you when the... incident occurred? We would like to hear it from you. To understand."

Hema blinked, an agonised expression coming over her face.

"I... I... don't know what you want me to say," she managed.

They all waited. But it seemed she wasn't going to say anything more. She just stared at Constable Gautami, mesmerised.

"Ma'am, I just need to know — were you there when your husband died?" Gautami asked gently. Harsha noticed that the policewoman was avoiding using definitive language, just making it sound like an accident had happened. She was giving Hema a way out, an easy explanation that would make it more likely that she confessed, he realised.

But there was no answer. Gautami sighed and leaned back in her chair again and rubbed her eyes wearily.

"You see, ma'am, we see these things every day," she said, finally. "Husband beats his wife for years. And one day, something snaps, and she fights back. An accident happens.

And sometimes, they don't beat them physically. They just put them in one corner. The man achieves great things, while the wife just watches. And cleans. And cooks. And brings up the children."

Gautami looked up at the ceiling reflectively and continued: "My mother was like that. And you know what was worse? The next generation is free. The daughters work. They dream. They achieve. And you are left in your prison. One day — you just can't take it any more. It happens."

Hema said nothing, but she was now breathing hard, staring at the constable with hard eyes, who leaned forward and assumed her alert pose once again.

"But you see, ma'am, we need to *understand* what happened and why. Then we can help. You want me on your side — not some old judge who just wants to punish you for fighting back against injustice."

Harsha's jaw dropped open. Who was this woman? She should be on stage, or in business, making millions of rupees. Another thought surfaced in his mind — Gautami was extremely dangerous. Her words were so powerful, that Harsha was starting to feel that it was completely understandable for Hema to kill her husband. And perhaps even justified, in some ways.

Gautami had eyes only for Hema. She placed her elbows on her knees and gazed keenly at her quarry. "Once again, ma'am, I ask you — where were you when your husband was killed?"

For one brief second, Harsha thought it was going to work. Hema was looking at Gautami with an expression of abject horror on her face.

Then, she seemed to shake herself. And then, she laughed. It was a cackle, an explosion of startled breath that rang unnaturally around the shaded room.

"All this from one book, Constable?" she asked and then shook her head. "I don't think so."

She stood up and stretched her arms. "I don't have time for silly games — I have a flight to catch," she said, impatiently and then strode towards the door heading further into the house.

Her hand on the doorknob, she turned and smiled mockingly at the inspector and said: "Unless you have any more questions about books and whatnot? Maybe there's a love letter written by my cousin which somehow proves I was in a certain place during the full moon or something?"

The police officers stood up and silently walked towards the front door of the house, apparently defeated. Senthil went out into the driveway and Gautami paused at the threshold.

Harsha looked up at Palanivel and bit his lip. What would they do next? Would the stain on the book really have any forensic evidence for them to go on? It seemed so unlikely that Harsha gave up hope altogether.

"Oh, just one question, madam," Palanivel said, just as Hema was about to retreat into the house, his strong Tamil accent and rough tone contrasting with Gautami's.

Everyone turned and looked at him. Hema paused, her brows contracting.

"When is your daughter coming home?"

Hema blinked, looking unsure for the first time.

"Neha? I don't know. Why?"

Inspector Palanivel glanced at Gautami and then muttered to her: "We will come back. Madam, have a good trip," he added in a louder voice.

The implication — that Hema would be on holiday while her daughter would face the music here — was so neat that

Harsha couldn't help admiring how it was done, distasteful as he found this strategy.

"What?" Hema asked, looking like an avenging angel again. "What has she got to do with this?"

The inspector turned and looked at her in surprise, his expression icily vindictive.

"If you know nothing about this book, madam, then it has to be her."

Hema was breathing deeply now. "What has to be her? You're not saying that she... Neha..."

"The book is the key," Palanivel responded, gesturing towards Gautami's bag.

Hema took a step forward into the centre of the living room. "You say you got the book from Neha. Why would she bring you evidence of her own crime? It makes no sense."

"Sometimes murderers want to be caught. I've seen it happen before," the inspector said, shrugging his shoulders. "At other times, they think they are too clever for the police, for the public."

Hema shook her head. "It isn't her. Feel free to waste your time, inspector," she said contemptuously.

"If she is innocent, she has nothing to fear," the inspector said, using a phrase designed to strike fear into the hearts of innocent people all over the world. "The investigation won't be too long — worst case, she gets arrested for a few days. If she has nothing to do with it, she will be fine. Maybe a little bad publicity," he glanced at Harsha at this point, who was standing by his sofa, "And she can get on with her life."

"What bad publicity?" Hema asked, her face paling, as she turned to Harsha.

Harsha cleared his throat. Much as he wanted justice to be done, he wasn't going to be a part of this grisly game being played by the inspector.

"I will not write anything based on speculation," he reassured the woman. "We would only cover facts."

"Such as arrests?" the inspector asked mildly.

Harsha glanced at him. "Well... yes," he said.

The inspector smiled in triumph. Harsha looked at Hema again and saw that this terrible future was flitting before her eyes — her daughter's name in the newspapers as the possible killer of her father. How could she ever recover from that? He wondered, if Hema actually was the killer — as he was now convinced she was — would she really throw her daughter to the dogs? He felt a plethora of emotions, which included a healthy dose of shame for his profession. What was he actually doing here?

"Let's go," Palanivel said to his Gautami, and they trooped out of the house and onto the driveway. Harsha followed them — what other choice did he have?

"Inspector!"

They turned and saw Hema standing on the threshold of her home in her faded sari and sensible shoes, an expression of great determination on her face.

"It was me," she said. "I did it. I killed him."

And then she crumpled to the ground.

Harsha turned away with a sense of horror from the scene. But Constable Gautami surged forward and propped the woman up.

"It's ok, ma'am. It's ok. It's for the best," Gautami said soothingly.

"I... that stupid award was just there... and he... he... I just... couldn't stop myself..."

"I understand, ma'am."

"I wanted him to *listen* and he just kept reading that...

perverted book... all he cared was about those dirty transgenders — *but what about me?"* she screamed out, scaring the birds in nearby trees.

They all stared at her.

"There was so much *blood*," she said, finally, blinking as though to try and banish the memory.

"And the book?" Gautami asked gently.

Hema's expression hardened. "I just wanted to get rid of that horrible book. Men acting as women! How disgusting! How did he not see how *wrong* it was? But... yes, I should have got rid of it elsewhere... Bringing it home... was obviously... a great mistake."

Harsha glanced up at the inspector for any sign of emotion, but he just stared stone-faced at Hema. Senthil wiped his face wearily with a pocket handkerchief. *How did they do this for a living?* How did they see the worst of humanity on a daily basis and still come to work the next day, Harsha asked himself.

Somebody suddenly flew past Harsha, and next thing he knew, the watchman was crouching on Hema's other side.

"What you have done?" he asked in broken English. *"What you have done to her?"*

"We caught a killer," Palanivel muttered, but softly, so that only Harsha could hear him. He then turned to Harsha and said: "Save your sympathy, Mr Dev... Harsha. She will have the best lawyers in the land. This is only the beginning."

Gautami and the watchman lifted Hema to her feet and she was now blinking and staring in front of her.

Inspector Palanivel stepped up towards her and said in a surprisingly gentle voice: "You will have to come with us, madam."

She looked at him for a second and then, surprisingly, smiled. "Of course. Paras, go fetch my mobile phone and handbag. It's on the kitchen table."

The watchman disappeared and Senthil took his place, helping to guide Hema down the driveway towards the police car.

"How did you know?" Hema asked Gautami as they shuffled down the driveway.

"About the book, ma'am? I believe your daughter gave it to Harsha here, and he…"

"No, no, no!" Hema said impatiently, leaning heavily on the policewoman as they hobbled down the driveway. "I meant about what he did to me. About the prison he had created for me. How did you know?"

There was a pause and then Gautami said: "Because I am a woman, ma'am."

Palanivel stepped forward and held out his hand to Harsha, barring the odd trio from his view. The inspector looked less tense, almost human, now.

"Thank you for your help," he said formally, though there was also a touch of warmth in his voice.

Harsha shook the proffered hand and said: "I only wish I had put two and two together sooner."

"Next time, you will," the inspector said to Harsha's gratification. The man then turned away and took a few steps down the driveway before looking back at Harsha. "Are you coming with us?"

Harsha hesitated and then shook his head. "It would be good to know exactly why she did it. But I have something else to do here."

Palanivel's eyebrows rose. "And what is that, may I ask?"

Harsha sighed and pushed his hair back with one hand. "Someone has to explain to Neha what happened. And be there for her when she hears."

Palanivel looked at him for a moment as the gate creaked open behind him, and then nodded. He said, surprisingly: "You are a good man. Call me if you need an update on the case."

Harsha nodded and watched the strange procession leave the compound. The watchman ran out after them, Hema's handbag in his hand.

And then, Harsha was alone in that beautiful garden, with just the searing sunshine and birdsong for company.

33. Journalism

Walking into the *Southern Echo* conference room the next day was one of the most anticlimactic moments of Harsha's life. Where earlier there had been five or six of the most powerful people at *Southern Echo* listening to his and Sampath's progress reports, this time there were just two of them — Venu, the news editor, and a distracted-looking Rahul Medappa.

The editor of Southern Echo was chomping on his nails when Harsha and Sampath sat opposite him and Venu, leaving a vast stretch of the conference table empty.

Harsha glanced at Sampath, who was wearing the same bored expression as always, as he slapped his famous spiral-bound notebook onto the table.

Rahul jumped, startled by the sudden noise, and then smiled humourlessly. Upon closer inspection, he had bags under his eyes and a hunted expression on his face.

"Should we wait for Jaishree?" Harsha asked, looking around hopefully for the proprietor of the newspaper.

Rahul blinked and Venu said crisply: "She has an important sales meeting with a corporate client."

Now why was Venu looking so satisfied with himself?

"So," Rahul said, putting his hands on the table. "The Gopinath case. Where do we stand? Have the police got any new leads?"

Harsha had to cough to hide his contempt. How could this man be so clueless?

Sampath said in his usual dry tone: "The police are confident that his wife was the murderer. They have a confession."

Rahul frowned. "Are we sure about this?"

Sampath nodded generously towards Harsha. "He was there when it happened."

Both pairs of eyes swivelled towards Harsha, one contracted in surprise, the other narrowed in calculation.

"Well... well done! How soon can you write a story?"

"It's all written up, Rahul. We can file it immediately."

"Excellent... excellent... good work," Rahul said vaguely, before turning to Venu. "I think we have a slot open on page 7, don't we? The Finance Minister interview fell through?"

Venu nodded sagely, leaning back in his chair in a rather oracular manner.

"But... but..."

Both editors looked at Harsha again.

"Page... page seven?" Harsha asked, trying not to sound petulant. "I mean... I thought this was a massive story for us? And this is a big scoop! We are first on this!"

Rahul shifted uncomfortably. "Well... you see... busy day, lots of political news... feature on the top pages..." he muttered, before turning to Venu for support.

The news editor smiled benignly at Harsha and said: "We will try and find space on the anchor story on Page 1."

The two reporters left the room, Harsha baffled and

Sampath as implacable as ever.

"Can you believe that?" Harsha demanded in disgust.

Sampath merely shrugged his shoulders.

The next morning Harsha sat at his desk, looking down in disbelief at the newspaper on his knee, his legs resting on the cabinet under his desk.

"How the hell is this word 'separate' spelled, *pa*?" Kalyan asked, eventually. When he got no response, he turned to see Harsha's arrested expression and smiled wryly to himself. He wheeled his chair up to Harsha and peered into the front page of the *Southern Echo* copy that was resting on Harsha's lap.

The top story on the front page was about the result of an important parliamentary byelection. The bottom, or anchor, story, was about...

"Salman Rushdie," Harsha said hollowly. "They put Salman bloody Rushdie on the front page. This new Midnight's Children movie or whatever."

"Where is your story?" Kalyan asked gently.

"Page 12," Harsha said hoarsely.

Kalyan pursed his lips, thinking. "Tea?" he asked, finally.

Harsha nodded mutely and the pair of them made their way down the now-familiar path out of the building and down to the tea stall.

They passed the newsdesk on the way and Harsha waved to Sampath, who was cradling a phone between his ear and his shoulder, scribbling furiously into a notebook. He gave Harsha a brief thumbs-up before resuming his note-taking.

He is already on to the next story, Harsha thought bitterly to himself.

Would his own career as a serious news journalist last beyond the past couple of months? Or was it just an interlude between skateboarding features and party pieces?

Kalyan didn't say anything until they both had steaming cups of tea in their hands, the derelict surroundings of the tea stall making an odd contrast with the fragrance of the brew.

"Tell me pa, what is the problem?" Kalyan asked.

Harsha clamped his lips together to keep from yelling in frustration.

"I don't understand, Kalyan," he said, finally. "I thought this was the biggest story of my career — and they just seem not to care any more! I thought... I thought this was going to be my life from now on — but I am simply back on features. I thought it... I thought it would all MEAN something."

Kalyan blew lightly on his tea, his brow contracted in thought. Harsha watched him as he delicately blew again on the surface of his tea before answering.

"It does mean something, Harsha," he said finally. "For you it does. For the police it does. For the family of this Gopinath, for the transgender community — it means a lot. Why are you second-guessing this?"

Harsha placed his tea on the crumbling wall beside the tea stall and kicked a stone moodily.

"It just *feels* meaningless," he mumbled. "I am back on features, getting a daily 'dose' from Namritha, Sampath has moved on to the next story and Salman Rushdie is more important than a murder case."

Kalyan chuckled. "You think this was all about a murder case?" he asked before sipping his tea, his bright eyes watching Harsha carefully.

Harsha stared at him. "Was it not?" he asked.

"Of course not! This was about politics. This was about

India's changing culture. If this Gopu fellow had been bumped off by a political opponent or by some shady corporation — then would have been a big story. Killed by his wife?" Kalyan shrugged his shoulders. "That's a story. But not a big one. People are always killing their spouses, man! It's a 'dog bites man' story."

Harsha nodded gloomily at the reference to the old journalistic maxim: if a dog bites a man, that's not a story, but if a man bites a dog — that's a story. The rarity of the occurrence made it newsworthy.

"I guess I foolishly thought we were doing something noble," he said, leaning against the crumbling wall and staring out into the distance.

Kalyan downed his cup and casually set his glass down on a dislodged brick.

"As long as you think that, you will only be disappointed, *pa*," he said. "Newspapers are not noble. They are businesses. But you can do noble work while you are here."

Kalyan suddenly stood in front of Harsha and put his arms on the younger man's shoulders, saying earnestly: "Make no mistake, Harsha — you did noble work in writing about this man. And about the transgender community. You should keep doing that. And as for the newspaper, now Jaishree knows you. She knows what you can do. Make no mistake, *pa* -— your time will come."

Harsha finally said: "Maybe the story is about a clash of generations — an old-fashioned, conservative version of Chennai clashing with a more modern, liberal one. About how rapidly India is changing, and how that change cannot happen without some turmoil and violence."

Kalyan smiled. "*Now* you're thinking like a journalist," he declared, clapping Harsha on the shoulder.

"Thank you very much for your time, Mithra," Harsha said finally, pushing his metal chair back and standing up. "All of that was really helpful. I'll send you back some quotes for you to review later today."

"My pleasure," Mithra said as she stood up from behind her desk at the tiny little head office of the Aravanigal Society of Chennai in Nungambakkam. She shook hands with Harsha and then eyed him beadily. "Can I ask what kind of a story you are planning? And when it will come out?"

Harsha took a second to admire his interviewee. She was dressed in a simple dark green sari with a gold border, contrasting brilliantly with her dark skin and her beautiful white hair. An ancient ceiling fan clanked and creaked above them and the sound of traffic seeped into the room from a long window on one side.

"I am writing about Gopinath as a champion of the transgender movement — and how it upset a lot of people, his wife included. To be honest, it's not quite clear in my head yet, but I will know more by next week," Harsha admitted. Sometimes you had to start writing a story before the angle became clear to you.

Mithra nodded. "You have to write something that your readers will appreciate. But it's my job to further my cause."

"Hopefully we will both be happy with the end result," Harsha said, and looked around the tiny office, the walls of which were plastered with pictures of various smiling people. All the transgender folk who had helped and had been helped by ASoC, he guessed.

She nodded, sat down again and began leafing through the papers on her desk — a clear dismissal.

He hesitated, and then said: "I wanted you to know that I am very glad that Nangai and Jamuna are no longer suspects in Gopu's murder. And I didn't mean to be a part of any witch hunt — quite the opposite."

Mithra looked up at him without saying anything. He couldn't help admiring her poise and calmness of manner. Nothing seemed to bother her at all. How old was she, he wondered to himself. Sixty, at least? Given that life was hard for transgenders now, he did wonder what it must have been like in the seventies and eighties.

"Why are you telling me this, Harsha? I never thought you were part of the problem, no matter what you may or may not have done," she said, finally, cutting into his thoughts.

Why *was* he telling her this? Was it his people-pleasing tendencies? His need for everyone to think of him as the good guy? All he knew is that he was hugely confused about what was right and wrong — and he wanted to feel like he had done the right thing.

"I... I guess I just wanted to make sure they are alright," he said.

Mithra sighed. "They are. We still need to find them work away from the sex trade and they have some other issues, but they are no longer afraid of being arrested. And I believe you played your part in that — for that I thank you," she said.

Harsha felt a huge weight off his shoulders and nodded and smiled. He looked down at the paperwork on her desk and blinked to see that she was dealing with a court summons of some description.

"Is this in relation to Nangai and Jamuna?" he asked.

"Oh no," she said, looking down at her desk and picking

up the piece of paper and holding it between her thumb and her index finger. "This is an entirely different case. One of our members has been accused of a robbery in Saidapet."

She looked at the sheet beneath that. "This is another member who was 'caught' speeding in Anna Nagar — and jailed for ten days."

"For speeding?" Harsha asked, shocked.

"Speeding, and for resisting arrest and causing a public nuisance," Mithra said, drily.

Harsha didn't say anything.

Mithra ran her finger across the thick sheaf of papers on her desk.

"I am very glad that Nangai and Jamuna are free," she said, bending over the papers again. "But the work goes on, Harsha."

Harsha stood up. "I have to go to another meeting. But let me know if I can help in any way. You have my number."

She nodded without looking up, though when he left the office, she did look up thoughtfully at the door that had just shut behind him.

34. Coda

It was fairly late in the evening when the doorbell rang. Paul twisted around from his vantage point on the floor and stared at Harsha, who was reclining romantically across the battered old sofa.

Paul pressed the pause button on his Playstation 3 controller and Harsha put Maya's copy of *Wuthering Heights* down on his lap.

"Shall I... Shall I get that?" Paul asked casually, though his stammer suggested he was feeling far from sanguine. The recent attack on Harsha had left them both a bit shaken and a little concerned about the security of their home.

Harsha hauled himself to his feet, his book clattering to the floor — it had been hard to concentrate anyway, while Paul was shooting arrows at dragons — and shuffled around the sofa towards the front door.

"Probably for me anyway. Azhar wanting to take me out clubbing or something," he added reassuringly.

He reached the front door and grasped the doorknob.

"Wait, wait, wait!" Paul called out in a panicked tone.

Harsha turned in surprise and saw Paul appear from the

kitchen with a chopping knife in hand.

"Just in case," he said, sheepishly.

Quelling a desire to laugh, Harsha opened the front door and blinked.

Harleen stood there, looking simple and lovely in a white kurta and with her hair pinned sensibly into a ponytail. She had a cloth Fabindia bag slung over one shoulder.

The knife clattered to the floor behind Harsha.

"Hi," he said.

"Er... are you busy?" Harleen asked, nervously.

"Not at all!" Harsha said emphatically, feeling immensely grateful that he had decided to shower just 20 minutes before.

"Can I come in?" she asked, peering cautiously behind him. The sight of their neat little living room seemed to reassure her, and she smiled slightly.

"Of course!" Harsha said, opening the door wide. "This is my flatmate, Paul."

"Hi," Paul said from behind the sofa, where he had retreated. "I'll just go into my room, Harry," he added quickly.

"No, no! Er... Harleen, is it ok if we go sit on the balcony?"

"Sounds good," she said, smiling a little uncertainly at him, as though she wasn't sure exactly what she was doing there.

They went out onto the balcony and sat on the patio furniture, with the moonlight rippling over the ocean waves. All they could hear was the sound of the waves and soft tinkling of the wind chime that Harsha had attached to the roof of the balcony entrance — one of his few contributions to the house's decor.

"This is a beautiful place," Harleen said. "And your flat is really nice."

She sounded slightly surprised — perhaps she thought all journalists were slobs. To be fair, a lot of the cleanliness of the flat had to do with Paul's fastidiousness, but still, every time someone visited and exclaimed over the flat, Harsha was struck anew at how lucky he was with his living situation.

"What is Skyrim?" she asked idly, looking out into the ocean.

Harsha smiled to himself. Clearly Harleen was working up to something.

"The game that Paul was playing? Just a fantasy video game. Quite good, actually," he said, as he leaned back on his chair and drank in the quiet of the evening air. A few of the locals from the nearby fishing community walked past on the beach in front of them, singing softly in Tamil.

When Harleen didn't say anything, he asked: "How are Nangai and Jamuna?"

She seemed to shake herself out of her reverie. She looked up at him and smiled her charming smile. "They are doing very well. That Mithra person — wow, she is a formidable one — has taken them both into the ASoC premises near Burma Bazaar and is trying to find them work, though I think they have strict controls over what substances they take," she said.

Harsha nodded. "I'm doing a wider piece on the transgender community — maybe you would like to give me a quote, as someone who has done some work in this space?"

Harleen blinked, surprised by this offer. "Well, I would have to clear that with my office, but I'd be delighted. I do hope to do some more work on human rights violations with

Mithra — and your friend Maya," she said, scanning his face as she said those words.

There was an unspoken question in the last part of what she had said and Harsha hesitated. How to let her know that Maya was no longer a romantic complication in his life without making it obvious? He finally decided to go for complete honesty.

"I think Azhar told you all about the history I had with Maya," he said, finally. "Listen — I hope you believe me when I say that is now behind me."

There was a pause. They had only been on one date, and though he felt there was strong chemistry between them, it was still ridiculously early for anything more serious than just a signal of interest.

Harleen cleared her throat and then leaned forward and fished something out of her bag.

"I wanted to give you this," she said, and handed him a book. He could make out from the light of the living room, which fell out onto the balcony through the glass door, that it was a beautiful hardcover edition of *High Fidelity* by Nick Hornby.

"This is the book I was telling you about," she said, with an indifference that he thought was feigned. "I brought it to your hospital room, but I was told you had left. The doctor was not happy!"

Harsha chuckled. "I bet she wasn't," he said, absentmindedly stroking the spine of the book.

"Anyway, I was passing by after meeting my auntie who lives further down ECR, and I thought I would stop by. Azhar gave me your address," she said, and then cleared her throat. "I hope that was ok."

And you gave him plenty to gossip about, Harsha thought

ruefully. He fully expected a call from his old friend the next morning.

But really, who cared? He held the copy of *High Fidelity* in his hand and felt immensely moved by the gesture. She had come all the way to the hospital and then all the way home. Another rare flash of insight hit him, and he realised that she must have really worried about him.

"This is so thoughtful of you, Harleen. So, so thoughtful," he said.

She smiled, showing her strong, even teeth and he felt his heart leap.

"Would you like a drink? I'm not supposed to have any, but maybe just one..."

"Oh no!" she stood up, alarmed. "I only came to give you this book, not to invite myself over for..."

"I didn't mean..." Harsha began, standing up himself.

"No, no!"

They both stood there in the balcony, a couple of feet apart, awkwardness flooding in like a moat between them.

"I'd better go," she said, finally. "You probably need to rest after all that excitement and, you know, the concussion and everything."

"Nah, it's fine. I feel ok now," he said, somewhat untruthfully.

"Well, I mean, you probably need to rest up before writing your next groundbreaking article on this murder mystery," she said, smiling.

"Not really," Harsha said bitterly. "Gopu's death is yesterday's news. No one cares about it any more."

"My clients care, Harsha," Harleen said, gently. She hesitated and then said: "Can I tell you something in complete confidence?"

"Always."

She hesitated and then said: "Nangai was in Gopinath's room the day he died. She went in to give him a piece of her mind, she says, but found him dying. She ran away very quickly, which is exactly what I would have done."

"I did get the feeling in the police station that she was about to admit that before you came in," Harsha said, nodding.

Harleen hugged herself as though shivering, even though the evening air was balmy. "I don't like to think what would have happened to her if it had gone to court. Even though she didn't kill the man, if that had come out in cross-examination, she would have been finished. And then think about what it would have been like for that whole community if a transgender person had been arrested or suspected of murdering a senior civil servant? So you see — your work was extremely meaningful," she finished, a little awkwardly.

Harsha was silent for a moment, trying to hold back the tears that suddenly sprung to his eyes. What was wrong with him?

"Thank you," he croaked. "That means a lot."

She smiled that lovely smile again and then said: "Goodbye, Harsha. Enjoy the book."

She stepped forward and leaned in to kiss his cheek goodbye.

He closed his eyes, drank in the aroma of her perfume and, almost without thinking, placed one hand on the small of her back and held her near him.

She did not resist, so he opened his eyes and found that she was looking up at him, their faces just inches apart now. A little shock went through his body, and he just looked at her, like that, for a moment. The light spilling out from the living room wasn't enough to illuminate her whole face, but he noticed that her eyelashes were long and her skin seemed to glisten in the moonlight. A smile was tugging at the corners of her lips and her body felt soft and warm against the palm of his hand.

Gently, he pulled her closer, felt her body against his and then leaned forward slightly to kiss her. The electricity was coursing through his body now, and every part of his body felt hyper-aware of every sensation — the sound of the waves and the wind chimes, the smell of salt and Harleen's floral perfume, and above all, the whispery softness of her lips. It was really quite astonishing. It felt like he was kissing a girl for the first time in his life, so novel was the feeling.

She put her arms around him, her elbows resting on his shoulders and her face turned slightly up towards him and they kissed like that for what felt like hours. Usually in these situations, Harsha felt a sort of impatience, wondering how much longer he would have to keep kissing before societal norms of courtship were satisfied.

But on this occasion, he just wanted to keep this electricity alive and running through his body, and to embed every memory of this moment in his brain. The tinkling of the wind chimes, the rushing of the waves, the perfume, the feeling of Harleen's lips. He almost felt like he could *hear* the moonlight rippling on the ocean in this elevated state.

Finally, Harleen let go and dropped back on her heels. Harsha thought to himself that it was nice that a woman had to tiptoe up to kiss him, as shallow a feeling as that was.

Harleen smiled up at him, put one hand on his chest and said: "It really is time for me to go."

Disappointment and relief warred with each other inside

Harsha's head. He wanted Harleen to stay, but he also wanted to take this slowly, to arrange everything correctly in his head.

"Will you have a drink with me this week?" he asked.

Her smile broadened, and he had a feeling that he had said the right thing.

"Let me check my calendar when I get back. Text me tomorrow?" she asked.

"Of course."

He walked her out to her car, shut the door on her and waved goodbye as she revved her sleek Skoda out onto the little lane that led back to East Coast Road.

Then he went back in, poured himself a glass of water and then went to knock on Paul's bedroom door.

"She's gone, Paul! You can come out now — it's safe," he said, grinning.

"Very funny!" he heard Paul yell back through the door.

Harsha was about to sit down in front of the television, but at the last minute, he dropped the remote control and walked back out towards the balcony. He put on the balcony light and made himself comfortable on the chair, his feet up on the parapet of the balcony, and looked out at the ocean. The fishermen were back, singing.

He listened, enchanted, to their song. After they passed, he picked up the copy of *High Fidelity* Harleen had given him, and opened it to the first page.

It wasn't just time to start a new chapter.

It was time to start a new book.

WANT MORE?

YOUR FREE BOOK IS WAITING

A gang of misfit English literature students. A despotic and racist professor. A strict Catholic university. Harsha and his friends master their growing pangs, love lives and struggles with Shakespeare to fight for change – with explosive results.

Get a free copy of *Joint Study,* the prequel to Last Resort, visit www.abhinavramnarayan.com or scan the QR code below with your smartphone.

AUTHOR'S NOTE

Throughout this book, I have tried to remain true to the soul of Chennai, or at least my experience of growing up in this incredible, sleepy and vibrant city of contradictions. That said, I have made up a lot of names and places in this novel. Don't waste your time looking for the Cloud Nine hotel or the Silk Road restaurant — they don't exist. And if you want to support worthy causes such as the Aravanigal Society of Chennai or Helping Hands, well I'm sorry, but they don't exist either (though the city is dotted with other similar organisations run by amazing people).

I did this mainly to avoid upsetting people. But as I said, I have tried my very best to try and convey what life in Chennai is like across the spectrum, and will continue to do so in my next few novels. Let me know how I've done by visiting my website www.abhinavramnarayan.com, where all my details and social media accounts are available.

Thank you for getting this far! You are the reason writers like me pour their souls into their work.

ABOUT THE AUTHOR

Abhinav Ramnarayan is a London-based Indian writer who has had a wide-ranging career as a journalist for publications including *The Guardian*, *Reuters* and *Bloomberg*. His debut novella, Joint Study, is a nostalgic journey through university life in India at the turn of the millennium.

The son of journalists and writers Gowri and V Ramnarayan and the great-grandson of renowned freedom fighter and Tamil novelist "Kalki" Krishnamurthy, he grew up on a diet of English and Tamil literature classics, Hindu mythology and epic tales from all over the world.

He took this one step further by studying literature at Loyola College in Chennai before getting his first job as a journalist at the *Deccan Chronicle* newspaper, also in Chennai. After working at a handful of Indian newspapers, he went on to study journalism at the University of Sheffield in England and subsequently secured the coveted graduate trainee position at *The Guardian* in 2008, out of a pool of over 400 applicants.

He went on to work for *Reuters* for several years, but along the way rediscovered his first love - story telling.

Abhinav currently works for *Bloomberg* as a journalist during the day and writes novels at night. He lives in East London with his wife Anne.

Printed in Great Britain
by Amazon